THE
BROTHERS
O'BRIEN

THE
BROTHERS
O'BRIEN

WILLIAM W. JOHNSTONE

with J. A. Johnstone

PINNACLE BOOKS
Kensington Publishing Corp.

www.kensingtonbooks.com

PINNACLE BOOKS are published by

Kensington Publishing Corp.
119 West 40th Street
New York, NY 10018

PUBLISHER'S NOTE
Following the death of William W. Johnstone, the Johnstone family is working with a carefully selected writer to organize and complete Mr. Johnstone's outlines and many unfinished manuscripts to create additional novels in all of his series like The Last Gunfighter, Mountain Man, and Eagles, among others. This novel was inspired by Mr. Johnstone's superb storytelling.

All Kensington titles, imprints, and distributed lines are available at special quantity discounts for bulk purchases for sales promotions, premiums, fund-raising, educational, or institutional use. Special book excerpts or customized printings can also be created to fit specific needs. For details, write or phone the office of the Kensington special sales manager: Kensington Publishing Corp., 119 West 40th Street, New York, NY 10018, attn: Special Sales Department; phone 1-800-221-2647.

PINNACLE BOOKS and the Pinnacle logo are Reg. U.S. Pat. & TM Off.
The WWJ steer head logo is a trademark of Kensington Publishing Corp.

ISBN-13: 978-0-7860-3301-0
ISBN-10: 0-7860-3301-0

First printing: February 2012

10 9 8 7 6 5 4

Printed in the United States of America

First electronic edition: September 2013

ISBN-13: 978-0-7860-3417-8
ISBN-10: 0-7860-3417-3

Chapter One

Texans are a generous breed, but they do not confer the title of Colonel lightly on a man. He has to earn it.

The two men who sat in the sway-roofed, sod cabin had earned the honor the hard way—by being first-rate fighting men.

Colonel Shamus O'Brien had risen though the ranks of the Confederate Army to become a regimental commander in the Laurel Brigade under the dashing and gallant Major General Thomas L. Rosser.

O'Brien had been raiding in West Virginia when the war ended in 1865, and thus escaped the surrender at Appomattox, a blessing for which he'd thank the Good Lord every single day of his long life.

He was twenty-three years old that June and bore the scars of two great wounds. A ball ripped through his thigh at First Manassas and a Yankee saber cut opened his left cheek at Mechanicsville.

By his own reckoning, Shamus O'Brien, from County Clare, Ireland, had killed seventeen men in single combat with revolver or saber, and none of them disturbed his sleep.

The man who faced O'Brien across the rough pine table was Colonel Charles Goodnight. He'd been addressed as colonel from the first day and hour he'd saddled a horse to ride with the Texas Rangers. A Yankee by birth, the great state of Texas had not a more loyal citizen, nor fearless fighting man.

"Charlie," O'Brien said, "it is a hell of a thing to hang a man."

Goodnight stilled a forkful of beans and salt pork halfway to his mouth. "Hell, Shamus, he's as guilty as sin."

"Maybe the girl led him on. It happens, you know."

Speaking around a mouthful of food, Goodnight said, "She didn't."

"She's black," O'Brien said.

"So, what difference does that make?"

"Just sayin'."

Goodnight poured himself coffee from the sooty pot on the table.

"Shamus, black, white, or in between, he raped a girl and there's an end to it."

O'Brien let go of all the tension that had been building inside him, words exploding from his mouth, his lilting Irish brogue pronounced. "Jesus, Mary, and Joseph, Saint Peter and Saint Paul, and all the saints in Heaven save and preserve us! Charlie, he's a Yankee carpetbagger. He's got the government on his side."

"Yeah, I know he has, but I don't give a damn. He's among the worst of the carpetbagging scum and I've got no liking for him. He called me a raggedy-assed Texas Reb—imagine that. I mean, I know it's true, but I don't need to hear it from a damned uppity Yankee."

"Is that why you're hanging him, because he called you raggedy-assed?"

"No, I'm hanging him for the rape of a seventeen-year-old girl."

"Charlie, you're not a Ranger anymore. You don't have the authority to hang anybody."

"So the government says. A Union general in El Paso told me my enlistment ran out at Appomattox. Well, I don't see it his way. The Rangers didn't tell me I'm done, so as far as I'm concerned I still have a sworn duty to protect the people of Texas, men, women, and children."

O'Brien was a big man, sturdy and well built, with the thick red hair and blue eyes inherited from his ancestor Brian Boru, the last High King of Ireland. His pine chair creaked in protest when he leaned back. "They'll come after us, Charlie, I'm thinking. And the gather just completed."

Goodnight considered that. He scraped his tin plate, the noise loud in the silence and stifling heat of the cabin. Finally he said, "By the time the Yankees give up their plundering and get around to investigating we'll have the herd across the Pecos and be well on our way north."

"They look after their own, Charlie," O'Brien said.

"And so do I, by God." Goodnight pushed his plate away, leaned back, and sighed. "That was an elegant meal, Shamus."

His poverty an affront to his Celtic pride, O'Brien said, "I am shamed that my poor house had so little to offer. Salt pork and beans is not a fit repast for such an honored guest."

Goodnight stepped lightly. "The food was excellent and freely given. You did indeed do me great honor, Shamus."

O'Brien and Goodnight were Southern gentlemen of the old school, and the mutual compliments were accepted without further comment.

"Will you hang him, Charlie?" O'Brien said. "I mean, after all that's been said."

Goodnight consulted the railroad watch he took from his vest pocket. "Yes, at noon, fifteen minutes from now."

O'Brien listened into the morning, his face grim. "He screams for mercy. You'll hang a coward."

"He's a carpetbagger. He was brave enough to throw women and children off their farms, but he's not so brave in the company of men." Goodnight's eyes hardened. "God, I hate his kind."

"What's his name?"

"Do you care?"

"Not really. I'm just curious."

"Dinwiddie is his last name. That's all I know."

"Ah, then he's not a son of Erin."

"No, he's a son of a bitch."

Chapter Two

His name was Rufus T. Dinwiddie, and he was not prepared to die well.

When Goodnight's drovers, Texans to a man, dragged him toward a dead cottonwood by a dry creek, he screamed and begged for mercy, and his broadcloth suit pants were stained by the loosening of his bowels and bladder.

Dinwiddie was a small man with pomaded hair and a black pencil mustache. His brown eyes were wild, filled with terror, and they fixed on Shamus O'Brien's wife, who stood beside her husband, a ragged parasol protecting her from the hammering sun.

"Save me, ma'am!" Dinwiddie shrieked, the dragging toes of his elastic-sided boots gouging parallel furrows in the dirt. "In the name of God, save me."

Saraid O'Brien was pregnant with her second child. Her five-year-old son Samuel stood at her side, frightened, clinging to her skirts.

She turned her head and glared at Goodnight. "Will you hang such a man, Charles?"

Goodnight said nothing, but the shocked, sick expression on his rugged face spoke volumes.

"He shames you," Saraid said. "He shames all of us here."

The rope was around Dinwiddie's neck and the little carpetbagger's screams had turned to hysterical shrieks that ripped apart the fabric of the young afternoon like talons.

Goodnight had seen men hanged before, but all of them, scared or not, had at least pretended to be brave before the trap sprung. A man who died like a dog was outside his experience and the last thing he'd expected.

He stood rooted to the spot as the drovers threw Dinwiddie on the back of a horse and then looked at him expectantly.

The man was no longer screaming, but he was heaving great, shuddering sobs. Still he pleaded for mercy.

Saraid rounded on her husband. "Shamus, if you hang that miserable wretch today you'll never again be able to hold your head high in the company of men."

She grabbed Goodnight by his upper arm. "And that goes doubly for you, Charles."

He looked like a man waking from a bad dream. "Saraid, he raped a girl."

"I know, and she stands over there by the cottonwood," the woman said. "She is the wronged party, so let her say what the justice is to be."

Goodnight shook his head. "I did not expect this, not in a hundred years."

If Saraid heard, she didn't respond. She said only one word that held a wealth of meaning—the name of her husband. "Shamus." Her green eyes glowed like emeralds.

O'Brien said nothing. He drew his .36 caliber Colt Navy from the holster on his hip and strode toward the cottonwood. "Take him down."

The hands were confused. "But, Colonel, the boss says to hang him."

"I know what he said, but this man isn't worth hanging," O'Brien said.

The punchers looked toward Goodnight, but the man stood frozen where he was, Saraid's slim hand still on his arm, as though she was holding him in place.

"Get him down from there," O'Brien said again.

The men did as they were told.

To O'Brien's disgust, Dinwiddie let out a loud wail and threw himself at his feet. He kissed the toes of O'Brien's dusty boots and slobbered his thanks. O'Brien kicked him away.

Rape was a serious offense and there was still justice to be done. "You men, put his back against the tree and hold him," the colonel said.

As he was hauled roughly to his feet, Dinwiddie cried out in alarm. "What are you doing to me?" he squealed.

"An eye for an eye, me lad." O'Brien's face looked like it had been carved from rock.

The black girl, slender, pretty, wearing a worn gingham dress, stood near the cottonwood. Her face was badly bruised. When O'Brien got closer he saw the arcs of a vicious bite on her neck.

He pointed the Colt at Dinwiddie. "Is he the man who raped you?"

The girl nodded. Her eyes were downcast and her long lashes lay on her cheekbones like ragged fans. "He hurt me, mister." She didn't look at O'Brien. "And now I'm afeared I'll be with child."

About two dozen men, women, and children had gathered from the surrounding shacks to see the hanging. They called the dusty settlement a town because of its single saloon and attached general store, but within a couple years the place was destined to dry up and blow away in the desert wind.

"Nellie works for me as a maid, Colonel," a fat woman said, stepping so close to O'Brien he could smell her sweat. "I examined her after she was undone, and she's tore up all right, fore an' aft if you get my meaning."

Tears trickled down the girl's cheeks and sudden anger flashed in O'Brien. Suddenly he wanted to smash his fist into Dinwiddie's face.

"Hey, ain't you gonna hang him?" the fat woman said.

O'Brien ignored her. He grabbed Nellie's arm and said, "Come with me, girl."

A breeze had picked up, lifting veils of yellow dust. Near where Saraid and Goodnight stood, a dust devil spun, then collapsed at their feet like a puff of smoke.

Insects made their small music in the bunchgrass and the air smelled thick of sage and the new aborning afternoon coming in clean.

Goodnight watched O'Brien, as did the crowd.

The residents of the town had come to see a hanging, but Dinwiddie's cowardice had spoiled it for everybody, especially the women. The ladies expected the condemned man to make the traditional speech blaming loose women and whiskey for his undoing, though he had a good mother. That always went down well at a hanging. It gave wives the opportunity to glare at their cowering husbands and warn darkly, "You pay heed, or this could happen to you."

But the spectators, their rapt attention fixed on Shamus O'Brien and the colored girl, had decided that not all was lost, for a fine drama was unfolding.

At least that's how it looked to Saraid. Why else would the people stay and brave the noonday sun to see a poor, cowardly wretch suffer for his sins, grievous though they were?

O'Brien led the girl called Nellie to within six feet of the cottonwood. A couple grinning punchers held Dinwiddie's arms, so his back was against the trunk.

The little man's eyes widened when he saw the Colt in O'Brien's fist. "What the hell are you going to do?"

O'Brien ignored him, thumbed back the hammer, and passed the heavy revolver to Nellie. "Shoot him."

Dinwiddie's expression went from fear to disbelief and back again. He glared at the girl. "Pull that trigger and I'll see you hang, missy."

The girl held the Colt in both hands. She started to lift the revolver, hesitated, and looked at O'Brien, her brown eyes afraid.

"Go ahead," O'Brien said. "He can't hurt you now."

Dinwiddie made an appeal to the crowd. "Stop this!" he screamed. "Are you going to stand there and see a white man get shot?"

No one moved or said a word, their collective stares on Nellie and the wavering blue Colt.

Goodnight stepped beside O'Brien. "This ain't gonna work, Shamus. Damn it, we'll put cotton in our ears and string him up."

But Nellie surprised them.

She raised the Colt in both hands and pointed it at Dinwiddie's head.

The man screeched and tried to break free, his eyes wild. The punchers held tight to his arms, strong men who quickly subdued his puny struggles.

The muzzle of the revolver trembled, then Nellie let it lower slowly, her skirt slapping against her legs in the hot desert wind.

O'Brien thought she was done. That she couldn't go through with it. He heard Goodnight curse under his breath and a collective sigh raise from the crowd.

The girl stopped the Colt's descent when it pointed at Dinwiddie's crotch, and pulled the trigger.

The ball slammed into the little man's groin and he screamed in pain, his mouth a startled O of shock.

Nellie fired again. Same place.

Stunned, the punchers dropped Dinwiddie's

arms. The man's knees buckled and he sank slowly to the ground.

"All right, he's had enough," O'Brien said. Almost gently, he took the Colt from the girl's shaking hands. "Go home now, girl."

She buried her face in her white apron and stumbled away. The fat lady stopped the girl, put her massive arm around her shoulders and led her toward home.

"You done good, girl," she said as they walked away.

Dinwiddie was traumatized, his pinched, narrow face white. But, no matter how shocked a groin-shot man may be, he'll always rip open his pants and check on his jewels.

Dinwiddie did—and what he saw made him shriek in horror.

Unbelieving, he looked around the crowd, then at O'Brien and Goodnight. "It's gone," he wailed. He looked down at his groin again. "All of it."

"Then you'll never again rape another woman," O'Brien said.

"Help me," Dinwiddie wailed. "Get me a doctor."

O'Brien deliberately turned his back on the man. He said to Goodnight, "I've got a bottle of Old Crow in the cabin if you want to get the bad taste of Dinwiddie out of your mouth."

"Shamus, we should've hung him," Goodnight said.

O'Brien smiled. "Well now, all things considered, I'd say he's suffered a fate worse than death."

Chapter Three

As a junior partner, Shamus O'Brien rode drag behind two thousand longhorns, a remuda of sixty horses, eighteen drovers and—

"What the hell does Charlie call that damned contraption, Colonel?" Luther Ironside said. He'd been eating dust for an hour and was even more cantankerous than usual.

O'Brien smiled under the bandana that covered his mouth. "A chuck wagon. And for heaven's sake call me Shamus. We're not in the army any more."

"Damndest thing I ever saw, Colonel," Ironside said. For a few moments he considered the vagaries of Goodnight's invention, then said, "It takes a score of oxen to haul the damned thing. He must've loaded up with a heap o' grub."

"We've got six hundred miles of hard country

ahead of us before we reach Fort Sumner," O'Brien said. "We'll need all the grub we can carry and more."

Ironside snorted. "Just wait until we hit the Staked Plains. Them drovers are gonna be too tired and too thirsty to eat." He grinned like an undertaker. "Or too dead from a Comanche arrow."

O'Brien had no illusions about what lay ahead. Texas longhorns never wanted to go anywhere. They preferred to stay right where they were, especially if grass and water were near, and that's why they had to be driven. On a good day the herd would cover twelve to fifteen miles, but there would be few good days. The relentless sun would dry up waterholes and bring drought and dust and flies and dead beeves. Sudden thunderstorms would mill the cattle and cause stampedes across a hard, unforgiving land miles from anywhere.

It was enough to make a thinking man wonder what the hell he was doing out there in the first place.

Saraid, young Samuel on the seat beside her, was up ahead driving O'Brien's Studebaker wagon and four-horse team. With her was a stowaway. Nellie, fearing retaliation from the Federals, hid in the back of the wagon and only revealed herself when there were fifteen miles of git between her and the settlement.

Ahead of Saraid rolled the chuck wagon. Goodnight and his partner Oliver Loving rode point.

Luther Ironside leaned over the side of his buckskin, spat, then rubbed off his mustache with the back of his hand. "How you figure Miz O'Brien and the younker are holding out, Colonel?"

O'Brien pulled down his bandana. "Just fine, I'm sure. Saraid is a strong woman. Why, back in the auld country she could plow a field as well as any man, and her only a slip of a girl."

Ironside nodded, pleased. "Young Sam will hold up. He's a quiet youngster, but he's got sand."

"He did all right back at the cabin," O'Brien said. "He was scared, I could see that, but he held his ground."

Ironside nodded. "He'll make a fine cavalry officer when the South rises again."

O'Brien replaced his bandana. Luther would never accept that the Confederacy had been beaten and beaten badly. It was an old argument between him and his former first sergeant, and one that O'Brien didn't care to renew.

Luther Ironside was forty-seven that summer, his black hair shot with gray, not from age but from four years of war. He was a man of medium height, stocky and strong, and he still wore his yellow-striped cavalry breeches, tucked into mule-eared boots. A buckskin shirt and a battered gray kepi completed his attire. Around his waist he wore a heavy black belt with a CSA buckle and a Colt Navy butt forward in a holster of the same color.

He was tough, enduring, and hard to kill. The new breed of Texas draw fighters who were making all the headlines in the Eastern newspapers stepped wide around him and called him Mister Ironside.

O'Brien and Ironside rode drag for several weeks to the herd's jumping-off place on the Concho. There the cattle rested on good grass, ready for the ninety-three-mile trek across the waterless Staked Plains.

They lost a hundred cattle to thirst and a dozen more to a band of Comanches who demanded tribute. Since the Indians were traveling with their women, children, old people, and slaves, they showed little inclination to fight nearly two dozen men armed with Henry rifles, and rode south without further incident.

Saraid and Samuel stood up well to the rigors of the drive and the boy was riding ahead on the back of Goodnight's saddle when the man caught his first glimpse of the Pecos.

When the herd reached Fort Sumner in mid-July, the army had eleven thousand Indians to feed, and beef was selling at a premium price, sixteen cents a pound dressed, eight on the hoof.

After paying his drovers, Charlie Goodnight realized a profit of twelve thousand dollars in gold. Shamus O'Brien's share was ten percent, the return on the money he'd invested, laboriously saved during the war by Saraid, who had traded Confederate scrip for Yankee dollars at exorbitant rates.

It was enough, O'Brien decided.

In his pocket was the foundation on which a man could build a dream.

Chapter Four

"That's my proposition, Shamus," Charlie Good-night said. "Is it to your liking?"

"Your terms are generous, Charlie," Shamus O'Brien said, "but it is not in my mind that I return to Texas."

"But only to pick up another herd, and next time we drive all the way to Colorado. I'm told the miners are willing to pay for beef with pokes of gold dust."

"It's a tempting offer, Charlie," O'Brien said. "I will not deny you that."

He and Goodnight sat in one of eight tents huddled under a painted canvas sign as big as a sail that proudly proclaimed:

THE BON-TON HOTEL
—Silas Meriwether, prop.

O'Brien's eyes moved to the open flap as an infantry company with slung rifles and full packs marched past, kicking up dust.

Apaches had raided the Navajo camp the night before, wounding two men before they made away with a woman and a dozen horses.

Patrols were out hunting the raiders, but O'Brien reckoned the Apaches were already long gone.

"How tempted are you, Shamus?" Goodnight said.

"Not much." O'Brien's blue eyes softened, like flowers opening in sunlight. "I want my own land, Charlie."

Goodnight nodded. "And you shall have it. There's plenty of land for the taking in Colorado."

O'Brien shook his head. "Saraid and I talked it over and we decided that we'll put down roots here, in the Territory."

"It will be hard, Shamus."

"It's hard everywhere." As though it made all the difference, O'Brien added, "Luther Ironside agreed to stay on with me."

Goodnight considered that. "He'll do."

Coming from Charlie, that last was a great compliment, and an endorsement of Ironside as a gentleman and a fighter.

O'Brien picked up his coffee, the tin cup almost disappearing in his big hand. "I'm pulling out tomorrow at first light."

Before Goodnight could respond, Saraid stepped inside. She still showed the rigors of the trail and

O'Brien had noticed little arcs at the corners of her mouth when she smiled that were not there before.

"Where's Samuel?" her husband said.

Saraid, big in the belly, sighed as she gratefully sat on the bench beside him.

"He's out with Nellie, watching the soldiers. I think he hopes the Apaches will come back." She smiled, her teeth strong and white. "He found a cartridge case over at the Navajo camp, and he's convinced it was fired by an Apache warrior."

"Maybe it was," O'Brien said.

"More likely by a Navajo," Saraid said.

Goodnight had listened to this exchange with growing impatience. Finally he looked straight into Saraid's face. "Can you talk some sense into this stubborn Irish husband of yours?"

She smiled. "I've been trying that for six years and haven't succeeded yet."

"Charlie wants me to head back to Texas with him and bring up another herd," O'Brien said.

"I thought we'd agreed to stay here in the New Mexico Territory?"

"We did, but Colonel Goodnight is a man who hates taking no for an answer."

"I'm due in two months, Charles," Saraid said. "I won't have my baby born in the back of a wagon."

"Hell, woman—" Goodnight snapped his mouth shut, appalled by what he'd just said. "I'm sorry, Saraid, I didn't mean to talk like that."

Her voice was calm. "Charles, we've all been under

a good deal of strain in recent weeks. You have no need to apologize."

Goodnight looked at O'Brien. "Shamus, I meant no disrespect to your wife."

O'Brien smiled. "Charlie, you couldn't disrespect a woman if you tried."

Goodnight smoothed his closely trimmed beard. "What I was going to say is that Saraid might be better off having her baby in a wagon than under a juniper in some godforsaken wilderness."

O'Brien rubbed the back of his wife's neck with the thumb and forefingers of his left hand. "Charlie makes a point."

"With luck and God's tender mercy, our baby will be born on our own land, Shamus," Saraid said. "I will hear no more about it. As for me giving birth under a juniper tree, there's no use building houses on a bridge we haven't crossed yet."

Charlie Goodnight smiled through a sigh. "You're as stubborn as your husband, Saraid. But there's steel in you and that I admire."

"When I was a girl, only the great English lords lived in their own houses. My mother and father paid rent for our poor cottage and a patch of dirt to the Earl of Sunderland, a man who never set foot in Ireland. After Shamus and I wed, we came to America and made plans to build a home of our own. It was our dream, you understand. But then came the war and Shamus went off to fight and our house was never built. The dream vanished like a fairy gift in the morning light."

Saraid was talking more to herself than Goodnight, her eyes searching the space between the two of them. "Our home will be built by Shamus and me, here, in the Territory, and we'll pay rent to no one."

Goodnight smiled. "Then I can see that your mind is made up."

"Indeed it is."

"Shamus, you'll need cattle to start a herd," Goodnight said. "I have a hundred head of mixed young stuff the army passed over, and they're yours if you want them."

"I'll pay you for them, Charlie," O'Brien said.

"No you won't. They're my gift to Saraid, and, unlike a fairy gift, they'll still be there in the morning."

"We're beholden to you, Charles," Saraid said. "For everything you've done for us."

Goodnight waved away the woman's thanks. "Where will you head to find your land, Shamus?"

O'Brien smiled. "Why, north, of course. When I was in the army I always enjoyed marching north and that's the course I'll set."

Goodnight rose and stuck out his hand. "Good luck to both of you." He smiled. "Come visit me in Texas sometime."

Shamus O'Brien was not yet finished with Fort Sumner.

Silas Meriwether, a giant of a man who'd worn the gray, had told him the army was selling off old Mexican land grants clustered around the Glorieta Mesa country that had been confiscated by the United

States under the Treaty of Guadalupe Hidalgo in 1848.

"If it's fertile farmland you seek, then the grants are not for you, Colonel," Meriwether had said. "But ranching is a different matter. The land will support longhorn cattle."

Later O'Brien walked to the fort, talked to a colonel who sent him to a major, who passed him on to a captain, who told him to talk to a first lieutenant, who palmed him off on a second lieutenant, who collared a civilian government employee who sold him the grant.

"We're now the owners of a deed to fifteen thousand acres southwest of the town of Santa Fe," O'Brien told Saraid, flourishing the document.

She was shocked. "Shamus, there's not that much land in all of Ireland. How did we pay for such an estate?"

"Six hundred dollars, my love. Half of all we own, but 'tis a fine bargain to be sure."

Saraid's quick brain made a calculation. "Shamus, four cents an acre seems a low price for so vast a tract of land."

For a moment, O'Brien's face shuttered, and his wife pushed him. "What are you not telling me, Shamus?"

"*A ghra mo chroi*, my heart's beloved, do not imagine the green fields of the auld country. 'Tis a wild, unforgiving land we have bought, fit only for the wolf and the buffalo and the Apache, but our cattle will thrive there, of this I am sure."

"It is our land, Shamus, is it not?"

"Indeed it is."

"Then we will tame it and make it our home and our children's home."

"And the Apache?"

Saraid did not hesitate. "Husband, we will fight for what is ours."

"Amen," O'Brien said.

Chapter Five

Glorieta Mesa, New Mexico Territory, August 1866

A cobalt blue sky arched over the top of Glorieta Mesa and a white cloud rested on the summit, pinned in place by the arrowhead canopies of ponderosa pines. Lower on the slopes grew thick stands of piñon, juniper, and mountain oak. Lower still on the flat, stretched brush flats and vast swathes of grama grass.

Borne on the hot August wind, the air smelled of cedar and of secret places in the high mountain meadows where mint-green frogs dived off ferns without a splash into mossy pools.

Saraid drove the wagon across rolling hill country, a new cast iron stove clanking in the bed. Samuel and Nellie were wedged on the seat beside her and a hundred yards back, Shamus O'Brien and Luther Ironside rode herd on ninety longhorn cattle, only a third of them beeves.

O'Brien had been silent for the last mile or so, and

looked around with quickening interest. "Luther, I think this is the place."

"Hell, it all looks the same to me," Ironside said.

He swung to his right and hazed a young cow out of a patch of brush and whistled it back to the herd, swinging his coiled rope. When he returned to O'Brien's side, the younger man was consulting the map he'd taken from his saddlebags.

After a few moments of head nodding, O'Brien said, "Yes, we're on our land." He pointed to the forested slope of the mesa. "You see the outcropping of rock shaped like the prow of ship?"

Ironside allowed that he did.

"According to the land agent's map, that's right in the middle of our acres." O'Brien grinned. "Damn it all, Luther, we're home."

He looked at Ironside. "You don't seem too excited."

The older man's face was grim. "I've got something to show you, Colonel."

"Where?"

"Come with me."

Ironside turned his horse and trotted back to the brush patch where he'd rousted the cow. When O'Brien drew rein beside him, Ironside pointed. He had no need for words.

Two skeletons lay on the ground, partially covered by brush and other debris. Several arrows that had lodged in bone still bristled from their rib cages. Scraps of leather from boots and belts, along with patches of cloth from plaid shirts, still clung to the bones like rotting flesh.

It took O'Brien a while before he could muster some words, but in the end he settled for only one. "Apaches."

"That would be my guess, Colonel. I'd say these were prospectors by the look of them." Ironside's eyes searched the surrounding ground. "Animals must've run off with some of the bones."

"How long ago, do you reckon?"

"Who knows, Colonel? Months, years. It's hard to tell."

O'Brien turned his head, his eyes fixing on his companion's face. "I don't want Saraid to know about this. Later we'll come back here and bury these men decent."

"That's fine by me."

O'Brien smiled. "This is a happy occasion, Luther, and I won't let some old bones spoil it for us." He swept off his hat, let out a wild rebel yell, and galloped his big sorrel toward the wagon. Even when he was still a distance away, he shouted, "Saraid, we're home! We're home!"

She reined the team to a stop as her husband drew up beside her. "This is it, Shamus? Are you sure?"

"According to the map, we're right in the middle of our land. We own this valley and a lot more beside."

Saraid crossed herself. "The Lord be praised. This is a green and pleasant land."

O'Brien nodded. "Better than I expected. 'Tis high desert country and I thought we'd see only miles of sand and cactus."

The herd trotted past on both sides of the wagon, followed by Ironside. "They've got their tails up, Colonel. There's water ahead."

O'Brien reached out his arm. "Behind me, Saraid, let's see where the cows lead."

Saraid stepped lightly from the wagon seat despite the encumbrance of her big belly and straddled the horse behind her husband's saddle.

Mindful of his wife's condition, O'Brien rode at a walk into the dust of the retreating herd.

The cattle lined the bank of a brawling creek about twelve feet wide, shaded by cottonwoods. The water ran over a sandy, pebbled bottom and fish the color of gunmetal hovered in the eddies.

Shamus O'Brien was mighty pleased. The spring melt was long gone, yet the creek flowed full and clear, an excellent sign in a thirsty land.

"Shamus, help me down," Saraid said. "I want to drink of our water."

He stepped from the saddle and assisted his wife to the ground. She ran to the creek, and with an effort kneeled on the bank.

Cupping water to her mouth with her hand, she swallowed, and then turned to her husband.

"The water is sweet, Shamus," She lifted her arms

and O'Brien helped her to her feet. "What shall we call this place?"

O'Brien took his wife in his arms, looking down at her from his great height. "If it pleases you, we'll call this place, our ranch, Dromore."

Saraid glanced over her husband's shoulder to the towering mesa. Knowing Dromore, in Gaelic meant the Great Ridge, she said, "It's a fine name, Shamus." She said the name again, tasting it on her tongue. "Yes, I will be happy here . . . at Dromore."

They made camp that night close to the creek, under a sky that glowed with stars. A rising wind whispered among the piñon and juniper and higher, an owl roosted in the pines and asked its eternal question of the night. A pair of coyotes hunted close by, yipping to one another in the lilac darkness.

"I'm afraid of coyotes," Nellie said, huddling closer to Ironside, the flames of the fire staining her face scarlet. "They come in the night and steal babies."

"Maybe it's the banshee," O'Brien said, smiling. "Oh, I heard the terrible cry of the banshee many a time during the war."

"Shamus, don't tell Nellie such things," Saraid said. "She's scared enough already, poor thing. And look at Samuel. He's white as a sheet."

"I'm not scared, Ma," the boy said. "Honest I'm not."

But Ironside was intrigued and wouldn't let it go. "What is a banshee, Colonel?"

"Ah, a terrible creature to be sure," O'Brien said.

"The *bean si* is a woman who lives in the fairy mounds by day and only comes out in the darkness of night." His eyes shone like jewels in the firelight. "She has the face of a skull and long white hair to her waist and she borrows her voice from the cry of the wolf."

Nellie gave a little yelp of alarm and buried her face in Ironside's shoulder.

"Shamus!" Saraid said. "I told you not to frighten the girl. Now, stop it at once, please."

Ironside grinned. "And what does all that crying amount to, Colonel?"

"Well," O'Brien said, "when you hear the cry of the banshee you can be sure that someone around you is going to die. She brings the bad news from the spirit world, you see."

"Oh Miz O'Brien," Nellie wailed, "I'm afraid. Are we all going to die?"

"No. No one here is going to die for a long, long time." Saraid smiled. "Come sit by me, Nellie."

The girl did as she was told and Saraid put her arm around Nellie's trembling shoulder.

Saraid glared at her husband, then Ironside. "Shame on you two, a pair of grown men scaring this child half to death, to say nothing of Samuel. Don't you think Nellie has been frightened enough recently?"

O'Brien looked contrite. "I'm sorry, Saraid."

"We were just funnin', Miz O'Brien," Ironside said.

"For heaven's sake, Luther, call me Saraid. You're one of the family now. As for fun, you and Shamus will have plenty of that tomorrow. I want you to do something for me."

"And what might that be?" O'Brien said.

"You'll find out in the morning, and this time tomorrow evening you'll both be so tired you'll have no appetite for funnin'."

Chapter Six

"There it is, on the slope," Saraid said. "See there, in the clearing between the junipers?"

"Saraid," O'Brien said, "it's a rock."

"I know it's a rock, and I want it."

"But it's halfway up the mesa."

"Then you'll have to bring it down, won't you?"

O'Brien drained the last of his morning coffee from the cup and stared at the slope over the rim. "Why do you want it? Is this another of your pregnant female notions?"

"Shamus O'Brien, bring me my rock," Saraid said. "Do it now before the sun rises higher in the sky."

"It's flat," Ironside said. "I mean, the rock is flat, at least what I can see of it."

"I know it's flat." Saraid's voice was tinged with impatience. "And it's a pink color, and I want it."

"Must weigh a ton, Saraid," Ironside said, with a noticeable lack of enthusiasm.

"Then hitch up the team, and haul it down here."

Saraid glared at her husband. "And don't you dare break it, Shamus."

O'Brien and Ironside exchanged the kind of glance men give each other when they come up against the unconquerable rampart of a woman's will and realize their only option is surrender.

"Hitch the team and get some rope, Luther," O'Brien said. "Let's go get the rock."

"It's sure gonna take a heap of gettin', Colonel."

O'Brien's shoulders slumped and he spoke through a long sigh. "Don't you think I already know that?"

Ironside grinned. "Yup, Colonel, I guess you already do."

Nellie and Samuel stepped beside Saraid. "I saw Mr. Ironside leave," Nellie said. "Are they getting you your rock, Miz O'Brien?"

"Reluctantly," Saraid said.

"Saraid, it ain't going to be easy," O'Brien said. "Like Luther told you, that's a ton o' rock."

"You'll have the horses, Shamus. If you get into trouble, let them do the thinking for you."

Saraid was on a tear and O'Brien figured talking to his wife in her present mood was like walking naked through a briar patch.

He looked from her to Nellie and was met with scowls, the female of the species banding together against the common enemy. Gathering what remained of his dignity around him like a ragged cloak, O'Brien tried for the last word. "When we come down from the mesa, we're going to be mighty hungry."

"You'll eat when you get my rock," Saraid said. "And not a minute before, Shamus O'Brien."

The pink rock was as large as a tabletop, about four inches thick, and the part that stuck out of the slope was roughly oval shaped.

The horses had declined to climb the rise. After a few tentative steps they'd backed away, deciding that the loose shale underfoot was too dangerous. But O'Brien and Ironside, lacking horse sense, made the ascent and attacked the dirt around the rock slab with pick and shovel.

After an hour, another foot of the rock was exposed with no end in sight. Ironside said, "Hell, Colonel, this here boulder might go all the way through the mesa and come out at t'other side."

"It might at that." O'Brien wiped sweat from the band of his hat with his fingers. "No matter, Saraid would still want it."

"Now tell me, what does she plan to do with it?" Ironside said.

"The hell if I know, Luther. Like I always say, pregnant women take on some strange notions."

Ironside spat on his hands and grasped his shovel again. "One reason I joined the cavalry in the war was because I don't like digging holes. Now I know why."

"It's never been one of my favorite occupations," O'Brien said.

"Didn't you dig holes in Ireland, Colonel?"

"Yes, plenty of them. It wasn't one of my favorite occupations there, either."

The sun rose in the sky and burned like a white-hot coin. Jays quarreled in the junipers and crickets played scratchy tunes in the brush. The mesa stood more than eight thousand feet above the flat, and on its wooded slope the air was sharp and smelled like fresh-sawn timber.

O'Brien and Ironside had stripped to the waist and the sun highlighted the sweat on their broad backs and strong arms, their bunched muscles shining as though they'd just been oiled.

By two in the afternoon, the pink slab was almost free, held in place by only a ledge of shingled dirt.

Now that it was visible, O'Brien figured the pink slab measured about eight by five feet, its thickness of four inches constant throughout its length and width. "Luther, 'tis indeed a mighty stone," he said, breathing hard.

"How do we get it down the slope, Colonel?" The expression on Ironside's face showed that he feared the answer.

"We'll rope the thing well, then hold on as its own weight slides it slowly down to the valley floor."

"That should work, Colonel, with you and me at the ends of the ropes to slow her some."

"Yes, I believe so." O'Brien crossed himself, glancing at the sky. "God willing."

After they looped the rock like a steer for branding, O'Brien laid out the ends of the rope where they'd be handy for grabbing.

"Chip away the dirt now, Luther, and easy as you go."

Ironside held the pick high up the shaft and gently scraped dirt from under the slab. The rock held stubbornly firm.

"Maybe you should dig deeper," O'Brien said.

Ironside swung the pick more forcibly. Dirt and shale flew as the pick sank again and again into the slope of the mesa.

"Now you're getting it, Luther," O'Brien said, pleased.

The front of the slab dropped an inch, then another.

"She's going," Ironside said, stepping to the side.

"Grab a rope, Luther. We'll guide her down, slow and easy does it, mind."

But the slab suddenly dropped onto the slope like a falling domino and touched off an unfortunate chain of events.

"Hold on!" O'Brien yelled, grasping the rope with both hands. "We've got her." He dug in the heels of his boots to give him traction, his chin set and determined. Opposite him, Ironside did the same, bracing himself to take the weight.

But, with the cussedness of inanimate objects, the pink rock stayed right where it was aslant the slope and refused to move.

"I'll give her a nudge, Luther." O'Brien reached out with his boot and shoved on the end of the slab.

That's all it took.

Suddenly the rock slid, gathered momentum, and then hurtled down the slope like a runaway freight train.

O'Brien and Ironside, taken unawares, stumbled after the slab, hauling on the ropes for dear life. But the weight and speed of the rock was too much for them and they were yanked off their feet and followed the hurtling slab downward. They bowled head over heels down the side of the mesa like shotgunned rabbits, scattering showers of shale.

O'Brien was vaguely aware of the world cartwheeling around him as he bounced down the slope. He yelled a wild Gaelic curse every time he slammed into the ground—until all the breath was knocked out of him when he hit the flat with a thud.

A moment later Ironside thumped beside him. He still had breath enough to let go a string of curses that turned the air around him blue.

"Where's the bloody rock?" O'Brien gasped.

"Hell, I don't know and I don't care." Ironside's left cheek was badly grazed, and he had a lump on his forehead the size of a pigeon's egg.

"We have to find it." O'Brien struggled to his feet when he heard Saraid scream.

She hurried toward her husband, her skirt hiked up, her face a mask of concern.

"I'm all right. Don't worry, Saraid, there's nothing broken."

"I'm worried about my rock. Is my rock all right?" Saraid wailed, rushing past him. She frantically looked around her. "Oh, there it is."

She stepped quickly to the pink slab. "It's fine. Oh my, that's such a relief."

She turned and looked at her husband. "Shamus, hitch the team to my rock, and I'll show you where I want it."

For a moment O'Brien was stunned. "Saraid, did you notice that I fell off the mesa?" He held up his hands. "Look, I've got a rope burn and cuts and bruises all over me. I could've broken my bloody neck, you know."

Ignoring him, Saraid walked to Ironside, who was arched backward, groaning as he worked out the kinks. "How are you, Luther?" Before the man could answer, she said, "Well, that's good. Now you and Shamus hitch the team to the rock and follow me."

"This way, Shamus, and please avoid the hole there." Saraid pointed to her right. "It's not far now."

O'Brien led the straining team around an old buffalo wallow and followed his wife. Ironside, muttering under his breath, walked beside the rock and Nellie and Samuel followed behind him.

Saraid smiled as she walked, looking behind her often to encourage the others. "We'll soon be there." Finally, exasperated, O'Brien said, "Saraid, where are we taking this thing?"

"To the creek," his wife said. "Well, close to the creek."

"What in heaven's name for, woman?"

"You'll see, Shamus."

A huge cottonwood spread its branches near a level area of ground, shading it like a vast parasol.

"This way." Saraid eyed her distance from the tree and the foot of the mesa where the piñon and juniper grew, then stopped. She pointed to a spot under her feet. "Shamus, here. Put the stone right here."

O'Brien maneuvered the slab into position, removed the ropes, and led the team away. When he returned he said, "All right, Saraid, now what?"

The woman didn't answer, at least not right away. She called everyone closer, and when they stood near she stepped onto the slab. "This is my hearthstone. Around it we will build our cabin and our lives, and we will call this place Dromore."

Chapter Seven

New Mexico Territory, October 1866

When Samuel O'Brien was old enough to have a past, two events would remain in his memory.

The first was when his mother gave birth to his brother Patrick. The second was when the Apaches came.

By the end of October, as winds sharked chill off the peaks of the Santa Fe Mountains to the north, the building of the cabin was almost complete. The bases of the walls were stone, rising to a height of four feet, then another five feet of logs and a sturdy sod roof. A pole corral with a lean-to was erected for the horses, and an outhouse was built well away from the river.

Inside, O'Brien and Ironside had built a stone fireplace, and Saraid, very big with child, loved to sit of an evening and watch the play of the flames reflected on her polished hearthstone.

What furniture they possessed was rough, made

from unplaned pine. Only the cast iron stove and an assortment of pots, pans, and crockery were store bought.

O'Brien, mindful of the Apache, had cut only two windows into the logs, both at the front of the cabin. Having no glass, they were closed by heavy wooden shutters with rifle slots.

The door was solid, made from mountain oak, the forged hinges of hammered iron.

Saraid had her hearthstone, and Shamus had his motto.

Above the door he nailed a painted sign that read:

Lamh laidir au Uachtar

The Gaelic words meant, "The strong hand from above," and were taken from the ancient heraldic crest of the O'Brien clan. Ironside said the motto looked like gibberish, but O'Brien was very proud of his sign and would hear no criticism of it, even from Saraid.

Winter came early to the valley that year, and on the morning of October twenty-eighth, snow flurries swirled in the chill air and ice stitched both banks of the creek like lace on a lady's collar.

By noon, the mercury in the outside thermometer dropped to twenty degrees. When O'Brien went out to check on the horses, his breath smoked.

Saraid went into labor at one o'clock that afternoon. She lay on the rope bed, her mattress stuffed with pinecones. Despite the cold, her forehead was damp with sweat, and the labor pains were coming at faster intervals.

O'Brien had been soldiering when Samuel was born, and seeing childbirth for the first time, he was beside himself with worry. He sat on the bed beside Saraid and took her hand. With a man's clumsy sincerity, he said, "How are you feeling, Saraid?"

His wife smiled. "Shamus, I'm not sick. I'm having a baby."

"Yes, yes I know." O'Brien tucked the sheet around his wife. "Can I get you something?" He thought about it for a few moments. "A bite to eat? Some fried bacon, maybe?"

Nellie put her hand on O'Brien's shoulder. Reflecting Saraid's smile, she said, "Colonel, I'll see to Miz Saraid. It's going to get cold and I reckon the fire needs more wood."

O'Brien jumped at that like a drowning man clutching at a straw. "First class idea, Nellie." He rose to his feet, and looked down at his wife. "Saraid, I'm going to get more wood for the fire."

A fresh spasm of pain helped Saraid hide her amusement. "Yes, Shamus, please do that. It's going to get much colder."

But O'Brien hesitated. When he looked at Nellie his eyes were questioning, but somewhere in their blue depths the girl saw a plea for assurance.

"Do you know anything about birthing babies?" he asked.

"My ma had nine," Nellie said. "I helped deliver the last three. A girl learns how to do a lot of things on a plantation."

O'Brien swallowed hard. "Nellie, take good care of her."

"I will, Colonel."

"And if you need me—"

"I'll holler."

O'Brien turned his attention to Saraid again. "I'm going now."

Before his wife could answer there was a knock on the bedroom door. Ironside called out, "Colonel."

It was a single word, but hearing it, sudden fear spiked at O'Brien. He'd heard Ironside's tone many times during the war, a mix of apprehension and anxiety as distinctive as a wrong piano note. It was the tone a soldier uses only when he sees the enemy advance in force on his position.

Without a word, O'Brien stepped to the closed bedroom shutters and bolted them in place.

Saraid watched her husband as he left the room, then her pained eyes moved to the black girl. "Nellie, when the baby appears, I will shift for myself. The men may need you to load rifles."

"How many?" O'Brien asked as he pulled Samuel close to him.

"Hard to tell, Colonel. They don't stay long enough in one spot to be counted. But I'd guess at least six."

O'Brien looked through the rifle slot. Outside, the spinning snow flew thicker, and small drifts had formed around the bases of the trees like wind-scattered white laundry.

"Why the hell are Apaches out on a day like this?" O'Brien said. "Damn it, they should all be home with their wives and youngsters."

Ironside nodded. "It's hard to tell why an Indian does what he does. But when Apaches ride out half-a-dozen strong it means they've got raiding and killing in mind."

"Are they just watching us, or will they attack?" O'Brien said.

As though in answer to his question, an arrow thudded into the shutter close to the rifle slot, then another.

Both men had buckled on their Colts, and each held a sixteen-shot Henry repeating rifle.

O'Brien peered through the rifle slot. "Damn it, Luther, I don't see them."

"I've heard that when you see an Apache it's too late because you're already dead."

"Samuel, you stay here with Luther," O'Brien said, his throat tight. "I'll take the window in the bedroom."

"Can I see Ma?" Samuel asked.

"No, not yet, son. Soon. When the baby is born."

O'Brien moved to the bedroom door. He stopped and said to Ironside, "Luther, may St. Patrick and all the saints and angels in Heaven protect you."

Ironside smiled and nodded. "Thank ye kindly, Colonel. But if it's all the same to you, I'll put my faith in this here rifle gun."

Henry in hand, O'Brien stepped to the bed. "How are you doing, Saraid?"

"It will be soon now, Shamus. The baby is trying to be born."

O'Brien looked at Nellie.

"She'll be fine, Colonel," the girl said.

A ball slammed into the bedroom shutter and it rattled noisily on rawhide hinges. The report of the gun echoed until it was borne away by the wind.

Saraid, her legs open wide, gasped as pain hit her. Through gritted teeth, she said, "Shamus, your place is at the window."

O'Brien nodded. He had five rounds in the Navy and those he would save. If the worst happened, he would not let the Apaches take any of his family alive.

Moving to the window, he peered outside, his view restricted to a narrow rectangle. The snow had thinned a little, but the keening wind had grown stronger. Piñon and juniper shivered, their limbs trembling. and the mesa was a vague, gray bulk behind a billowing white curtain.

He heard the crash of Ironside's rifle, then the disappointed curse he hurled through the rifle slot when he missed his target.

An arrow slammed into the shutter where O'Brien stood, and he eased up his Henry. He caught a glimpse of a bent figure, bow in hand, sprinting along a deer trail leading to the creek. O'Brien fired, but he shot at a shadow. The Apache disappeared like a puff of smoke into the underbrush by the trail, and O'Brien thought he heard the man's derisive laugh.

He dusted a few more shots into the brush where

he'd last caught a glimpse of the Indian, but he was certain he did no execution.

His anger flaring, O'Brien cursed, boiling mad at the savages for not being true blue and acting like white men. They should come at him in an orderly rank, ready to take their medicine.

He didn't know it then, but the War Between the States had taught him one kind of fighting and the Apaches were about to teach him another.

Behind him, O'Brien heard Saraid cry out, a long, drawn-out paean of pain and hope that struck him to the heart.

"Good girl, Miz Saraid," Nellie said. "The baby's comin' just fine. Now push, lady, push . . ."

O'Brien didn't turn. He pretended to himself that he had to keep his eye on the Apaches, but in reality, he didn't want to see his child come into the world. He or she would have one quick glimpse at life and its wonders and then . . .

He touched the revolver on his hip, but immediately shook his head, refusing to look at the pictures in his mind. Staring through the slot, he saw nothing but the snow and wind.

"Colonel, it's a boy!" Nellie yelled above the shriek of a newborn. "You have another son."

O'Brien turned and looked from the baby to his exhausted wife. Strands of hair lay damp across her flushed forehead, but her eyes shone, the look of a woman who has just experienced a miracle.

Bullets hit the cabin with a noise like hammered nails.

He looked outside again. Three Apaches were moving to his left at a quick trot, in the direction of Ironside's window. "Is Luther down?" he mumbled to himself.

"Saraid!" O'Brien said aloud.

"Go, Shamus," she said. "Look out for Luther. Patrick and I will still be here when you get back."

O'Brien opened the door and dashed into the main room of the cabin.

"Colonel, they're after the horses," Ironside said.

Horses were the difference between life and death in the wilderness, the reason why the theft of one was a hanging offense. Without horses O'Brien and his family would be marooned in the high desert country and the dying would begin very quickly.

"Luther, stay here and protect the cabin. I'm going after them."

Samuel stared at him, his eyes wide. The boy was very pale, but he seemed unafraid. Only then did O'Brien see the scarlet splash of blood on his son's left arm.

"Are you wounded, Samuel?" O'Brien said, on a rising note of horror.

Ironside spoke quickly. "He got grazed by a ball, Colonel, came clean through the door. One of them Indians using a Sharps Big Fifty, I reckon."

O'Brien stepped to the door, then looked back. "Samuel, are you sure you're all right?"

"I'm fine, Pa."

O'Brien had no time to express the pride he felt. He spoke to Ironside, who had his eyes fixed to the rifle slot. "Luther . . ."

Without turning, the man said, "I know what to do, Colonel."

There was nothing more to be said. O'Brien slid back the door's wooden bolt and charged into the tumbling snow and the wild wolf wind.

Chapter Eight

O'Brien, his rifle up and ready, moved to the corner of the cabin in a crouching walk. His eyes searched into the snowstorm, but his visibility was limited to a few yards around him. He saw no Apaches.

Walking carefully, his eyes never at rest, he stepped toward the corral.

A rifle roared and a ball kicked up a startled exclamation point of dirt and snow at his feet. He swung the rifle to his right, seeking a target. The snow-blurred shape of an Apache was not twenty feet away. The Indian frantically rammed a fresh ball into the barrel of an old muzzle-loader, his eyes on the white man.

O'Brien shouldered his Henry. Snow and ice stung his eyes and he knew his aim would be an uncertain thing. But before he could take a shot, he heard the flat report of Ironside's rifle. The Apache took the hit square in his chest and staggered back a step before thudding onto the hard ground.

Luther had made a good shot, and O'Brien vowed to thank him—if they both lived that long.

He stayed where he was and got down on one knee, his gaze reaching out to the corral. One of the draft horses trotted to the rail opposite the lean-to. The animal lifted its head, then looked behind it, as though troubled by something—or someone.

Despite the cold, O'Brien's right hand sweated on the Henry's stock and his heart hammered in his ears. He recognized the symptoms of fear. He'd felt them many times during his four years of war.

He knew the kind of men he was about to face. Resolute, ruthless, and relentless, superb guerilla fighters, the Apaches wanted him dead. They'd never leave until they had his scalp and his horses.

O'Brien moved again. Reaching the corner post of the corral, he took a knee again. Toward the lean-to his big sorrel whinnied, alarmed by a man smell he'd never encountered before.

Planning his every movement, O'Brien rose carefully to his feet.

The snow no longer relented, but came down thicker and faster, tossed this way and that by the gleeful wind. He shivered, suddenly cold. He could no longer make out the lean-to, and the horses were agitated, prancing shadows. He bent to slip under the top rail of the corral, a movement that saved his life.

An arrow thudded into the fence post where his head had been a moment earlier and the shaft thrilled a few moments before it stopped.

Footsteps pounded toward him. He completed his duck into the corral, and then straightened. His eyes barely had time to register the charging Apache before the man was almost on top of him. The Indian had tossed away his bow, but held a war lance high, ready for a killing downward thrust. The steel head was two-and-a-half feet long, made from the blade of a Mexican cavalry saber, rawhided to a painted and feathered shaft.

The Apache's lean brown face was close to O'Brien's, the features contorted into a mask of hate. Separated as they were by the poles of the corral, the Indian didn't stab the lance at the white man. He drew back his arm and threw it.

Shamus O'Brien was young and his reflexes were good. He twisted away at the last moment, but the hurtling lance still found him. The blade entered his back low, an inch or two from his spine, and he cried out in pain as the honed saber bit deep.

As he staggered a step or two, trying to bring his Henry to bear, all the weight of the bobbing lance shaft stressed its carbon steel blade. The Apache had ground the thick back of the saber to give it an edge and the blade was thin. It snapped somewhere in O'Brien's back and the shaft dropped to the ground.

Waves of agony slamming at him, O'Brien knew he was weakening fast. The horses were more nervous, meaning there had to be another Apache somewhere behind him in the corral, hidden behind the swirling snow. He figured he could count the remainder of his life in seconds.

The Indian who had hit him with the lance made no attempt to climb into the corral. He drew a Joslyn

.44 from a rawhide holster on his hip and shoved the big revolver out in front of him at eye level.

Crazed with pain, O'Brien fired from the hip, levered another round, and fired again. His first shot missed, but the Apache, hit hard, rode the second bullet into eternity.

An arrow hissed like a spiteful snake past O'Brien's left ear. He turned, levered the rifle, and searched for a target. He saw the Apache almost instantly, a stocky warrior wearing a Union army greatcoat with corporal's chevrons on the sleeves.

The day was cold and the Apache's numbed fingers fumbled as he attempted to nock a second arrow. The delay cost him his life.

Levering the Henry as fast as he could, O'Brien pumped three bullets into the Indian, the last two hitting him as he fell.

Beside himself with rage, O'Brien's vision narrowed to a black tunnel shot through with searing streaks of flaming scarlet. He staggered to the dead Apache and slammed bullet after bullet into his face.

"You bastard," he screamed. "You try to kill me on the day my son is born." Shots racketed into the icy wind-lashed day, then the *click, click, click* of the hammer falling on an empty chamber.

O'Brien threw down the Henry and his boot thudded again and again into what was left of the Apache's bloody face.

"Colonel!"

The voice came from behind him. He turned, his

face still twisted and ugly by a mindless rage. Ironside stood in front of him.

"It's over, Colonel. The Apaches are dead or gone."

But O'Brien didn't see Ironside. He saw an Apache warrior with a rifle in his hands, coming at him.

He took a step back, snarling, clawing for his Colt.

Samuel saved Ironside's life that day.

"Pa!" He ran to his father and threw his arms around his waist. "It's me. It's Samuel."

O'Brien looked like a man waking from a dream. He blinked, and then looked down at the boy. "Samuel?"

"Please come home now, Pa. Ma needs you."

The snow did its dervish dance around father and son and the cold air smelled like raw iron. O'Brien's sorrel whinnied and danced on its toes, and white arcs showed in its eyes, made uneasy by the presence of dead men.

"Saraid," O'Brien whispered, as the madness fled his eyes.

Samuel dropped his arms from his father's waist, then stared at his hands, glistening, stained red with blood. "Luther." He held them up for the man to see.

Ironside stepped to O'Brien's side and placed his strong right arm around him. "Time to go home, Colonel."

Shamus O'Brien didn't hear. His eyes closed as he descended into darkness.

Samuel walked a few steps behind as Ironside carried his father into the cabin. He did not take his eyes off his bloody hands . . . a sight he'd remember for the rest of his days.

Chapter Nine

"No, Miz Saraid, you must stay in bed," Nellie said. "You don't have your strength back yet."

Saraid eased back on the pillows, her newborn suckling at her breast. She smiled at the black girl. "Nellie, you're an angel in a man's mackinaw."

She turned her attention back to Ironside. "Tell me again, Luther." Saraid looked exhausted, but her eyes were alive, shadowed with concern. "The truth now. How is my husband?"

Ironside shuffled his feet, not knowing where to cast his gaze. Saraid sympathized with the man and his discomfort, but said nothing.

"Well, ma'am," he said, looking down at his feet, at the ceiling, anywhere but the bed, "the Colonel has a chunk of steel in him that I can't get out." He suddenly looked old, the lines of his face deepening, tight as drawn wires. "It's buried deep and too near the spine, you understand."

"Oh, Miz Saraid," Nellie said, burying her face in her hands.

"What does it mean, Luther?" Saraid's voice was calm, level, a fact that spoke of her inner strength.

The man hesitated a few moments. "If the steel stays, the Colonel will get well again, or he won't."

"Will the lance head move closer to his spine when he moves?"

"I don't know."

The wind talked low around the angles of the cabin, spreading sly lies to the falling snow and shivering trees.

"What can we do, Luther?" Her voice was less calm, less certain.

"There's nothing to do except pray, I guess."

"Will you pray with me, Luther?"

"Saraid, I'm not exactly on speaking terms with God, but if you think it will help, then I surely will."

Samuel stepped through the open door and Ironside forced a smile, pretending a confidence he didn't feel. "How's your pa, boy?"

"Luther, he's hot. I put my hand on his forehead and Pa's real hot."

"Maybe I should damp down the fire," Ironside said. "I'll take a look."

But a different kind of fire burned inside Shamus O'Brien. It was five hours since he'd battled the Apaches and now he fought once more, in single combat against a raging fever.

O'Brien was no longer in the New Mexico Territory. He'd returned to another place and time, as a boy again in a greener, more ancient land. He muttered, smiled, and laughed, bringing substance to memories as faded as mist.

Despite Nellie's protests, Saraid rose from bed, settled the baby, then stepped out of the bedroom and walked to the table where Ironside had laid out her husband. O'Brien lay on his right side so his wound wouldn't come in contact with the rough timber.

A glance told her that Ironside had indeed dug deep. The wound was raw and bloody, open and obscene, like the scarlet mouth of a painted whore.

"Saraid, you get back to bed," Ironside said. "There's nothing you can do here."

The woman, aware of the milk that stained the front of her nightdress, pulled her shawl tighter around her. "My place is here, Luther, at my husband's side."

"The baby—"

"Is asleep. Nellie is with him."

Saraid touched O'Brien's forehead with the back of her fingers. When she looked at Ironside her eyes were bleak. "Luther, Shamus is too hot. If we don't get the fever down it could kill him."

O'Brien raved and jerked on the table, refighting an old, forgotten battle. "Sound retreat!" he muttered. "Cannon . . ." He shook his head. "Too strong . . . cannon . . . retreat . . ."

Ironside listened intently. "I remember that fight. The Colonel was ordered to charge Union batteries, cavalry against cannon. We lost our whole brigade that day."

"Luther, now we have another battle to fight, and

this one, we can't afford to lose." She touched her husband's forehead again. "He's burning up."

Ironside looked lost. "What do we do, Saraid?"

"We must break the fever, quickly, before Shamus dies of it."

Ironside had nothing to offer but another question, so he kept his mouth shut, his eyes on Saraid's face.

"The creek," she said. "And quickly."

Ironside's troubled eyes asked the question that Saraid answered. "It's the quickest way to break the fever, Luther."

"But it could kill him."

"I know. But if we do nothing, he'll be dead by sunrise anyway."

The snow had stopped and the clouds had cleared, revealing a waxing moon that rode night herd on the stars. Patches of wind-drifted snow lay in places and the trees wore virginal mantles of frost. An opalescent light illuminated the way to the creek and beyond in the hills, silvered the coats of a pack of hunting wolves slipping through the pines like phantoms. The night air smelled sharp and of the hard winter.

Shamus O'Brien was a big man and heavy, but Ironside carried him effortlessly. Even through his blanket mackinaw he felt the searing heat of O'Brien's naked body. Beside him Saraid huddled in her husband's army greatcoat and battered campaign hat, her feet shuffling along in a pair of oversized boots.

She carried a folded blanket over her arm she would not wear. It was for Shamus.

To her relief, the bodies of the dead Indians were gone, and their blood no longer stained the ground. As was their custom, the Apaches had taken away their dead.

Try as she might, she could not bring herself to hate the Apaches for what they'd done to her husband. They were a primal force of nature, like the wind or the falling snow, and she did not hate those. Even as she reached the creek, she thought of the Indian women grieving for dead sons on the very day her own son was born.

Ironside stood by the icy bank and glanced at Saraid.

The bottom of her nightdress was wet, and she shivered in the barbed cold.

"Saraid, I think—"

"Put him in the water, Luther. There"—she pointed to a runnel close to the bank—"where the creek runs deeper."

"You should be home, Saraid," Ironside said.

"Do it, Luther."

Gently, like a mother laying her baby in a bath, Ironside lowered O'Brien into the water. The creek ran fast and the icy flow cascaded over the big man's head and body.

Saraid kneeled and helped support her husband's head and chest, making sure his mouth stayed above the surface and his wound did not contact the pebbled bottom of the creek.

He cried out several times, but from the numbing cold of the water or in a dream, neither Saraid nor Ironside knew.

Visible even in the darkness, the creek flowed pink over Ironside's hands for a while as blood from O'Brien's wound stained the water. Then it stopped as suddenly as it had begun.

"Look at the Colonel," Ironside said. "He's white as bone."

"I know," Saraid said. "But I don't believe his fever has broken yet."

"Saraid, we're killing him."

"A while longer, Luther. Just a while longer."

Suddenly Patrick opened up his lungs in the cabin, and Saraid felt the milk start in her breasts.

Ironside looked at her, his face concerned. "Go to the baby. I'll stay here with the Colonel."

Saraid shook her head. "The baby can wait for a while."

The wind had dropped, but it picked up again and rustled restlessly in the trees. One by one the stars winked out as clouds reclaimed the sky, then covered the moon. Snow flurries spun around Saraid and Ironside, and the cold night took on a sharper edge.

A fallen tree branch bumped against O'Brien's shoulder and Ironside reached out and pushed it away.

Saraid pulled her hat further down on her head as the rising wind threatened to steal it, and she huddled deeper into the thin cloth of the greatcoat. Leaning over, she placed her hand over her husband's chest, feeling for his heartbeat. After a while she detected it, faint, but regular, no longer faltering.

Behind her, at the cabin, Patrick loudly screamed his outrage, and Saraid fervently wished she could be in two places at once.

"How much longer, Saraid?" Ironside's mustache and eyebrows were white with snow, giving him the look of an old man.

"I think it's time. If we stay much longer all three of us will freeze to death."

Ironside lifted O'Brien from the icy water. "He's quiet now."

"It's because the fever is down." Saraid wrapped the blanket around her husband, and Ironside carried him to the cabin.

"Saraid, I could stitch up the Colonel's wound," Ironside said. "During the war I saw it done plenty of times."

"No, he must heal from the inside, Luther."

While Ironside held her husband in a sitting position on the bed, Saraid bandaged the gaping wound with strips torn from an old petticoat.

"Lay him back down now, Luther."

"Ma," Samuel said, "will my pa live?"

"Yes, he'll live," Saraid said. "Because I want him to live."

Chapter Ten

New Mexico Territory, 1876

There were some who said Shamus O'Brien was never the same man after the Apaches left their steel in him.

Certainly, he was not as ready to laugh. As the years passed he grew graver, and pain was never far from his eyes, a thing four years of war had not accomplished.

Doctors came and went at Dromore, one of them a famous surgeon from Boston who was on a tour of the western territories. But none would consider cutting for the lance head.

"Too near the spine," they said. "You could be paralyzed for life, Colonel O'Brien, so best to let it stay where it is."

The wound slowed him physically, but his spirit was as strong as ever, and his ranch prospered.

During the ten years that passed after the Apache fight, Saraid gave birth to two more sons, Shawn and

Jacob. She'd badly wanted a girl, but after Jacob was born she was told she could have no more children. She did not grieve for what might have been, but put all her energies into raising her sons well.

A bigger cabin, then a small house, a larger house, then a grand mansion with four white pillars in front grew around the pink hearthstone, which was never moved. O'Brien added a bunkhouse for his hands, and a sprawling complex of outbuildings that gave Dromore the look of a medieval Irish fiefdom.

As his herds grew, he expanded his ranch, adding another two hundred thousand acres of open range to his original land grant. He had twenty men riding for him, all of them tough and good with a gun. Luther Ironside became foreman, and a partner in all but name.

Nellie supervised the household staff, ruled the Chinese cook with a rod of iron, and domineered the punchers every chance she got, insisting on clean hands at the table and please-pass-the-potatoes manners.

Saraid had had a piano delivered to Dromore, hauled by wagon all the way from Santa Fe. To her disappointment Samuel showed no interest, nor did Patrick, though Shawn took to it and Jacob revealed a great deal of talent.

On a Saturday in July, Samuel, now fifteen and man-grown by frontier standards, acquired a third memory that would stay with him to haunt his dreams for years to come.

It began on a morning of glittering heat when a

Dromore puncher by the name of Danny Anderson rode up to the ranch house more dead than alive.

Luther Ironside caught the man as he fell from his horse and eased him gently onto his back. Anderson's shirtfront was splashed with blood, and he had a second lesser wound on his forehead.

"What happened, Danny?" Ironside said, aware that Shamus O'Brien, supported by a cane, had just joined him.

"Rustlers, Mr. Ironside," the young cowboy said. "Hit us south of Starvation Peak an' run off, fifty, maybe sixty head." Anderson winced as a wave of pain hit him. "They shot Shack Caldwell off his horse, an' I don't know if he's alive or dead."

That last gave O'Brien pause. Caldwell was a top hand and a man with a gun rep. Over to the Nations a couple of years back, he'd outdrawn and killed the Texas gunfighter Ryan Buck, a man nobody considered a bargain. If the rustlers had gotten the drop on Shack, they weren't amateurs.

"How many of them were there, Danny?" O'Brien said.

"Five I saw, Colonel." The young puncher hesitated a moment. "I ain't real sure, but I could swear one o' them was Tom Platt."

O'Brien and Ironside exchanged glances. Platt had been fired the week before for stealing a barlow knife from another puncher. An easygoing bunch, there were two classes of men cowboys would not tolerate, cowards and thieves. Platt qualified as the latter. There were some who said he was also in the running for the former, so nobody was sorry to see him go.

O'Brien looked at the wounded puncher, then at Ironside, a question on his face. His foreman gave a barely perceptible shake of his head.

"Luther, carry Danny inside the house and make him comfortable. Then mount up. We're going after those damned animals. I want Isham Banks as scout, and Samuel will ride with us."

A scant ten minutes later Ironside had a dozen armed men mounted, including Samuel, who rode a lanky, American stud, a gift from his father. Banks, a black former mountain man and army scout, had pulled out ahead of the rest, riding across the mesa in the direction of Starvation Peak.

Saraid stepped out of the house and stood by O'Brien's stirrup, looking up at him. "Shamus, I think Samuel is too young to go off chasing rustlers."

"And I think he's old enough, Saraid. The ranch will be his one day, and the sooner he learns how to fight for his land and cattle, the better."

There was gray in Saraid's hair, deeper lines in her face, but she was still a beautiful woman. O'Brien's heart always leapt at the sight of her.

"Will there be a battle, Shamus?"

"That depends on the rustlers."

"You will not leave Samuel behind?"

"No, I won't, Saraid. Today, he'll prove he's a man, and an O'Brien."

Saraid stepped to Ironside and put her hand on his knee. "Luther, take care of my boy." Much overcome, the man said nothing. He touched his hat to Saraid, and then kneed his horse in the direction of the mesa, waving on the rest of the riders.

"Take care, Shamus," Saraid said to her husband.

As Ironside had done before, O'Brien made no answer, but he smiled and nodded. Ahead of him the mesa bulked large against the morning sky and birds sang in the trees.

Standing more than seven thousand feet above the flat, Starvation Peak was a steep-sided mesa that looked like a truncated cone in the distance. Years before, the Apaches had marooned the survivors of a wagon train on the summit, where they all starved to death, hence the name.

Isham Banks, the Dromore horse wrangler, waited until O'Brien and the rest arrived on the bank of a dry creek, a mile west of the peak. "There were more cows taken than Danny reckoned, Colonel. I'd say five men driving a hundred head." He pointed. "Shack's body is over there by the piñon trees. I covered him up the best I could to keep the flies off him."

O'Brien felt that like a blow, and his face stiffened. "Where are they headed, Isham?"

"West, Colonel, toward Apache Mesa. I'd say an hour ahead of us."

"That's rough country, Isham. I don't want to lose them."

"We won't lose them, Colonel. Hell, they've left a trail a hundred yards wide."

"All right, let's get it done."

Chapter Eleven

Samuel O'Brien rode beside his father. They didn't talk, each busy with his own thoughts.

The day's heat lay like a mailed fist on the land. In the distance Apache Mesa was a hazy bulk behind a shimmering veil. The only sounds were the creak of saddle leather and the soft thud of hooves. A couple hands bantered back and forth for a while, but soon fell silent, as though the effort to talk was suddenly too much for them.

The high desert air smelled of piñon and sage, faintly tinged with the musky odor of the cattle that had passed that way only a short time before.

Finally, O'Brien turned to his son. "How are you holding up, boy?"

Samuel nodded. "As well as anybody else, I reckon."

"You scared any?"

"I don't know. Yeah, I guess a little." Samuel gave his father a weak smile. "I'm scared of being scared, Pa."

O'Brien smiled and nodded, and for a moment the pain left his eyes. "That's how I feel and that's how it should be. If it starts to get rough when the guns start shooting, say a Hail Mary. That always works for me when the Apaches are out."

"I'll remember that, Pa." Samuel kept his face straight.

O'Brien nodded. "Now, see to your guns. We should sight those damned bandits soon."

"It's a pity about Tom Platt," Samuel said. "I kinda liked him."

"It's a pity about Danny Anderson and Shack Caldwell," O'Brien said, his mouth a hard tight line under his mustache. "I liked those boys too."

Isham Banks had ridden ahead again. He cantered back, and O'Brien halted his column.

"They hazed the herd into an arroyo, Colonel, and them boys are still in there."

"Isham, is it a box?"

"Looks like, Colonel. I reckon they plan to hold the herd in the arroyo until their buyer shows up." Banks wiped his face with a red bandana. "It's as hot as hell down there near the mesa."

O'Brien's face was grim. "And it's going to get a lot hotter. Lead the way, Isham."

The arroyo cut into the treed hills at the base of Apache Mesa. The ground O'Brien and his men had just crossed, a wide area of brush and cactus flat, stretched in front of it.

He halted the column a hundred yards from the mouth of the arroyo, and Ironside deployed the punchers in a skirmish line on each side of him.

Most carried a Henry, but a few had the new model '73 Winchesters.

"Isham, I'm not going in there after them," O'Brien said. "But you've gotten cows out of slot canyons before, huh?"

"Sure have, Colonel, a heap of times."

"Good. Take Samuel and get up on the top of the arroyo and roust those damned murderers out of there, only use lead, not rocks."

"What about the cattle, Colonel?"

"We'll lose a few, but that can't be helped." He looked at Samuel. "You game, son?"

Samuel nodded, but said nothing. He felt a strange niggling sensation in his belly, a mix of excitement and apprehension.

"Say a Hail Mary, Samuel, remember?"

"I'll remember, Pa."

"Well, that's fine then, just fine. Isham, take my son and go do it."

O'Brien watched Banks and Samuel ride away, his face troubled. The boy had to prove himself, that was necessary for the future of Dromore, but his thoughts kept drifting to Saraid. Rather than bring her home a dead son draped across his saddle, he'd willingly die himself . . . a hundred times over.

"Colonel." Ironside passed field glasses to O'Brien. "I reckon you'll want to keep an eye on Isham. And Sam."

O'Brien nodded. He met Ironside's gaze. "You think I'm asking too much of the boy?"

"Did we ask too much of fifteen-year-old boys at Chickamauga, Chancellorsville, Gettysburg, and all the others?"

After a moment's hesitation, O'Brien said, "Yes, I believe we did."

"Then there's your answer, Colonel."

"Did Saraid put you up to this, Luther?"

"No, I did it my ownself."

"The boy's got to prove himself."

"I think he's already done that, Colonel. Maybe you set too high a standard."

The reports of rifle shots echoed across the flat and stilled the retort on O'Brien's lips. He stood in the stirrups and yelled, "Get ready, boys. They'll be coming."

Ironside's remarks forgiven, O'Brien said, "Makes me wish I had my saber, Luther."

The other man smiled. "Be just like old times, huh, Colonel?"

"Damn right."

Dozens of longhorns boiled out of the arroyo, five riders galloping behind them. Up on the rim, Samuel and Banks fired steadily, and O'Brien saw a man go down.

He motioned with his rifle. "Charge 'em, boys!"

The Dromore riders followed O'Brien, the Texans among them hollering rebel yells. The longhorns split, leaving the surviving rustlers exposed. Firing from the shoulder, O'Brien and his punchers unleashed a storm of lead. Another rustler went down, then a horse.

O'Brien's men surrounded the two mounted outlaws. Both had their hands in the air, grabbing for handfuls of the blue sky. The man whose horse had been shot rose unsteadily to his feet, his boyish, beardless face pale and frightened.

"Tom, I'm sorry to see you in such company," O'Brien told him.

"Sorry, Colonel," Tom Platt said. "Whiskey and loose women drove me to this pass."

"Greed drove you to it, Tom," O'Brien said. "The greed for what belonged to another man, a man who was once your employer."

The two other rustlers were older, one of them with gray in his hair that looked like he'd lived some hard years. The second man was younger, his bold blue eyes defiant.

O'Brien stared at the older rustler. "What's your name?"

"You go to hell," the man said. "If I'd had any kind of fair show with you, I wouldn't have been taken so easily."

"And you?" O'Brien asked the other man. The rustler spat over the side of his horse and said nothing.

O'Brien glanced around his milling riders. "Any of you boys know these two?"

A puncher said, "Yeah, Colonel, I know one of them from when I was a peace officer down Lordsburg way." The man smiled. "The ranny who told you to go to hell is Sonora Steve Warren, a bank and train robber by profession. But times must be hard because he don't usually ride with amateurs." The cowboy nodded at Warren. "Fur piece off your home range, ain't you, Steve?"

"Some, Luke," Warren allowed.

"Anybody recognize the others?" O'Brien said. "Take a look at the dead men."

The two dead rustlers were strangers, not recognized by anyone.

Samuel and Banks rode up and O'Brien said, "You two did well, cleared them out of there just fine. Whose shot killed the one as he left the arroyo?"

Banks shook his head. "Don't rightly know, Colonel. Me and Sam was both shooting."

O'Brien seemed disappointed, but he recovered and smiled. "In any case, what you did was true blue. Well done to both of you."

After the rustlers were disarmed, Ironside said, "Tom, you mount one of the dead men's horses."

"Where are you taking us, Mr. Ironside?" Platt asked, his words thick from a dry mouth.

"To the law, Tom. And that goes for your pals."

"No, I don't think so." O'Brien's face looked as though it had been chiseled from a block of granite. "This is my range, and my cattle that were stolen." His eyes were cold on Ironside's face, all the Irish laughter having fled from them years before. "I'm the law here."

"Colonel, the county sheriff—"

"Has nothing to do with this." O'Brien's horse

tossed its head, the bit chiming. "Isham, find me a tree."

Banks hesitated, his gaze searching O'Brien's face, looking for the smile, the twinkle in the eye that would betray the joke. There was neither.

"Damn you, do it, Isham!"

"Yes, Colonel, right away."

After the wrangler left, Ironside said, "We should let the law deal with these men, Colonel."

"We, Luther? Who are we? Do you see the brand on my horse, the same one as is on the flanks of the longhorns over there?"

"I see it."

"What does it say?"

"It's the Shamrock-D."

"Then there's no 'we,' Luther. The brand is mine and mine alone."

"And I ride for it, Colonel."

"You always have, Luther. Will you back away from it now?"

"As I said, I ride for the brand."

"I did not expect you to say anything less."

"Sam," Tom Platt said, fear chasing across his face like cloud shadows on a prairie, "old times, huh? Remember old times, Sam?"

Samuel O'Brien felt sick. He couldn't meet Platt's eyes.

"Say the words, Sam. Say them to the Colonel. Say you remember the good old times. Let me ride away from here for old times' sake, Sam."

"Tom Platt," Shamus O'Brien said, "make your

peace with God, then take your medicine like a man. My son can do nothing for you now."

Dismounted Dromore hands stood around a dying cottonwood by the bank of a dry wash. The three rustlers sat their horses under a thick, white limb, nooses around their necks.

O'Brien, still in the saddle, looked from one to another. "Sentence has been passed. Do any of you men want to say anything before justice is done?"

"Yeah," Warren said. "You go to hell."

O'Brien's face didn't change. "Anyone else?"

The silent rustler remained silent, his head tilted, his eyes on the sky. Platt, who realized that any hope he might have had was gone, tried his best to die game. "Sam," he said, smiling through tears, "recollect the day we chased them wild turkeys? That was—"

Tom Platt finished that sentence in whatever place awaits dead rustlers. Ironside, sick of the entire business, slapped the horse out from under him, then did the same with the other two.

Shamus O'Brien stared at the swinging bodies for a long time and listened to the creak of the tree limb. Finally he reached into his pocket and withdrew his tally book. He wrote the same two words on three pages: *Cow Thief.* He tore out the pages, rolled each into a tight cylinder, then pushed them one by one into the shirt pockets of the dead men where they'd be seen by others.

Without a word he rode away from the tree and his men followed.

Samuel rode beside Ironside and neither of them felt like talking.

But Samuel O'Brien knew he'd lost something that day. His boyhood had died with Tom Platt and the others.

And he would never get it back again.

Chapter Twelve

Santa Fe, New Mexico Territory, later that year

By the middle of September, the aspens in the Sangre de Cristo Mountains had turned yellow and the skies above Santa Fe were a clear, cobalt blue.

When Samuel O'Brien and Ironside rode into the town, the fiesta season was well under way, and the streets thronged with people. The sporting crowd had already arrived. Elegant gamblers, painted whores on their arms, rubbed shoulders with miners, soldiers, punchers from the surrounding ranches, dance hall loungers, frontier toughs, and the dark, laughing, ever-present Mexicans and their sloe-eyed women.

Huge freight wagons, drawn by ox teams, jostled for space in the clamoring streets. A couple bull-whackers, in a bid to determine who had the right of way, pounded each other in a rolling fistfight in the dust that drew a cheering crowd.

The sharp tang of dried peppers hanging in the

booths lining the streets competed with the musky aromas of perfume, human sweat, spilled beer, and cigar smoke. The stink of fly-blown oxen and horse manure overlaid it all.

Samuel was fascinated by the town's sights and sounds, his eyes wide. "I didn't know there were this many people in the whole world."

Ironside smiled. "It will get busier, Sam. We'll make the deal for the Hereford, then get back to the ranch."

"But we'll stay for a while, huh?" Samuel said.

"Long enough to make a deal with the Scotsman." Ironside looked around him. "Place like this crowds in on a man after a while."

"Not me, Luther," Samuel said. "I would never get bored with this. Not ever."

Dressed in dusty range clothes, they led their horses through the crowds, their eyes searching for the Bon Chance saloon. In his letter, the Scotsman, a cattle broker by the name of McKenzie, wrote that he made the saloon his headquarters and could be found there most times of the day.

Ironside stopped a miner in the street and asked the whereabouts of the Bon Chance. The miner, bearded, belligerent, and already half-drunk, pointed farther along the street. "Down thataway, and be damned to ye fer stopping a Christian man going about his business."

"Friendly town," Ironside said.

But worse, much worse, was to come. And for

Samuel, the day's events would complete the farewell to childhood that began at the hanging of Tom Platt. The man he was destined to become was born that early fall in Santa Fe.

The Bon Chance occupied an entire street corner, with wide tinted glass windows on each side. A porch ran the entire length of the building, held up by ornate iron pillars. A dozen horses stood hipshot at the hitching rails, drowsing in the heat along with the old-timers who sat in rockers on the porch. Nursing beers, they gravely consulted nickel watches the size of saucers, as though their time mattered a damn to them or anyone else.

"Sam," Ironside said as he led the way up the wooden steps to the saloon door, "stay close to me."

"I can take care of myself, Luther," Samuel said with a teenager's confidence.

"Just stay close, is all." Ironside glared at the boy. "And you heed me."

The saloon was crowded with miners, townspeople, mule-whackers, businessmen in broadcloth and high celluloid collars, and a few drovers who were as dusty as Ironside and Samuel. The place had a fair-sized stage and a top floor where cribs were lined up in a row behind the carved wooden rail. A dozen girls in knee-length red, blue, and yellow dresses mingled with the crowd, laughing loud and false at the men's dirty jokes.

The mahogany bar ran the whole length of the saloon. Five exquisite, pomaded bartenders, diamond stickpins glittering in their cravats, served up drinks behind it.

What Ironside saw and Samuel didn't were two young men affecting the fancy garb of professional gamblers sitting at a card table near the far wall. They had a bottle on the table but seemed to drink little, their insolent, challenging eyes constantly scanning the crowd. Both wore tooled cartridge belts, ivory-handled Colts in the holsters.

Ironside recognized them for what they were, wannabe gunmen on the make, eager to kill a man to add to their reps. He decided then and there to step wide around them. Such youngsters would be mighty sudden and quite dangerous.

Angus McKenzie had not exaggerated when he wrote that the saloon was his headquarters. He sat in a far corner behind a huge desk, papers and ledgers spread out on the top. Behind him stood a filing cabinet and an oil lamp. Close at hand was a bottle of whiskey and a glass.

The man himself was small, wizened, his wrinkled face shaded by a green visor. He wore a broadcloth suit, much frayed at the cuffs, and a collarless shirt that had, years ago, been white.

"I think," Ironside said to Samuel, "that's our man."

The ringing of their spurs as they stepped toward McKenzie attracted the attention of the two young men at the card table. The eyes of the taller of the two lingered on Ironside, perhaps noting the older man's graying hair and his high, horseman's way of wearing a gun. One of them said something, making the other laugh, and Ironside became aware. Both men had the cold, reptilian eyes of predators, and he knew he was being targeted.

He ignored the gunmen, his mind on the Hereford bull.

"Are you Mr. McKenzie?" he said when he stopped in front of the desk.

"Who wants to know?" The Scotsman's voice sounded like a rusty gate opening.

"My name is Luther Ironside, foreman of the Shamrock-D. If you are Mr. McKenzie we exchanged letters about—"

"I'm McKenzie and know what we exchanged. Get chairs and sit yourselves down."

The Scotsman waited until Ironside and Samuel were seated, then said, "Are ye sharp set?" Without waiting for an answer he pushed a plate of dried-up cheese and crackers across his desk. "It'll cost you a dollar, though."

Ironside and Samuel declined.

"A drink?" McKenzie lifted his bottle. "That will cost you a dollar as well."

Again the two men refused and the Scotsman didn't try to hide his disappointment. "Weel then," he said, scowling, "since I can see you're all business, Mr. Steelside—"

"Ironside."

McKenzie ignored that and continued, "We'll discuss the Hereford bull."

"Where is he?" Ironside said.

"Weel, he's no in my back pocket, is he? He's biding at a farm a mile out of town. The farmer is charging me ten cents a day for board, the damned robber."

"I'd like to see him. The bull I mean."

"And so ye will, and you'll no see its like again, I tell you that." McKenzie's face grew crafty. "Do you have the siller with ye?"

"I have the money, if that's what you mean," Ironside said, not liking the man.

Though Samuel was interested in the bull, he was much more fascinated by the deep, blue-veined cleavage of the plump woman in a red dress who stood at the bar, smiling at him.

He was vaguely aware that McKenzie was saying, "If I had the bull in Scotland, I'd ask no less than five hundred pound sterling for him, and I'd be taking a loss at that . . ."

The woman winked at Samuel, and he blushed and glanced away.

Filled with a strange urge he'd never felt before, Samuel forced himself to become aware of the conversation again.

"Surely, sir, ye jest," McKenzie said. "Three hundred dollars for a fine bull like the one I have not a mile from here? I'll take six hundred, and at that such a loss I'll end up in the poorhouse."

As the bargaining went back and forth, the plump woman walked to Samuel and stood by his chair, her small, rounded belly just inches from his face.

Ironside glared at her. "Beat it, Rosie. We're talking business here."

"My name's Chastity," the woman said.

"He's too young," Ironside said, smiling. "He's fifteen and he's been raised gentle."

The woman took off Samuel's hat and ran her fingers through his hair. "I've never seen hair like this, as yellow as sunlight."

Samuel blushed, and for the want of anything else to say, he managed, "My ma cuts it."

"Well now," the woman said, her voice too loud, "isn't that a good boy."

Over at the card table, the two young men laughed, and Samuel blushed a deeper red.

"Have you ever thrown a leg over the bucking pony before?" Chastity said.

Samuel was unaware of the reference, but was smart enough to understand its meaning. He shook his head, his ears bright red.

McKenzie leaned across the table, scowling. "She's talking about the carnal pleasures of the flesh, boy, sinful pleasures to be sure."

"I know," Samuel said, still blushing.

Ironside had been watching intently, and then made up his mind. "How much, Rosie?"

"For you or the virgin?"

"For him."

The woman's eyes hardened. "Two dollars. It will be quick."

Ironside reached into his pocket and brought out a coin. "Here's five. Teach him all you know."

"That's a lot."

"Teach him. I don't ever want to see him get red in the face with a woman again. It ain't manly."

"Then it's agreed," Angus McKenzie said. "Four hundred and fifty dollars for the bull, and you've robbed me."

Ironside smiled. "Mr. McKenzie, I don't think you've ever been robbed in your life."

The Scotsman grinned for the first time that day. "Yer no tellin' a lie, Mr. Ironside, but you paid a fair price for the bull. Now I'll give you a bill of sale."

McKenzie pretended to busy himself with the papers on his desk. Without looking up, he said, "Beware, Mr. Ironside."

"I see them."

His eyes still on his desk, the Scotsman said, "The laddie on the left killed a man a couple days ago, right here in the saloon. He's very skilled with the revolver."

Ironside nodded. "I would guess he is."

"And the other lad is just as quick."

"I have no quarrel with them."

"But I think they have with you." He looked up for the first time. "Those old breeks you're wearing are

Confederate cavalry issue. I know, since I wore the gray myself."

"I reckon their heads are full of strange Yankee notions," Ironside said. "I'll step clear of them."

"You and the boy, if he ever gets done with that fancy woman."

McKenzie dropped his head again, picked up a pen, and scrawled a bill of sale. Then he told Ironside how to get to the farm.

"Now, if ye don't like the bull for any reason, you just come back here and I'll refund your money," the Scotsman said. "Of course, I'll have to deduct a hundred dollars for expenses, you understand."

"What expenses?" Ironside said.

"Oh weel, wear and tear on the bull and the extra paperwork. It all adds up, you know."

"Mr. McKenzie, I have the feeling you'll end up a millionaire."

"And what makes you think I'm no one already?" The Scotsman's eyes twinkled.

Fifteen minutes later Samuel came down from a crib upstairs, Chastity hanging onto his arm.

"Sam did just fine." She smiled. "As a teacher, I'm a credit to my lousy profession."

"How are you feeling, Sam?" Ironside said.

The boy grinned. "Good, real good. It was fun."

"It usually is. Now let's get the Hereford bull and head home." Ironside rose from his chair and stabbed a finger at Samuel. "Don't tell your mother what happened or she'll skin us alive, then have us doing penance for the next year."

"Aye, that's right, because in the female mind there's no greater sin than fornicatin' with loose women," McKenzie said.

"There are some things Ma doesn't have to know," Samuel said.

He and Ironside shook hands with McKenzie and stepped toward the saloon door.

Then big trouble came down.

Chapter Thirteen

"Hey, cowboy!"

It was not a friendly greeting, it was a challenge. The edged words cut through the clamor of the saloon like a knife.

Ironside, a man with nothing to prove, would've kept on walking, leaving the threat to hang in the air and wither like a leaf. But Samuel, younger, less wise, turned.

Ironside realized the boy had made a mistake and cursed under his breath, but he stood by Samuel's side, his eyes on the two grinning young men walking slowly toward them. He knew there was no way out of it. Maybe there had never been.

Both men had killed before, and they were eager to stack up against somebody and kill again. He could read that in their eyes. Their white-handled Colts hung lower than most, and the younger man on the left was pulling on skintight black gloves, a tinhorn's trick used to scare and intimidate. It might have worked on farm boys, but not on Luther Ironside.

"Are you talking to me?" he said.

"Yeah, you, and your boy there." The man's eyes shifted to Samuel. "What the hell were you doing with my woman, boy?"

"I'm not a boy," Samuel said, his anger flaring.

"My woman says you are, says you pecked away at her like a scared little chicken."

"Take it easy, Sam," Ironside said. To the grinning gunmen he said, "If you're trying to pick a fight, pick it with me. I'm the one who paid the whore."

"You calling my woman a whore, old Johnny?"

Ironside smiled. "Yeah, I took you for some kind of Yankee, all gab and no guts." He was sick of this; sick of the two wannabe bad men, sick of the pre-gunfight ritual they felt was necessary. "My talkin' is done, boy. Now let's open the ball. Skin your iron and get to your work."

The youngster knew he'd made a mistake. The big man with gray hair showing under his hat was not scared, but was standing easy, confident, waiting to make his move, almost relaxed. The thought clamored into the gunman's head, *Damn it, he's been through this before.*

His voice thick, the man said, "My quarrel's not with you." He looked at Samuel, an easier target. "It's with him, the damned woman-stealer."

Samuel stood still, as though he'd absorbed the insult and had decided to let it go. But he was Shamus

O'Brien's son, descended from a people with an ancient fighting tradition, and he would not back off. Samuel would take only so much sass and he'd reached his limit.

He drew and fired.

Shock. Horror. Disbelief. One by one the emotions registered in the young gunman's face. When Samuel made his play, the gunfighter had gone for his own gun. Too slow. Samuel's bullet crashed into the man's chest, high center, and he staggered back a step, then dropped to his knees, stunned at the time and manner of his dying.

"I'm out of it! Don't shoot!" The second gunman's hands were in the air. He looked like he'd just been punched hard in the belly.

"Unbuckle the gun belt, let it drop," Samuel said, gun smoke wreathing around him.

Beside him, his own Colt still in the leather, Ironside stared at Samuel as though he was seeing a complete stranger.

The thud of the gun belt hitting the floor was loud in the hushed room.

"Take him out," Samuel said, nodding at the dead man on the floor. "Find him an undertaker."

A couple men stepped to the body, but Samuel's cold voice stopped them. "Not you." He pointed to the gunman. "Him."

The man hesitated; saw something in Samuel's eyes he didn't like, then bent to his task. He dragged his friend out the saloon door, and a rush of conversation began.

Ironside silenced it. "All of you saw it. He was notified."

"What was his name?" Samuel asked. When nobody answered he asked again. "Anybody know his name?"

Chastity stepped forward. "Yeah, he called himself the Blue Springs Kid. He'd told me he'd seen the elephant and had killed seven men, and that's all I know about him." She looked at Samuel. "You learn everything fast, don't you, my boy?"

"I'm not your boy or anybody else's boy," Samuel said.

The woman nodded. "No, I guess you're not."

Ironside and Samuel were on Dromore land, the big Hereford bull plodding in front of them. Between them there had been little talk since Santa Fe, both men marooned on an island of their own thoughts.

When Samuel saw the mesa and the big house of Dromore in the distance, he said, "Will the bull live through the winter?"

"Yes, Sam, I believe he will," Ironside said.

"He must if he's to improve the herd. Four hundred and fifty dollars is a considerable capital investment for one bull."

"He's not a longhorn, but he's tough."

"I want to see Hereford crossbreeds come spring," Samuel said.

Ironside smiled. "I can't guarantee it, but I'm pretty sure you will."

Samuel turned his head and stared at the older man. "I don't want pretty sure, I want certain."

"Then, I'm certain you'll have calves on the ground."

"You will see to it, Luther."

"Yes, boss."

The word had come out unbidden, and the wonder of it was that neither Ironside nor Samuel thought it amiss.

Chapter Fourteen

Dromore, Fall 1885

The circle of the years rolled on at Dromore as the O'Brien brothers grew to manhood. Despite blizzards, years of drought, and the depredations of the Apache, the ranch continued to prosper. By 1885, Shamus O'Brien had shipped sixty thousand cattle north to feed the burgeoning cities and very few of them were longhorns. The backbone of his cattle operation was a dozen vaqueros up from the Mexican border who worked for him full-time, half of them settled on Dromore land with their families. Fifty seasonal cowboys were hired every spring.

Saraid had been ailing for years, but had managed to educate her sons and turn Jacob into an accomplished pianist. She worried constantly about her youngest son. The strange darkness hidden deep in the Celtic soul had manifested itself in him. He was a startling contrast to his brothers, physically and mentally. Whereas Samuel, Pat, and Shawn were blond and blue eyed, Jacob was black of hair and eyes, a throwback to the ancient people of Ireland who were there before the arrival of the fair Celts.

Samuel was twenty-four, a serious, driven man who took over more and more of the day-to-day operations of the ranch as his father aged. The old injury caused by the Apache had finally taken its toll. Shamus could no longer walk far, and used a wheelchair most of the time. But Samuel smiled often, something Jacob rarely did.

Shawn was handsome, happy-go-lucky, with a fine singing voice and an eye for the ladies, who adored him in turn. He was fast with a gun, and displayed his shooting prowess often, something that irritated Jacob, who was even faster and more accurate, but never revealed it to anyone.

Patrick, bookish and bespectacled, was also an easygoing man. With a love of literature, he worshipped at the altar of Sir Walter Scott, but claimed Mr. Dickens knew more about the human condition than anyone else on earth.

All four brothers were top hands and had earned the respect of the vaqueros, an honor they did not bestow easily or often. But they were always wary of Jacob, their laughing, carefree Hispanic nature at odds with a man of black moods and deep depressions, capable of explosive rages and brooding silences.

Settlements had grown up between Dromore and Santa Fe and other ranchers had moved into the area. For a while, people had come from miles around to hear Jacob play Chopin, but the young man's hair-trigger temper and the threat of the violence that seethed just under the surface of his nature soon drove them all away.

Saraid, her dazzling beauty destroyed by the cancer that consumed her, refused to confine herself to her bedroom. She lay on a couch in the living room where she could see her pink hearth, now supporting an ornate marble mantel and fireplace where a huge log burned.

"Is he gone again, Shamus?" Saraid asked.

Her husband nodded. "He rode out just before sunup."

"Where does he go?"

O'Brien smiled. "Wherever the trail goes, I guess. Jacob is like a ship. He sets sail and the wind blows him this way and that."

"I worry about him, Shamus. I worry about him constantly."

"Yes, we all do."

O'Brien rolled his wheelchair closer to the bed. "I have good news, mavourneen."

Saraid smiled. "And I can see that you're impatient to tell me."

"This morning I made Samuel the new master of Dromore."

"And his brothers?"

"They'll each have a share, though Jacob told me to give his portion to the others. He wants no part of the life his brothers have chosen."

Saraid thought for a while. In a tired voice, she asked, "And what of you, Shamus?"

"You mean what of *us*?"

"Yes, what of us?"

"This is our home and here we will stay." He held his wife's hand. "I'm an old man, Saraid, but I can still give advice."

She laughed, and for a fleeting moment she looked like the girl she'd been when they first came to the valley. "You're forty-three, Shamus, hardly an old man."

"Well, I can't ride and I can barely walk. Are those not the traits of an old man?"

Saraid shook her head. "Shamus, you'll never be old." She pointed. "Go over there and stand on the hearthstone."

"I'll do it, if I can."

"You can, Shamus."

O'Brien rolled over to the fireplace and struggled out of his chair, the old Apache lance head slowing his movements.

He stood on the hearth, facing his wife. "Well?"

"Get your pipe from the mantle and hold it."

"'Tis strange things you're asking me to do, Saraid," he said, smiling.

He got his pipe and stood wide-legged on the hearthstone, a gray-haired, stocky man, with eyes that were still a piercing blue.

Saraid smiled. "Yes, that is how I will always remember you. Shamus, you are still the squire of Dromore and all the land around."

Saraid died a month later, just as the first snow of winter drifted past the windows of Dromore.

As fate would have it, Jacob returned to the ranch on the day of his mother's funeral. He stood by her grave at the base of the mesa, his head bowed in the falling snow. But he shed no tears, though his grief was immense.

He'd always been his ma's favorite and he'd bonded with her, as he had with no other person. His love for his mother went deep. Her death devastated him, plunging him into a depression as black as night.

He stood next to Lorena at the graveside. Pregnant, she swayed and almost fainted. He put his arm around her and held her, though he did not utter a word of comfort.

People had come long distances for the funeral. The women were dressed in unrelieved black; the menfolk wore mourning garments over their clothes, as was the custom of the time.

The vaqueros and their wives and children kneeled in prayer on the icy ground, whispering to each other that Saraid had died a *Santisima Muerte*, a Most Holy Death.

As the coffin was lowered into the ground, in his fine tenor voice, Shawn sang "Abide with Me" and his mother's favorite Irish hymn, the old folk song "Be Thou My Vision."

Luther Ironside, snow flecking his mustache and

beard, stood like a graven statue, a hard-living man who did not know how to give expression to the grief that tore at him.

At the wake, Jacob drank little, spoke less, and was relieved to quit the crowded living room when his father called him into his study. He pushed his pa's wheelchair beside the fire, and sank into the leather chair opposite.

The death of Saraid had worn on Shamus and he looked years older. His movements were slow and two kinds of pain showed in his eyes, the pain of Saraid's passing and the constant agony of the Apache lance head.

Jacob rose, stepped to the drinks cabinet and poured brandy into two crystal glasses. He passed one to his father and sat again. He raised his glass. "To my mother, the kindest, most wonderful woman who ever lived."

"Amen," Shamus said, drinking, hiding the tears in his eyes with the rim of his glass.

Jacob had became a man that winter, a tall, muscular man with the dusky face of an Indian. Craggy black brows overhung his dark eyes, and under his great beak of a nose grew a thick dragoon mustache, his only vanity. Even dressed in broadcloth, he looked out of place amid the fussy Victorian splendor of his father's study. Restless, fierce, lonely, he was a man more suited to the wild mountains or perhaps life on a trading schooner, sailing halfway around the world to far countries.

Shamus, who had spent his life among strong and violent men, recognized that, young as he was, his son was a man to be reckoned with.

"Your mother asked for you before she died," Shamus said.

"Yes, Samuel told me so," Jacob said. "I'm sorry I wasn't here."

"So was your mother," Shamus said.

Jacob made no answer, for he was not a man for excuses. He lit a cigar and waited for his father to speak again.

"Where were you, Jacob?"

"South of here, seeing places I'd never seen before. I go wherever my will takes me."

"You go to places where no one is glad at your coming or sad at your leaving. Unless, that is, you consort with whores."

"Unlike Shawn or Patrick, I don't have the face for any other kind of woman."

"You should be like Samuel. He has never been attracted to loose women and now he has a fine wife, who's already bearing him a son."

Jacob nodded. "Sam is like Ma's hearthstone. You've built this ranch around him." He smiled. "He's the rock of Dromore."

"I want you to stay, Jacob," Shamus said. "A share of Dromore is yours."

"I don't want it, Colonel. I'm man grown and I go my own way."

"How will you live?"

"I'll get by. My needs are few."

Shamus held out his glass, and Jacob rose. He refilled it, and his.

Talking to his son's back, Shamus said, "I was speaking to John Moore, the Santa Fe lawyer. He says you could go east to the big cities and become a concert pianist."

Jacob handed his father's glass to him. "I play for my own enjoyment, Pa. Besides, I'd go crazy in a city."

"You'll go crazy anyway if you continue to drift aimlessly like a rudderless ship."

Jacob again retreated into silence.

To the Colonel, life and all it represented was Dromore. But the ranch stifled Jacob O'Brien, and even as he sat in his father's study, the portrait of Robert E. Lee above the mantel staring down at him with faint disapproval, he felt the walls closing in on him.

Shamus sighed, a long, drawn-out exhalation that signaled pain and resignation. "We should get back to the others. Saraid would expect it of us."

Jacob rose to his feet and put his hands on the back of his father's wheelchair.

"No," Shamus said, his hands on the rubber-rimmed wheels. "Open the door for me, the rest I'll do for myself."

Jacob felt like a puncher who'd just been fired before the spring roundup was over. An hour later, after saying good-bye to no one, he saddled his horse and rode away from Dromore.

Chapter Fifteen

Dromore, Spring 1886

"There's three of them, Colonel, that I saw anyway," Luther Ironside said.

"Any sign of Nellie?"

"No sir, unless she was in the cabin."

"What about the surrey and the Morgan?"

Ironside shook his head.

Shamus O'Brien sat in his wheelchair on his porch in the morning light, and his eyes ranged over Ironside's exhausted vaqueros. They'd been searching for Nellie for five days and were totally used up.

"I claim the open range up by Lone Mountain, Luther," he said. "You figure those three are nesters?"

Ironside shook his gray head. "They didn't look like nesters to me, more like outlaws or rustlers. Those boys wore guns like they were born to them."

"You were right not to tackle them by yourself, Luther," Samuel O'Brien said.

"Well, boss, the hands were scattered, searching all

over, and I reckon I could've rounded up a few, but they're worn out. They set store by Nellie, and none of them has slept in days."

"For sure they don't look in any shape for a gun-fight, if it came to that," Samuel said.

Ironside was covered in dust, and his face was drawn tight with exhaustion.

"Luther, dismiss the men and get some rest," O'Brien said.

"What about Nellie, Colonel?" Ironside said.

"Nellie is part of Dromore and Saraid loved her like a sister. If she's in the cabin, I'll get her."

"A few hours' sleep and we'll be ready to ride, Colonel," Ironside said.

"Yes, sleep for a while and we'll talk about this again."

After Ironside and his vaqueros left, Samuel said, "I sure hate to lose that amount of time. If the three men Luther saw kidnapped Nellie, they could move on and take her with them."

"We won't lose time, Samuel. You, Patrick, and Shawn are going after her." O'Brien rolled his chair closer to his son. "When they stole Nellie, they stole from Dromore, and I won't let that go unpunished."

"Pa, Patrick and Shawn are pretty well used up themselves. They scouted all the way to Camaleon Draw and didn't get in until well after midnight."

"They are my sons. They will be ready to ride. Now go rouse them and tell them to arm themselves."

Samuel stepped toward the door into the house, but his father's voice stopped him. "Samuel, if those three men took Nellie and have harmed her in any way, I don't want them brought back to Dromore alive."

Samuel heard and nodded, his face stiff. He walked into the house to wake his brothers.

Shamus remained on the porch, drinking the strong coffee his black butler had brought him. To the east the sun had just cleared the El Barro Peaks and its light lay on top of the silent mesa like a blessing. The sky was barred with bands of purple, scarlet, and jade, and he smelled pine in the cool air. Some of his Herefords were drinking at the creek, ripples of water circling out from their soft muzzles.

His butler returned with a thick sandwich of sourdough bread and sizzling bacon, cut in neat triangles, carefully arranged on a china plate. He made to lay a napkin on O'Brien's lap, but the colonel waved him away.

"Colonel, you must eat. As it is, you barely eat enough to keep a bird alive."

"I'll eat when Nellie is back at Dromore," O'Brien said.

"But, Colonel—"

"Go away, John, and stop fussing."

"But . . . but . . ."

"Damn ye for a pest, John," O'Brien said. "Leave the bloody sandwich on the table beside me and I'll eat it later."

"Make sure you do, Colonel. I'll be back to check on you."

"I'll eat it. Now scat."

O'Brien glared at the man as he left, then worried some more about Nellie. She'd taken Saraid's death hard, but had continued to rule the household staff of Dromore with a rod of iron. Nellie had also gained a reputation as a midwife, and was on her way back from delivering a baby at a ranch near Big Draw when she disappeared.

O'Brien felt a spike of anger. If Nellie had indeed been kidnapped, it was a direct attack on Dromore and an affront to himself. In the past he'd hanged men for less.

Patrick and Shawn led their horses to the front of the house, their faces puffy from lack of sleep. Shawn, who always slept late, was in a sour mood, forced to postpone a trip to Santa Fe where he was sparking a brewer's pretty daughter. Samuel followed with his own horse.

"Bring Nellie back, boys," Shamus O'Brien said. "Dromore is not the same without her."

The O'Brien brothers were mounted and ready to leave when a Mexican boy astride a skinny, mouse-colored mustang rode up to the house and slid off the pony's bare back.

Looking up at the three riders, he said, "*Tengo un mensaje para el Señor O'Brien.*"

"Give it here, boy," Samuel said.

The boy withdrew a note from inside his shirt

and handed it to Samuel. He read it, and wordlessly passed the note to Patrick.

"Hell, what does it say?" Shamus said.

Patrick kneed his horse closer to the porch and handed the note to his father. "Read it for yourself, Pa."

Shamus took a pair of round glasses from his vest pocket and laid them on his nose. His face turned black with rage as he read the scrawled words.

"What's it about, Pa?" Shawn said, temporarily forgetting the brewer's daughter.

Shamus's face was like thunder. "It says, 'Bring thirty thousand dollars or the woman dies.'"

"Do you speak any English, boy?" Shawn asked.

"Some. But I don't like to."

"You're a damned little bandito." Shawn tossed the boy a silver dollar, which he deftly caught. "Now do you speak English?"

"Yes, I remember," the boy said.

"When did you get this?"

"A man came to my parents' farm last night and said to take this message to the Dromore ranch. I told him I knew the way and he gave me a dollar."

"You'll get rich one day, kid," Shawn said. "Where did the man say we should take the money?"

"He has a cabin near Lone Mountain. I can show you the way for a dollar, no, two dollars."

Shawn looked at his father. "What do you say, Pa?"

Beside himself with anger, Shamus yelled, "John! Come here, damn your eyes!"

The butler hurried onto the porch.

Shamus, his anger making him louder still, roared, "Get a carpetbag and fill it with newspaper or whatever else you can find. Bring it here."

The butler hesitated, his face puzzled.

Shamus roared, "Now, damn it!"

After John scurried away, Shamus said, "Samuel, saddle the buckskin. I'm going with you."

"Pa, you can't ride." Samuel was horrified.

"Then you'll rope me to the horse."

Samuel sat his saddle, staring numbly at his father.

"Jesus, Mary, and Joseph," Shamus cried out, "does no one at Dromore obey me any longer?"

Like a man waking from sleep, Samuel said, "I'll get the horse, Colonel."

"Smartly now," Shamus called after him. "By God, Dromore is at war."

Chapter Sixteen

Shamus O'Brien, roped to his saddle, led the way northwest across the rolling country under a high, scorching sun. Ahead of him rode the Mexican boy, who occasionally turned and pointed the way to Lone Mountain, a place the O'Briens already knew.

The peak was surrounded by hill country covered with piñon, wild oak, and juniper. Ponderosa pine and aspen grew on the taller ridges. Here and there Dromore cattle grazed in shaggy meadows, often joined by small herds of antelope.

The land around Shamus was glorious, but he had little eye for its wild beauty, nor did he heed the heady scent of the spring wildflowers.

He rode deep in thought, the pain in his lower back gnawing at him like a rabid beaver. The ransom note had come late, probably when Nellie eventually revealed that she was from Dromore. The kidnappers had suddenly seen their chance and taken it. The carpetbag, bulging with paper and empty burlap sacks, hung on Shawn's saddle horn. Shamus smiled to himself, his face grim. He'd pay all right, but in lead, not gold.

The four riders took a cattle and game trail that climbed upward toward a pine-covered saddleback, a clearing about twenty-five yards wide at its crest. Had the Apaches not been far to the south raiding with old Geronimo, the O'Briens would've approached the gap in the trees with more caution. But, led by the colonel, they rode into the clearing . . . and into an ambush.

"Hold it right there."

A man wearing a black-and-white cowhide vest stepped out of the trees, a Greener in his hands. A second man, also holding a shotgun, walked out of the pines opposite.

Vest Man read something in Shamus's eyes and said, "Don't get any ideas, Pops."

"I don't argue with scatterguns," he said.

"You got the money?" Vest Man was a tall, gangling drink of water, and he grinned constantly, something that always put the colonel's teeth on edge.

"I have the money," he said. "All of it. Do you have the woman?"

"We've got her. She's back at the cabin with the boss."

"And who might he be?" Samuel spoke for the first time.

"Maybe it's best you don't know, cowboy," Vest

Man said. "I don't want to scare you away afore the money is paid."

"Mister," Samuel said, "I don't scare easily."

"All right. Does the name Jesse Tanner mean anything to you?"

"Not a damn thing," Samuel said.

But Shawn had heard the name before. Jesse Tanner was an outlaw and sometime lawman out of Deaf Smith County, Texas. He was a named gun hand of reputation, and the talk was that he'd killed six men in draw fights. Shawn didn't know if that was true or not, but he'd no doubt that Tanner was a bad one, and lightning fast with the Colt.

Samuel's answer to the outlaw's question had irritated the man, and it showed. "Let's see the money."

"You'll see the money when we see Nellie," Shamus said.

"You're difficult," Vest Man said.

"Uh-huh, can't argue with that," Shamus said.

"Only a damned Irishman would be difficult."

Shamus nodded. "Yes, that is so."

Vest Man thought it over for a while, and then became more aggressive with the business end of the Greener. "You boys shuck your guns." He pointed into the trees. "See that boulder there? We'll pile 'em up for you on top of that, and you can pick them up on your way back."

"Leave us our rifles," Samuel said. "The Apaches are out."

"There ain't an Apache within miles of here," Vest Man said. "Now shuck them guns like I told you."

The outlaw saw the O'Briens hesitate and he pinned his grin back in place. "Boys, if'n you don't drop your guns it will lead to a shootin'. An' ol' Jesse says to tell you that if he hears a gunshot, just one, he'll gut that woman like a hog." He moved the muzzle of the shotgun until it pointed at Shawn. "I'm pegging you for the gun hand, handsome. You'll git it first."

"Drop your guns, boys," Shamus said. "I won't endanger Nellie's life."

"But, Pa—"

"Do as I say." Shamus unbuckled his gun belt and let it drop to the ground. His rifle followed. The O'Brien brothers did the same.

Vest Man's grin stretched. "Now that's what I call bein' right sensible." He looked at his companion. "Lem, pick up them guns and stack them over there where I said."

"Mister," Shamus said to Vest Man, "you're a sorry piece of trash."

"Yeah, and you may be a damned foreign Irishman lording it over half of creation, but I can still blow you clean out of that saddle if I hear any more of your sass."

"Pa," Patrick said, "let it go. We came here to rescue Nellie, remember."

"Since I'm a sorry piece of trash, maybe I don't

understand the words real good, but it seems to me you should've said ransom. Not rescue."

"Yes," Patrick said. "You're right, and I stand corrected."

"Rescue sets better with me," Shawn said.

Vest Man gave him a mean look. "Don't get any fancy ideas, handsome. I can gun you an' spoil them good looks real easy."

The hogback led down into a canyon about a hundred yards wide. After a mile or so, the walls opened into a flat and Lone Mountain came into view. Behind it the peaks of the saw-toothed Ortiz Mountains stood purple against the sky.

A cabin stood near the base of the mountain, near what looked like the entrance to an abandoned mine shaft. The cabin was a windowless log structure that probably dated from the 1850s, when hard-rock miners had moved into the area. They'd moved on after they failed to hit pay dirt.

Shamus kneed his horse closer to Shawn. "In the carpetbag," he whispered.

Shawn nodded, knowing instantly what his father meant.

Shamus had seen Shawn use a gun and he reckoned of all his sons, only Jacob was better, and not by much, though that narrow margin was the difference between life and death.

The outlaw named Lem rode on ahead. He drew

rein at the cabin and yelled, "Jesse, it's me. We got the money."

The door opened and a tall man stepped outside. He wore a frilled white shirt and tight riding breeches tucked into English boots. His hair was long and fell over his shoulders in cascading black waves. His crossed gun belts held a pair of Colts, the holsters low on his thighs.

This was a flashy, tinhorn rig, a fact that did not escape Shawn O'Brien.

Tanner was a draw fighter all right, and Shawn knew he'd be almighty sudden. Such men went into a gunfight like coiled springs, their nerves taut as violin strings. It was the very source of their speed. The sudden release of this tension manifested itself in explosive motion, giving them the edge. But facing unarmed men, Tanner was relaxed, smiling, his fast draw distant from his mind.

When Shamus and his sons drew rein, Tanner said, "Why, Colonel O'Brien as ever was. It is indeed a great honor to meet you, sir. You are a true hero of the South."

Shamus ignored that. "Where's Nellie?"

"In the cabin, of course."

"If you've harmed her, Tanner, I'll—"

"You'll do nothing, Colonel. I can't abide threats from a man in no position to make them. Can you, sir? I mean, really?"

Tanner affected the costume and manners of a Southern gentleman, but Shamus considered him white trash, and he was not a man to hold back his opinions.

"Get Nellie out here, you damned thief."

"Thief, am I?" Tanner said, his face reddening.

"When you took Nellie you stole from Dromore, and that makes you a common thief and criminal. Now get her out here."

Tanner's men had dismounted. Rifles at the ready, they flanked him, tense.

"Since you wish for no courtesy between us," Tanner said, "I'll get right to the point—show me the ransom money."

Shawn O'Brien held up the carpetbag. "I have the thirty thousand here. You'll get it when we see that Nellie is unhurt."

"We had some fun with her, is all," the man in the cowhide vest said. "She's a mite wore out, but she ain't hurt." He grinned. "You know how it is when men pass a woman around."

"No, I don't." Shawn opened the carpetbag. "I have the money, now show me Nellie."

Tanner stared hard at Shawn, his instincts clamoring. The O'Brien brother had the look and self-assurance of a gun hand. He'd be dangerous in a fight, if he were armed.

The outlaw relaxed a little. Without looking away from Shawn, he said, "Hank, get her out here."

The man in the vest said, "You sure, Jesse? We don't have to show these people nothing."

"You heard me, Hank, get her out here."

His face ugly, Hank stepped into the cabin and

returned with Nellie. He threw her onto the ground. "There you are, good as new. Now you 'uns can wear her out."

"Nellie, get over here," Shamus said.

The woman rose to her feet and stumbled toward him, but Tanner's voice stopped her. "You stay right there, woman. First, the money, Colonel, then we'll parley some more."

"My talking is done, especially to a lowlife like you, Tanner," Shamus said.

"Yeah, well maybe I've decided to keep her. If that turns out to be the case"—Tanner smiled—"it'll cost you a heap more than thirty thousand to get her back."

"Are you reneging on our deal, Tanner?" Shamus said.

"Seems like, don't it?" Tanner turned to Hank. "Get the bag." To Shamus he said, "While we count the money I'll decide if you can have the woman back or not."

Shawn tensed, his hand near the open top of the bag. He was ready to throw the dice. But the Mexican boy decided it was the moment to cut and run.

All three outlaws turned their heads to look after the fleeing boy. Shawn plunged his hand into the bag and found a three-inch barreled Colt. It was a gun for close work, but it would do.

Hank carried his rifle, unhandily, in his right hand. His eyes widened in horror as Shawn brought his revolver up and fired. The bullet crashed into the middle of Hank's forehead, and before he hit the ground, Shawn had already kicked his horse toward Tanner, the more dangerous of the two surviving kidnappers.

Tanner was surprised, but he recovered quickly. His Colt cleared leather as Shawn swung his mount to the right and lashed out at the gunman with his left boot. The kick caught Tanner square in the chest. He made an "*Oof*" sound as the air drove out of his lungs and he fell back against the cabin wall.

The man named Lem stepped to the side, his rifle coming up to his shoulder. He and Shawn fired at the same time. Lem's bullet split the air beside Shawn's right ear, but the outlaw staggered back a step when Shawn's bullet hit him low in the belly. The man sank to his knees and Shawn was vaguely aware that Samuel had charged his horse at Tanner.

Samuel launched himself from the saddle and tackled the gunman. Both men fell to the ground, Samuel punching hard on his way down.

Screaming obscenities, Lem tried to get to his feet and Shawn shot him a second time. The man went down and stayed down.

Shawn controlled his rearing horse and turned in time to see Samuel haul Tanner to his feet and connect with a tremendous right hook to the jaw that sent the outlaw crashing to the ground, his chin hanging slack.

"Samuel, get that piece of trash to his feet," Shamus said. He yelled to Shawn, "Bring me the Colt, Patrick."

Patrick kneed his horse to Shamus's side and handed him the revolver. "Samuel, stand clear there," his father said.

Samuel picked up the gun Tanner had dropped, jerked the one from his left-hand holster and stepped aside.

"Jesse Tanner," Shamus said, grim and terrible, his eyes on fire, "you stole from Dromore when you took this woman captive. That is a thing I cannot forgive or forget. An attack on Dromore is an attack on me and my kin and it can't be allowed to stand. I've hanged better men than you for stealing a single cow, not because they were thieves, but because the theft of just one steer weakened Dromore in the eyes of men and God."

His eyes locked on Shamus's terrifying, merciless face, all the self-assurance went out of Jesse Tanner. Without his guns, the man seemed to shrink, becoming less significant.

"Have you anything to say?" Shamus said. "I will wait if you wish to bow your head in prayer."

Tanner said nothing. Then he salvaged some dignity and stood tall, his eyes defiant. "Get it over with, damn you."

"Then go to your Maker with a curse on your lips."

Shamus fired, and shot again. Tanner fell, and all the life in him fled.

The Colonel turned and looked one by one at his sons. "I will not tolerate any attack on Dromore, and when I'm gone, neither will any of you."

He waited, got no answer, and said, "Samuel?"

After a moment's hesitation, Samuel said, "It will be as you say, Colonel."

"Patrick?"

"As you say, sir."

"Shawn?"

"Dromore will always be, Pa. And I will do my best to make it so."

Shamus smiled. "Then I am well content. Let us go home now."

Chapter Seventeen

Dromore, Winter 1886

The terrible winter of 1886 that devastated the cattle industry from Montana to Texas spared Dromore, a blessing Shamus O'Brien ascribed to the will of God.

The O'Brien brothers and the vaqueros were out all winter long, checking on range conditions and their herds. Luther Ironside put the die-off at no more than ten percent, and, unlike many others ranchers who lived constantly on the edge of bankruptcy, it was a loss Dromore could absorb. Shamus turned a profit in December of that year when he shipped a thousand head by boxcar from Santa Fe to the San Carlos Indian reservation on an army contract.

But on Christmas Eve came bad news, the arrival to the south of a four-legged plague that threatened the very existence of Dromore and the O'Brien family.

A cowboy riding the grub line showed up at the

ranch house and was immediately invited to set and eat, as was the custom.

During the meal around the great table in the dining room, the vaqueros and their families were dressed in their Christmas finery. Even Luther Ironside and the local ranchers had been persuaded to take off their chaps and spurs and wear broadcloth and white linen.

Patrick, a more sensitive man than any of his brothers, felt a reserve in the drifting puncher, a Texan by the name of Jim Lawson. The young man played his part in the festivities and even pulled an English Christmas cracker—the first one he'd ever seen—with Nellie. Although he happily wore the paper hat he'd found inside, he seemed a little distracted the entire evening, as though he was holding something back. Patrick was sure Lawson had a secret of some kind he didn't want to tell the others.

At least not yet.

After the ladies retreated to the drawing room for bonbons and sherry, the men settled down to port and cigars, and Patrick made a point of sitting next to Lawson.

As the conversation at the top of the table turned to the great blizzard and its devastating effect on cattlemen, Patrick held a match to Lawson's cigar and said in his quiet way, "Are you on the scout, Jim?"

The cowboy blew out a cloud of blue smoke, then shook his head.

"Then what's on your mind?" Patrick said.

Lawson was quiet for a while as though dabbing a

loop on his thoughts, then he turned guileless blue eyes on Patrick. "I came up through the Estancia Valley yesterday and stopped at a sheep camp a mile east of the salt lakes." He smiled. "First time I ever ate sheep meat stew. It ain't half bad."

Patrick nodded, letting the man tell his story at his own pace.

"Well, anyhoo, I got to talking with a greaser and he said a couple gringos showed up in the valley last week," Lawson said. "Seems they were this lawyer feller from Boston by the name of Joel Whitney and his brother James. They claimed they'd bought a land grant for the entire valley from the government of these United States, said they'd been to Albuquerque and got a court order of eviction, and that the sheepherders were squatters and they'd have to get off the land, pronto."

"How many sheep are we talking about?" Patrick said.

"Thousands. Hell, maybe tens of thousands. Too many for a body to count, I reckon."

Lawson studied the end of his cigar, then said, "All them woolies got to go somewhere and from what the herder told me, somewhere is north where there's still open range."

"That's Dromore range," Patrick said.

"Well, it's wide open as far as them herders and their sheep are concerned."

Lawson poured port into his glass from the decanter. "I never tried this before. What's it called?"

"Port. It's a kind of wine."

"Sure beats forty-rod to a pulp." Lawson sipped his port. "There's worse to come."

"Hell," Patrick said, "I reckon it couldn't get any worse."

"It does."

Patrick suddenly became aware that there was a silence at the head of the table. He turned and saw his father's eyes locked on Jim Lawson. Sitting beside Shamus, Zebulon McCoy, a hard-bitten old rancher from the Conchas River country, looked as though somebody had just shot his favorite dog.

"Tell us about them woolies, son," McCoy said.

Lawson was flustered. In the crystal and polished wood room with its silent servants, he was a far piece from the bunkhouse.

Patrick smiled at him. "Just tell it, Jim. How did things get worse?"

Lawson swallowed hard, and fortified himself with a slug of port. "The original owner of the valley through a Mexican land grant is a feller by the name of"—the cowboy took a tally book from his shirt pocket—"I wrote this down when the greaser told it to me, because it's a right fancy handle. Yeah, the feller's name is Don Manuel Antonio Otero." Lawson smiled at Patrick. "Don is a funny handle for a Mex, ain't it?"

"Well, it's a title," Patrick said, "like duke or earl."

Zebulon McCoy thumped the table so hard, the glasses jumped. "Damn it, boy, tell it straight, I want to know about them woolies."

Beside him, Shamus's face was like stone, a man who didn't like the writing on the wall.

"Well, the dook or don or whatever the hell he was, asked for a parley with the Whitney brothers to settle who really owns the valley," Lawson said. "Joel Whitney arranged the meeting. Don Manuel didn't come in person, but he sent his son Felipe along with a couple vaqueros. The Whitney boys invited their brother-in-law, a pretty fair gun hand, as it happens. I don't know his name."

The cowboy talked directly to Zebulon McCoy. "It turns out that somebody at the meeting figured his talking was all done because he started shooting. When the smoke cleared, James Whitney was dead, the brother-in-law gasping his last, and Joel was wounded in the wrist." Lawson consulted his tally book again. "Don Manuel's son was as dead as he was ever going to be and so were the vaqueros."

"And what about them woolies?" McCoy said. "That's what I want to know."

The port gave Lawson confidence. "All I can tell you is what the Mexican herder told me. He said Joel Whitney, after seeing his relatives lying there in a welter of blood, sent to Texas for hired guns. On account of how times are hard, he got some of the best. Felipe's sorrowing Pa armed his vaqueros and a war is brewing. It ain't about sheep, it's about land, and if the Mexicans lose, them herders will be forced out of the valley and move their woolies north."

Shamus suddenly looked concerned. "Sheep will cover the range like locusts and poison the grass for hundreds of miles around."

Lawson nodded, his face flushed from the wine.

"Seems like it's time for you to take sides, Colonel O'Brien."

Normally Shamus would have called that last statement impertinent and jumped all over the cowboy, but worried as he was he let it go.

Patrick voiced his father's thoughts. "We must side with the Mexicans, Colonel. Or make a deal with Whitney to move the sheep south if we help him."

"Damn it," McCoy said. "I ain't a one for making deals. I say a pox on both their houses and we chase them *all* out of the valley, Whitney *and* the Mexicans." He looked at Shamus. "We'll graze cattle on the Estancia."

"Your range will not be affected, Zebulon," Shamus said.

"Shamus, if ten thousand woolies move north, everybody's range will be in danger. They'll spread across the high country like a plague." McCoy refilled his glass. "I can bring five hands, all of them good men."

"Didn't you hear what young Lawson said, Zebulon?" Shamus demanded. "This Whitney person, a carpetbagging Yankee by the sound of him, has recruited Texas gunfighters. I will not send cowhands against such men."

"My riders will stick," McCoy said.

"They'll stick because they'll all be in the ground," Shamus said.

"Pa, I'll go," Samuel said.

"And me, Colonel," Ironside said.

"I'll tag along as well," Shawn said, smiling. A

rancher's giggling daughter, who preferred the company of a handsome young man to that of the gossiping ladies, sat on his knee.

"Samuel, you'll bide here at Dromore. Your wife is nursing my grandson and I won't see her widowed. Luther, you're a tough man, but you're too old for gun work."

Ironside opened his mouth to object, but Shamus held up a silencing hand. "Shawn, you're better with a gun than most. You will ride south."

"What about me, Pa?" Patrick asked.

Shamus thought for a few moments, and then said, "Yes, you will go with Shawn. But you will keep your wits about you, and your nose out of a book."

He looked again at Ironside. "Who among my vaqueros is best with the iron?"

Before the man could answer, a slim, handsome vaquero said, "That would be me, Colonel."

"You have a wife, Andre," Shamus said.

"I ride for the brand, Senor."

"Well said. Then you will go with my sons." Shamus stared at Shawn, a mildly disapproving look on his face. "Where is your brother?"

Shawn smiled. "Which one?"

"You know the one."

"Jacob is in El Paso, Pa."

"Can you wire him and bring him here to Dromore?"

Shawn hesitated, and his father said, "We need his fast gun. The future of Dromore is at stake."

"I'll wire him."

"He'll come?"

"Of course he'll come."

"Then, when Jacob gets here you will ride south. You will make sure the sheep don't move out of the valley." Shamus looked hard at Shawn. "Beyond that, you must use your own judgment and do what you think is best for Dromore. Do you understand?"

Shawn nodded. "I understand, Colonel."

McCoy stabbed his cigar in Shawn's direction. "Just remember, young feller, ain't nobody gonna blame you for shooting a Yankee or a sheepherder or two."

Shamus sat back in his chair and smiled. "Now, enough long faces on Christmas Eve, the night of Our Savior's birth. We will rejoin the ladies, and, Shawn, we'll have a song with you, a good old Irish song if you please."

"It will be my pleasure," Shawn said aloud. Inwardly he said something else entirely. *Please, Jacob, don't let me down.*

Chapter Eighteen

El Paso, Texas, Christmas Eve, 1886

The north wind bit cold, and snow dusted the rugged peaks of the Franklin Mountains as Jacob O'Brien stepped along the frosted mud of El Paso's Main Street, then turned right onto North Oregon toward the steamed-up door of the Columbia Restaurant.

Many of the residents of the town were celebrating at home, but scores of tipsy revelers crowded the public park opposite the restaurant. Farther down the street a crowd had gathered outside the Star of Texas Saloon. For what purpose, he had no idea.

The short day was already shading into night and lamps were lit all over town. Jacob smiled when the thought came to him that El Paso boasted more twinkling lights than the evening sky.

He heard a soft, low mew behind him and stopped. *What the hell?*

Turning, he saw nothing, then heard the sound again, this time from the direction of his feet. He glanced down and met the green eyes of a tiny calico kitten staring up at him. "Well, who are you?"

The kitten mewed again and coiled around his feet like a furry snake.

"You go back to your ma," O'Brien said. "You'll catch your death of cold out here."

He turned and stepped away, but the calico followed him, raising a ruckus for attention.

O'Brien stopped, picked up the little cat in both hands, and held it at eye level. "All right, you're as skinny as a rail, so maybe you don't have a ma."

The kitten kicked its legs and mewed, showing tiny white teeth in a pink mouth.

"What am I going to do with you?"

The calico mewed a suggestion, but O'Brien shook his head. "That's no good. I don't talk cat."

He looked down the street. The crowd outside the Star of Texas had grown larger, and people chatted with each other, and pointed to the saloon's closed glass doors.

"What do you suppose is going on down there, cat, huh?" O'Brien said.

The kitten showed little interest in speculating on that point, and O'Brien said, "You can come into the restaurant with me and get some grub, because I reckon you're starving. Just be aware of three things— be on your best behavior, remember that I don't take sass, and thirdly, this isn't a permanent arrangement. I don't want a cat. I've a hard enough time keeping myself fed."

O'Brien opened a button of his canvas mackinaw

and shoved the kitten inside next to his chest. The little animal shivered for a few moments, then began to purr.

O'Brien smiled, oddly pleased. "Well, if that don't beat all." He pulled the door open, and entered the restaurant.

"Where are all your customers, Joe?" O'Brien said.

The restaurant owner shrugged. "It's Christmas Eve, Jake. Everybody's to home, where I'll be real soon." He shook his head. "Well, everybody but the drunks and the crowd down at the Star of Texas."

"Saw that. What's going on?"

"It's that damned Jasper Rhodes. Crazy man has the piano player and a girl inside the saloon with him. He says he'll kill 'em both if'n he doesn't get five thousand dollars, a hoss, and safe conduct out of town."

"I never knew Jasper to be violent before," O'Brien said. "He's a real good blacksmith. Be a pity if he gets himself gunned tonight."

"I don't know about that, but sometimes the festive season does strange things to a man." Joe smiled. "Five thousand dollars be damned. Hell, I don't think there's that amount of money in the whole town."

O'Brien took the kitten from inside his mackinaw. "Burn me a steak and put half-a-dozen fried eggs with it, Joe. And do you have something for this little feller? He's hungry."

"He ain't a feller, Jake. He's a girl cat. I seen her hanging around the past couple days, making a damned nuisance of herself."

"Must've lost her ma, I reckon," O'Brien said.

Joe nodded. "Seems like." He stepped toward the kitchen. "Steak an' eggs comin' up, then I'm shutting shop."

O'Brien set the kitten on the table. "I'm calling you Eve, on account of how this is Christmas Eve and I don't know what your mama named you." The calico mewed and he said, "Good, Eve sets all right with you, huh?"

Joe laid a small plate filled with chopped egg and scraps of beef on the table. "That ain't for you, Jake. It's for the cat."

"Glad you told me. I thought it looked real tasty."

"Yours is coming right out," Joe grinned when he saw the kitten dive on the food.

But before O'Brien's dinner was served, the door opened, letting in a gust of cold air and a few flakes of snow. A small, worried-looking man wearing a bearskin coat stepped to the table.

"A feller told me he saw you come in here," the man said.

O'Brien recognized him as Bill Andrews, the owner of the Star of Texas. "What can I do for you, Bill?"

"It's Christmas Eve and I'm losing money," Andrews said. "Jasper Rhodes is drunk and has my piano player and a hostess in the saloon, threatening to kill them."

"So I was told," O'Brien said.

Andrews gave the younger man a despairing look. "If people can't get into my saloon, they aren't buying drinks and I'll go broke."

"What do you want me to do?"

"Get the crazy bedbug out of my place."

"Why me?"

Andrews looked surprised. "Because you're good with the iron and you don't scare worth a damn."

"Why me?"

"I told you why"—realization dawned on Andrews' face—"because I'm paying you—"

"Fifty dollars."

The saloon owner was shocked. "That's highway robbery."

"Take it or leave it. If Rhodes doesn't get out of your saloon, you'll lose a lot more than that."

Andrews' shoulders slumped. "All right. Fifty dollars."

"In advance."

"You drive a hard bargain, Mr. O'Brien."

"It's a hard world, Mr. Andrews."

The saloon owner paid O'Brien just as Joe put his plate in front of him, the smoking steak still sizzling.

"I'll be right down just as soon as I eat dinner," O'Brien said, fending off Eve as he picked up his fork and knife.

"Eat it fast," Andrews said. "Time is money."

"Here, take the kitten," O'Brien said. "Her name is Eve."

Andrews gingerly took the calico, then yelped. "Hell, it's like holding a roll of barbed wire."

"I'll take her," a saloon girl in a bright red dress

said. She had a man's coat thrown over her shoulders against the cold. "Cats like me."

And Eve did, preferring the woman's sure and gentle touch to Andrews' timid fumbling.

About sixty people, mostly men with a scattering of women, including a couple of El Paso's respectable matrons, were assembled outside the Star of Texas to see the fun. Whiskey flasks passed from hand to eager hand and the evening air was blue with cigar smoke.

O'Brien opened his mackinaw and eased his Colt in the holster.

"If you hear shooting," he said to Andrews, "come a-running. I could be the one who's down."

He stepped to the front of the saloon, took a deep breath, and opened the door.

Chapter Nineteen

Jasper Rhodes stood in the middle of the saloon floor, a bottle to his lips and a revolver in his hand. Pinned to the far wall, like butterflies to a board, stood the piano player and a pretty, terrified saloon girl.

Rhodes turned as Jacob O'Brien stepped inside, his Remington coming up.

"Don't, Jasper," O'Brien said, his hand hovering over the butt of his Colt. "Or I'll drop you right where you stand."

Rhodes blinked, peering into the smoky distance between him and O'Brien. "Jacob?"

"It's me all right, Jasper."

"Are you here to kill me, Jacob?"

"Only if I have to."

The black man, dressed only in pants and a torn, collarless shirt, took a staggering step toward O'Brien who tensed, ready for the draw and shoot. Rhodes had the huge chest and shoulder muscles of a blacksmith, and he wouldn't be easy to drop.

"It's Christmas Eve, Jacob, an' nobody gives a damn about me," Rhodes said.

"Put the gun on a table and we'll talk," O'Brien said.

"Jacob, they was gonna throw me out of here on account of me being a colored man. " Rhodes' face took on a look that O'Brien interpreted as a strange kind of disappointment. "It's Christmas Eve and they was gonna throw me out." He blinked again, trying to bring O'Brien into focus. "Why would they do that?"

"I guess they don't think you belong, Jasper."

"They don't think you belong, either, Jacob."

O'Brien smiled "No, most times they don't."

"Are you gonna kill me, Jacob?"

"If you put the gun down, I won't have to."

Rhodes sat in the nearest chair and laid the Remington on the table, but it was still close to hand.

O'Brien looked past him to the saloon girl. "What's your name?"

"Laura," the girl said.

"Bring us a bottle of Bill Andrews' best brandy and three glasses," O'Brien said. "Oh, and a few of his Havana cigars." He moved his eyes to the piano player. "Play us some Christmas music."

The man nodded and hurried to the piano. "Yes, sir, anything you say." His fingers found the keys and he began to play *Angels from the Realms of Glory*, with its message of angels, sages, and saints.

The girl returned with a dusty bottle of Hennessy and the glasses.

"Sit with us, Laura," O'Brien said.

After throwing Rhodes a single half-worried,

half-scared look, she did as she was told. She chose the chair farthest from him.

O'Brien poured the brandy into the glasses and held his high. "Happy Christmas, Jasper," he said.

The girl was smart, caught on quickly and did the same. "And may you have many more, Jasper," she said, smiling.

The big blacksmith was taken aback. He lifted his glass and smiled, "It's Christmas Eve and we're celebratin'."

"Hell, yeah, a time to be with friends," O'Brien said. He stuck a cigar in Rhodes' mouth, thumbed a match into flame and lit it.

Rhodes looked from O'Brien to Laura. "You are my friends."

"Yes, we are," Laura said with a smile in her blue eyes.

It suddenly reminded O'Brien of his mother, and he felt a pang of loss.

"I did something wrong, Jacob," Rhodes said. "Didn't I?"

"You were lonely, Jasper, that's all. You didn't kill anyone."

"I wouldn't have killed anybody, Jacob."

"Of course you wouldn't."

O'Brien poured a brandy and took it to the piano player. "Play 'Hark the Herald Angels Sing.' It's by Felix Mendelssohn and it was one of my mother's favorites."

"I sure will," the piano player said. "Just so long as I get out of here alive."

"You will," O'Brien said. "It's all over."

When he returned to the table, Jasper Rhodes' face shone like a piece of polished ebony, a wide grin almost splitting his features in two. Beside him, Laura, well used to men of all kinds, had her arm around his shoulders and soon she began to sing the beautiful words of the Mendelssohn carol into Rhodes' ear. O'Brien soon joined in, his strong baritone adding a harmony, and Rhodes sat entranced.

> *"Hark the herald angels sing,*
> *'Glory to the newborn King!*
> *Peace on earth and mercy mild;*
> *God and sinners reconciled.'*
> *Joyful, all ye nations rise,*
> *Join the triumph of the skies;*
> *With angelic host proclaim,*
> *'Christ is born in Bethlehem!'*
> *Hark the herald angels sing,*
> *'Glory to the newborn King!'"*

After the carol ended, Rhodes jumped to his feet, held his glass high, and yelled, "This is the best Christmas of my life!"

It was also destined to be his last.

The saloon doors burst open and Bill Andrews stormed inside, followed by five men, one of them wearing a star on his mackinaw.

"There he is," Andrews said. "Constable Tate, do your duty."

O'Brien saw that one of the men, a lantern-jawed redhead with reptilian eyes, carried a rope.

"It's all over here," O'Brien said. "Jasper Rhodes is going home." In an attempt to head off a lynching, he added, "And he'll answer to a charge of disturbing the peace."

"He don't have a home," Constable Tate said. "At least in El Paso, he don't. He's coming with us."

O'Brien stepped in front of Rhodes, a Colt suddenly in his hand. "If you want this man, you'll have to go through me."

He heard Laura's sharp intake of breath, then felt something hard hit him on the back of his neck just under his hat brim. O'Brien saw the saloon floor rush up to meet him, then something else—Tate's huge fist coming at him in a swinging uppercut. The lawman's knuckles crashed into O'Brien's face and suddenly he was falling . . . tumbling headlong into a pit of darkness.

Jacob O'Brien woke to morning light drifting through a small barred window. A few flakes of snow, like pale moths, fluttered in the angled beam.

It took him a while to realize where he was—in a jail cell that smelled rank of urine and vomit—lying on a filth-encrusted mattress on an iron cot.

He moved his fingers to his face. Dried blood smeared his mustache and his lips were cut and swollen. He was sure his nose was broken, for maybe the third or fourth time in his life, and he had a splitting headache.

The cot squealed in protest when he rose and put his feet on the floor and his aching head in his hands. He heard nothing of the outside, but a sly wind whispered around the roof of the adobe jail, its breath iced by frost. As solemn as a courthouse clock, a leak ticked in the adjoining cell and rats scuttled and squeaked in the corners.

He lay back down and an hour passed while he dozed the time away without moving. But he woke with a start when the iron door to the cell opened and Constable Tate stepped inside, holding a smoking cup of coffee.

"Ah, you're awake, O'Brien," he said. "For a while there I figured you was dead."

"Not hardly," O'Brien said.

"Well, a good Christmas Day morning to you," Tate said, smiling. He held out the cup for O'Brien to take. "I brung you coffee." He reached inside his mackinaw. "And the makings, if you're a smoking man."

Angry as he was, O'Brien wasn't about to cut off his broken nose to spite his face. He took the cup and makings without comment. After he'd built a cigarette and flamed it alight, he said, "Where is Jasper Rhodes?"

Tate, a big-bellied man with a blue-chinned, brutal face, shrugged as though O'Brien's question was of little importance. "The negro gentleman is no longer with us."

"You ran him out of town?"

"No, I hung him."

That last hit O'Brien like a fist. "Damn you, you murdered the man."

Tate shook his head slowly and seemed to take no offense. "No, I hung him legal, like. He was accused of stealing a Remington revolver from Tom Wright's rod and gun store, the theft of bonded bourbon and Havana cigars from Bill Andrews' saloon, vagrancy, and the attempted rape of one Laura Higgins, saloon employee and prostitute. All of those crimes are hanging offenses in El Paso."

"I took the cigars and whiskey, damn you," O'Brien said. "And Jasper Rhodes didn't try to rape anybody. Hell, I was there."

"Maybe what you say is true, but the law decided otherwise."

"You mean the vigilantes decided otherwise."

"They're the law in this town, so it was all done legal like, as I said."

O'Brien opened his mouth to speak, but Tate cut him off. "If I hear another word out of you, I'll forget you're Colonel Shamus O'Brien's son and keep you locked up until spring."

"My father's got nothing to do with this," O'Brien said.

"I know. But he's a rich and powerful man with friends in high places. Jailing his son for months might create a problem."

"Why don't you hang me, like you did Jasper Rhodes?"

Tate nodded. "Well, I thought about it, but that

might create even bigger problems." He leaned forward and clanked a key in the lock. "No, O'Brien, you're getting out of El Paso today, you and your damned cat that's out there in my office hissing at everybody. I mean, you're both leaving this very minute." He reached inside his coat. "Hell, I almost forgot. This came for you this morning."

He passed O'Brien a telegram that read simply:

COME. SHAWN.

"Not bad news, I hope," Tate said, "this being Christmas Day an' all."

"You've already read it."

"Yeah, I guess I did. But it didn't mean much to me."

O'Brien said nothing. He folded the telegram and shoved it in the pocket of his mackinaw.

"Follow me," Tate said.

After they stepped into the office, cold despite the potbellied stove that glowed cherry-red in a corner, the constable took O'Brien's gun belt and holstered Colt from the gun rack and laid it on his desk.

"Before you get any fancy notions about gunning me, look out the window," he said.

O'Brien crossed to the frost-laced window and glanced outside. Eight men carrying shotguns stood outside, bundled up to the eyes against the cold and flurrying snow.

"Those gentlemen will accompany you to the livery and then the railroad station," Tate said. "Your train leaves at three after ten, and there's a branch line from here to Santa Fe, though the conductor might let you off closer to home."

"You don't take chances, do you?" O'Brien said, buckling on his gun belt. "You must think I'm a real dangerous hombre."

"Live longer thinking that way," Tate said. "You're a draw fighter, O'Brien. You are dangerous, and I hate your kind, seed, breed, and generation of you."

"I'd say the feeling is mutual in that respect." O'Brien stepped to the door, and then stopped. "Who hit me and with what?"

Tate's smile was not pleasant. "Lou Hunt, the piano player. Said you forced him to play Christmas carols, and he despises them things. He hit you with an Old Crow bottle, empty, of course."

O'Brien nodded. "Lou Hunt, a name to remember. I may ride back this way and put a bullet in his belly."

"That would be a pity," Tate said. "He's the only piano player in town."

O'Brien loaded his horse into a boxcar and then settled into the cushions in the passenger car with Eve on his lap, the lynching of Jasper Rhodes weighing heavily on him.

A nice English lady sat next to him. Middle-aged and motherly, she asked him if he was leaving El Paso to visit dear parents.

Not eager for conversation, he replied, "Brother."

"Then we must get your face cleaned up, young

man," the woman said. "One can't visit loved ones with a bloodied countenance, can one?"

"I'm fine," O'Brien said. What he really wanted to say was, *Leave me the hell alone, woman.*

"I can't in all conscience, as a good Christian on this most blessed day of the year, let you continue on your journey looking like you just went ten rounds with Tom Cribb." The woman frowned at O'Brien as though she'd fairly stated her case and would brook no opposition.

Her face apologetic, she said, "I'm afraid I don't have any water, but I do have a bottle of rosewater and that will serve splendidly."

"When the train stops to take on water, I'll stand under the hose," O'Brien said. He was desperate now.

"You will do no such thing," the woman said. "Stand under the hose indeed. You'd catch your death of cold, and then what would your dear loved ones think?"

She touched the kitten's head with elegant white fingers. "What a pretty kitty. What's her name?"

"Eve."

The woman smiled. "Ah, Eve has found her Adam."

"As I recall, the last time that happened, it didn't work out so well," O'Brien said.

The woman had an honest laugh, clear and light as a ringing silver bell. "Why, how deliciously droll. I declare, you Western men have such a wonderful sense of humor."

Before he could say anything else, the woman

poured rosewater over a scrap of handkerchief and began to dab blood from his mustache and nose.

"I know this must sting, and I do apologize," she said. "But sometimes one must be cruel to be kind, mustn't one?"

He surrendered to the Englishwoman's ministrations, figuring it was best to endure her for a few minutes and get it over with. In fact, it took almost half an hour, and by that time the train was speeding through a howling, cartwheeling snowstorm.

Finally the woman leaned back, her bloody handkerchief poised, and admired her handiwork. She rode the pitching floor of the railcar expertly, like an old salt in a nor'easter.

"Yes, we do look so much better," she said. "Your dear brother will hardly recognize you."

"Thank you," O'Brien said. "Now I figure I'll catch up on some sleep."

"Wait." The woman rummaged in her drawstring purse, and found a scrap of mirror. "Look at yourself and see the difference Christian charity can make in the lives of others less fortunate than ourselves."

O'Brien was not a man for mirrors, but he glanced at his reflection to please the woman. His right eye was puffed, already turning a purple shade, his lips were split and swollen after Tate mashed them against his teeth, and he was certain his nose was busted.

"Yes," he managed a smile, "I look much better."

"If you need more administrations of rosewater—"

"I'll let you know."

The woman smiled and went back to her seat, but

she continued to glance at him as though anxious for an opportunity to impart yet more Christian charity.

Aware that he smelled like a two-dollar whore, to the apparent distaste of the grizzled miner who sat in front of him, O'Brien closed his eyes. Eve climbed onto his lap, curled up, and was asleep in seconds.

The train hurtled through the iron gray morning, the locomotive's chimney white with frost. In the cabin, the fireman and engineer sweated, the glow of the firebox scarlet on their faces. Snowflakes swept past the passenger cars like birds in flight, and ahead the rails vanished into a steel-mesh curtain where the land and sky became one.

Jacob O'Brien slept . . . and dreamed of Dromore.

Chapter Twenty

The snow followed Jacob McBride from El Paso to Dromore, as though reluctant to take leave of him.

Sitting his horse in sheltering pines, he gazed across the timeless land. The mesa still dominated the skyline, as though defying the lowering clouds to obscure its savage beauty. Beyond, rose the peaks of the Santa Fe Mountains, but those were lost in snow and distance.

O'Brien breathed in deeply, enjoying once again the air of Dromore, a heady mix of pine, piñon, sage, and the bubbling waters of the creek where the silver trout swam.

He lit a cigarette and smoked, taking his time. It was good to be home. The big house with its plantation pillars had not changed, looking as though it would endure for centuries at the foot of the mesa, just as it was. O'Brien saw no movement around the house, but then, who would be out on such a cold morning, three days after Christmas?

He was strangely reluctant to enter the house. Perhaps he feared the disappointed, slightly disapproving look the Colonel would lash at him, or the marital happiness he'd see in Samuel, such a sharp contrast to his own lot, the echoing loneliness of the long-riding man who could live no other way.

O'Brien built and lit another smoke, a shivering wind shaking snow from the pines around him. His horse, eager to be going, pawed the ground and tossed its head, breath snorting from its nostrils like plumes of smoke. Eve emerged from under his mackinaw and jumped to the ground, eager to explore.

"Don't you go far," he said. "Or the coyotes will get you."

The kitten paid no heed and nosed into a clump of brush, tail up, interested.

It wasn't a trick of the wind. O'Brien was sure of that. He was certain there was somebody, or something, close.

Slowly he turned his head and glanced behind him. The pines were set close together, the ground at their roots carpeted with needles, and flakes of snow drifted in the air from the high branches.

Nothing. Not even a shadow moving.

But he was aware. A man was close. O'Brien could feel his presence, the eyes on his face crawling over him like snails. He reached down with his right, freed his gun from the mackinaw, ready for the draw.

"Too slow, little brother, I could've plugged you for sure."

The voice came from Jacob's right. He turned as his gun came free and saw Shawn grinning at him. His brother sat an Appaloosa horse among the trees. He wore a sheepskin coat and the brim of a gray Stetson was pulled low over his eyes.

"Damn it, Shawn," Jacob said, fright making him angry. "You know better than to sneak up on a man."

"Saw you from a ways off, Jacob," Shawn said. "I came at you slow. This palouse steps through the trees like a deer."

"How the hell did you know it was me?"

"Who else dresses in old rags, sits his saddle like a sack of grain, and stares at Dromore like a frightened child?" Shawn looked at the kitten rustling around, searching for bugs. "Is that yours?"

"Yeah, her name is Eve."

"You look thin, Jacob. Did you have a hard time on the trail, driving the cat all the way from El Paso?"

Jacob shook his head. "Shawn, how come nobody's shot you yet?"

"Just lucky, I guess." He smiled. "A farmer once took a pot at me when he caught me in the barn with his wife, but that was a couple years back."

Jacob said nothing. He holstered his gun, reached into his mackinaw, and produced the telegram. Silently he held it up for his brother to see.

"We've got trouble, Jacob," Shawn said.

"What kind of trouble?"

"Well, you could call it sheep trouble, but it'll more'n likely turn into gun trouble"

"And that's why you sent for me?"

"Uh-huh. You're fast with the iron, little brother, and you don't scare worth a damn."

Jacob laughed, a rare thing for him. "How can you say that when you just scared the hell out of me?"

"I reckon you knew I was kin, Jacob. It's only kinfolk who scare you."

Jacob let that go. "Tell me about the sheep."

"Later. We'll go to the house and I'll tell you then." Shawn looked at his brother, his face concerned. "Damn, you're as skinny as a rail. Haven't you been eating good?"

"I eat when I have money."

"It looks like you don't have money too often."

Jacob nodded. "That's about the size of it."

"Better get your cat," Shawn said. "Then we'll go talk to the Colonel."

"I'm missing my last six meals," Jacob said.

Shawn grinned. "Nellie will see that right off and she'll stuff you so full of grub you won't be able to move for the rest of the day."

"She's my kind of gal," Jacob said.

He retrieved his kitten. Then he and Shawn rode to Dromore.

* * *

"You have had breakfast, Jacob?" Shamus O'Brien asked.

"Nellie filled me up with pancakes and bacon, to say nothing of eggs, steak, and a gallon of coffee."

"That is good. You look thin."

Jacob nodded. "I can't say I've been eating real regular."

"Your coat is ragged, your boots have no heels left, and your hat is fit only for a scarecrow," Shamus said. "What has become of you, son?"

"I live, Pa. Hard times have come down recently, but I live."

"But not well."

"Well enough. My needs are few and I go where I choose. As you used to say, I have a free foot and a fellow for it."

"We heard you killed a man."

"He needed killing."

"Down on the Brazos we were told."

"He was a drunken lout who abused his woman and her daughter. He was notified, but went for his gun."

"A mistake, as it turned out."

"One he made."

"You're gaining a reputation, Jacob."

"It's not of my choosing."

Shamus rolled his wheelchair to the fireplace, where a great log burned, and seemed to take much interest in the oil portrait of Saraid that hung above the mantel.

Without turning, he said, "You know what is happening, the direst threat to Dromore that ever was."

"Samuel told me. Sheep, he said."

"They could destroy us, Jacob, if they move north."

"I'm aware of that, Colonel."

Shamus turned. "God forgive me for saying this, but we need your gun."

"In other words, you need a killer down on the Estancia."

"None of your brothers has that qualification." Shamus sighed; a shuddering proclamation that what he was about to say disturbed him greatly. "It's much I'm asking of you, Jacob, since you are no longer part of Dromore."

"I'll always be a part of Dromore, Colonel. I was born and"—he glanced at his mother's portrait— "raised here. Dromore stays with me constantly, awake or asleep."

Shamus absorbed that and decided it needed no comment. "Samuel told you what needs to be done?"

"Yes, he has."

"You and your brothers will go only as observers," Shamus said. "You will only take action if and when the sheep herds move north."

"I understand," Jacob said.

"A man named Joel Whitney claims he has title to the whole valley, and he plans on moving the sheepherders off his land. He has hired Texas gunfighters and that could be a complication."

"Texans on the prod usually are," Jacob said.

"I want you to move out tomorrow at first light."

Jacob nodded, but said nothing.

Shamus smiled. "In the meantime get acquainted with your new nephew. He's named for me and he'll be master of Dromore one day."

Jacob rose to his feet. "I'll do that, Colonel."

"Your hand, son," Shamus said. "I want no ill-feeling between us."

Jacob shook hands with his father and started for the door.

"Will you play the piano for me tonight?" Shamus asked after him.

"Of course I will," Jacob said.

Chapter Twenty-one

Snow fell, dimming the morning. Ice frosted the trees, the grass, and the rock faces of the mesa, and gleamed like polished iron on the roof of the house. The creek was frozen and a couple vaqueros were already busy with picks, chopping holes for the cattle. A gray sky hung low over the steely land and the air was hard, snapping in the mouth like stick candy.

Shamus, wrapped in a blanket, sat in his wheelchair at the door of the big house and watched his sons leave. Patrick gathered up the rope of the pack-horse and followed Shawn, Jacob, and the vaquero Andre Perez. His stiff-kneed mount walked slowly, unsure of the footing.

The snow swirled around the riders, and Shamus, fearing they'd soon be lost to sight, called out after them, "Return alive to Dromore, all of you."

Shawn raised a gloved hand, acknowledging that he'd heard.

The brothers O'Brien rode in silence for a while, then Jacob said, "Hell, I forgot Eve."

"She's in the barn," Patrick said.

"Why did you put her there?" Jacob said.

"She has to learn to be a cat. The other cats will teach her."

Jacob considered that, then said, "She's real little."

"Cats grow fast," Shawn said.

Jacob's eyes above his woolen scarf looked worried. "I hope a rat doesn't get her."

"It would take a brave rat to tackle your cat," Shawn said. "Pick her up and suddenly she's all claws and fangs."

"She doesn't do that to me," Jacob said.

Shawn laid a hand on his brother's shoulder. "Jacob, that's because you're her daddy."

"Damn right," Jacob said, after thinking about it for a moment.

The O'Briens had planned to reach the settlement of Estancia, which had first appeared on the map in 1779 and had given its name to the valley, but the night closed in on them and they made camp a mile north of McGillivray Draw.

Standing rocks and a few juniper provided shelter from the worst of the snow and razor-sharp wind. Jacob, who had a whole range of woodsman's skills, soon had a fire going. He also took on the cooking chores, and prepared a meal of thick salt pork and sourdough bread sandwiches, followed by wedges of apple pie that were half-frozen but tasty.

The brothers were drinking coffee, Jacob smoking

a cigarette, as was his habit, when a voice hailed them from the darkness.

"Hello the camp!"

Jacob stood, moved out of the firelight, his Colt up and ready. "Come in real slow and smilin', like you are visiting kinfolk."

"Hell, is that you, Jacob? I guess I didn't paddle your butt enough when you was a younker, or teach you how to be sociable." Luther Ironside, muffled in sheepskin, a wool scarf over his hat and ears, rode into the pale orange glow of the fire. There was frost on his eyebrows and mustache.

Shawn rose to his feet. "Luther, what are you doing here?"

"I'm joining you," Ironside said. "Ain't that kinda obvious?"

"But Pa ordered you to stay home," Shawn said.

"Yeah, I know he did. The Colonel's a fine man, but sometimes his orders don't make a lick o' sense."

Breaking the speechless silence that followed, Ironside said, "Are you going to keep a man sitting his horse all night, or are you gonna invite me to light and set?"

"Step down, Luther," Jacob said, grinning. "There's coffee and grub if you need it."

"Right now hot coffee would be welcome. Damned wind's as cold as a stepmother's breath."

Perez took Ironside's horse as the man sat stiffly by the fire. Jacob handed him a cup of steaming coffee, and Shawn said, "The colonel will skin us alive if we don't send you back, Luther."

"Well, you have a problem, because I ain't a-goin' back." Ironside fished inside his canvas coat, found a cigar, and lit it with a brand from the fire. "I'm not going to stand by and let you young hellers ride into what's shaping up to be an all-out range war. Hell, without me you'd all end up dead, seeing as how there's not a lick o' sense atween you, except what little I drilled into you. Well, me and your ma, God rest her soul."

Shawn smiled. "Luther, you're what? Near sixty years old, I reckon. Pa already told you that you're too old for gun work."

For a moment Ironside's face was hidden behind a cloud of cigar smoke. When the smoke cleared, he was scowling. "Listen, Shawn, the day I can't out-shoot, out-ride, and out-drink the three of you is the day I hang it up for good."

His expression despairing, Shawn looked at his brother. "Jacob, what are we going to do with him?"

Jacob smiled. "Well, I'm not going to tackle him, are you?"

"Hell, no."

Ironside nodded. "That's the first smart thing you boys have said all night. I'm riding with you, and there's an end to it." He slapped his hands together. "Now, Jacob, rustle me up some of that grub you was talking about."

The few buildings that made up the town of Estancia huddled together as though trying to keep warm in the morning cold. Feathers of smoke rose from a dozen scattered cabins that looked as though they'd decided to wander off into the prairie but had lost their way. Surrounded by rolling flats, only the crooked spine of the Manzano Mountains to the west offered relief to the eye of the traveler.

"Ain't much, is it?" Ironside's gaze wandered over the town's business district, a two-story hotel and a short row of stores. Presiding over the stores like a dowager queen was a false-fronted saloon with a porch in front and a small barn out back, painted rusty red. "I don't see much sign of a range war."

Jacob turned in the saddle and looked at him. "I don't, either, but I feel it, like the town is holding its breath, waiting for something to happen."

Shawn smiled. "Nothing ever happens in this town, it seems to me." He looked around him. "And not a pretty gal in sight."

But Patrick's face was solemn, his mouth a tight line under his mustache. "There's danger here, all right. Hell, my back is crawling."

Ironside kneed his horse into motion and said over his shoulder, "We'll check into the hotel before you boys start spooking yourselves all the way back to Dromore."

The snow had stopped, but now and then flurries drove through the morning, pushed by a gusting wind. A brown sky loomed over the valley like a brooding, mad monk, and the smell of wood smoke and burning kerosene hung heavy in the air.

They tied their horses at the hotel hitching rail and stepped into the close heat of the lobby. A clerk with slicked-down hair parted in the middle and a pencil-thin mustache adorning his upper lip smiled and picked up his pen, as though poised to do business.

"Welcome to the Prince Regent Hotel, gentlemen," he said. "Do we require rooms?"

"We do," Ironside said.

"And how many do we need?"

"Hell, make it five," Ironside said. "I don't want to sleep with a ranny who snores."

After they'd signed in, Shawn said, "I smell coffee."

"Ah yes, in the dining room. There's always a fresh pot on the stove. Help yourself. Should you require food, let me know and I'll inform Mrs. Hazel, the cook and owner of this establishment."

The combination dining room and parlor, decorated and furnished in the Victorian style of the day, would have done credit to a better hotel in a better place. It looked as though it had been built for diners who'd never arrived.

The O'Briens, Ironside, and Perez poured coffee into china cups and sat at a table covered with a clean white cloth. Salt and pepper shakers were located so squarely in the center, Ironside reckoned somebody using a ruler had placed them there.

Patrick laid his cup on the saucer, and then looked around the table. "Well, we're here. Now what?"

"We wait," Jacob said, lighting a cigarette.

"For what?"

"For something to happen."

"Jacob, we have to make it happen," Shawn said. "I say we speak to both parties, stop a war, and the woolies stay right where they are."

"You make it sound easy," Jacob said.

"I didn't say it was going to be easy. But the way I see it, talking is a sight better than shooting."

"I never come across a range war yet that was settled by talkin'," Ironside said.

"There's always a first time," Perez said. "Isn't that right, Patrick?"

But Patrick said nothing. His eyes were on the door and the two men who'd just stepped inside. The taller of the two wore a black overcoat that reached his ankles and a bowler hat of the same color. The fringes of the scarf wrapped around his neck fell to his knees. His eyes roamed around the room, seeing everything. Beside him, the younger man wore a canvas coat—the wool collar pulled up around his ears—shotgun chaps, and expensive, Texas-made boots. His spurs, as large as teacups, chimed when he walked. He had a wild, reckless look that boded ill.

Jacob rose to his feet, his hand away from his gun. He wasn't smiling, but he wasn't frowning, either.

"Hell, Jacob, I thought that was you." The man in the overcoat grinned, revealing good teeth.

"Howdy, Clay," Jacob said. "It's been a while."

The man named Clay stepped closer to the table.

"When was it? Down on the Brazos, right? The day you killed Big Bill Anderson."

"He was notified."

"He sure was, but he drew down on you anyhow." Clay smiled. "Bill was fast and I didn't think you could take him. You surprised the hell out of me that day."

"I took him too high. He got a shot off."

Clay nodded. "That does happen sometimes." He smiled again, blunting the barb. "But mostly to amateurs."

He waved a hand at the young man beside him. "This here is Charlie Packett, sometimes called the Memphis Kid, other times called one mean son of a bitch."

Packett took no offense, smiled, looked around the table, and touched his hat. His eyes lingered on Ironside for a moment, then a little longer on Shawn, but longest of all on Andre Perez.

"Aren't you going to introduce me to the others, Jacob?" Clay said.

"Sure." Jacob mentioned everyone at the table by name, and then said, "Meet Clay Stanley out of Fort Worth, Texas."

"Seems we have a gathering of the O'Brien clan here," Stanley said, smiling. "What brings you all to this dung heap?"

Ironside said, "Stanley, why don't you and Packett sit? You're making me nervous."

Stanley looked at Packet. "Charlie, get us some

coffee, huh?" He sat down across from Ironside and said, "You've been through it, old-timer."

"I've been up the trail and back a few times," Ironside allowed.

Stanley nodded his approval. "Well, what about it, Jacob, what brings you here?"

"I won't ease in to it, Clay," Jacob said. "I don't want sheep moving north onto our range."

Stanley seemed surprised. "Why would you care?"

"My home range is that way."

"I didn't know you had a home range."

"It's my father's range."

Stanley accepted his cup from Packett, taking his time as he sorted out his thoughts. "Jacob, Joel Whitney wants the greasers off his land. He has a claim to the whole valley."

"I know. I just don't want the herders moving north."

"You're here to stop that?" Stanley said.

Ironside answered for Jacob. "That's right, Mr. Stanley. It's why we're here."

"I'll talk to Whitney, see what I can do. How does that set with you, Jacob?"

"Sets with me just fine, Clay. But if a single wooly steps any farther north than Lobo Hill, we'll take sides."

"Whose side, Jacob?"

"That I don't know yet."

"Then choose carefully." Stanley rose to his feet. "Jacob, I like you, always have. But if this goes bad and we end up on opposite sides, I'll gun you like any other man. Do you understand?"

Jacob O'Brien nodded. "I think you've made your position clear."

"No hard feelings, Jacob. It's business."

"I understand that as well, Clay."

The Texan nodded. "Then I'll bid you gentlemen good day."

"Seems to me a man who isn't carrying a gun shouldn't be making threats to those who are," Shawn said after Stanley left.

"Clay had a gun all right," Jacob said. "He carries two Russians in shoulder holsters. He's fast, and he hits what he's shooting at. He's been a bounty hunter, peace officer, and railroad detective, and he'll probably be all those things again. Last I heard, he'd killed eight men, all of them in fair fights."

"What about the other one, the Kid?" Patrick said.

"I don't know him personally, but he's a Texas draw fighter and that's all I need to know."

"Is that all Whitney has, just those two?" Shawn said.

Jacob smiled. "Those two are a handful all by themselves. But he'll have more. A businessman like Whitney likes his insurance policies."

"Jacob, will Stanley talk to Whitney about keeping the woolies off our range?" Ironside said.

"Clay is a killer, but by his own rights, he's an

honorable man," Jacob said. "When he says he'll talk to Whitney, he will. But Whitney's a carpetbagging Yankee and all he wants is the Mexicans out of his valley. He's doesn't care where the sheep go, and he sure as hell won't lose a night's sleep over Dromore."

"Then where do we go from here?" Ironside said.

"Well, we've talked to one side, now we'll talk to the other. What's the Mexican's name again, Patrick?"

"Don Manuel Antonio Otero."

"Maybe we can make medicine with him," Jacob said.

"Don Manuel is a proud man, and Whitney, or one who was with him, killed his son," Perez said. "He will not back down from a war."

"Andre, do you think we can convince him to keep the sheep herds off Dromore range?" Ironside said.

"The winter blizzards killed the grass to the south, east and west," Perez said. "The only lands that escaped were that of Dromore and the Estancia. If the sheep are forced out of the valley they will starve if they do not move north."

Shawn shook his head. "Damn, it seems like we're wading through duck crap."

Ironside's face was gloomy. "It'll get worse if we have to take on both Whitney and the Mexican don."

"We're building a bridge over a river we may never cross," Patrick said. "As Jacob said, we should talk to Don Manuel."

Perez's sharp intake of breath attracted the others' attention and they watched as a dark cloud passed over his face. "Don Manuel has a daughter, the Donna Aracela, and she is very beautiful. But she"— Perez hurriedly crossed himself—"*es una Civatateo*. She is what the Aztecs call 'blood-eater.' It is said she bites with her fangs, then drinks the blood of the living."

Patrick smiled. "Then maybe we can get her to bite Whitney and his Texans."

Perez shook his head. "Please, señor, do not mock. Only noblewomen who died in childbirth then returned to life become Civatateo. Donna Aracela can summon all the powers of darkness, and to kiss her lips is death, as many men have found to their cost."

"Well," Shawn said, "that's one way to keep her virtue intact."

"It sounds like an interesting family," Jacob said. "Let's mount up and go talk to them. I guess the desk clerk knows the way."

"Figure you'll kiss Donna Aracela, Shawn?" Patrick said, grinning.

"I don't know. I'll wait and see what she looks like first."

Andre Perez did not smile. His face was grim and there was fear in his black eyes.

Chapter Twenty-two

The Hacienda Ortero lay a mile to the east of the Rayo Hills, built in the lee of a mesa that reminded Shawn O'Brien of Dromore. Like the peasant farmer casas that surrounded it, the hacienda was constructed of adobe, but there the similarities ended. The peasant shacks were small, had only one room, and had lattice and straw roofs. But the hacienda, with its airy, fountained plazas and arched walkways, was roofed in red Spanish tile and sprawled over a quarter acre.

"I thought Dromore was the biggest house in the world, until I saw this place," Patrick said.

"It's impressive, all right," Shawn said. "But the Colonel would never allow any of his employees to live like the people around here are living."

Scrawny chickens pecked around the shacks and a huge pig was doing its best to dig a wallow in the frozen ground. There were children everywhere, thin, ragged urchins with coal-black hair and huge eyes. Their slack-breasted mothers looked up at the

O'Brien group as they rode past, revealing only a dull, defeated interest.

The village smelled of smoke, dung heaps, disease, and poverty. The few trees in the area spread skeletal limbs and looked like the bones of ancient slave masters, herding the peasants back into their rightful places.

"It's medieval, this place," Patrick said, looking around him. "Like a castle surrounded by Saxon peasant hovels in one of Sir Walter Scott's novels."

Andre Perez overheard. "The Mexican peons have lived like this for hundreds of years, even before the Spanish came. The priests tell them this is their lot and they must accept it or there will be no salvation for them in Heaven."

"Andre, if God has any sense of justice at all, they'll go to Heaven," Patrick said. "It seems to me that they're already living in hell."

"As you say, Patron," Perez said. His eyes shuttered, as though he had no desire to witness the poverty around him.

A whispering maid led the O'Briens and Ironside into the don's study, leaving them there and then departing on silent feet.

Perez, who had no wish to meet Donna Aracela, remained outside with the horses.

The four tall men, made huge by winter coats, spurred high-heeled boots, and leather chaps, stood hat-in-hand in the middle of the oak floor. They were left to admire the honey glow of the don's polished furniture, ornate wrought iron ornamentation, and the vivid colors of the expensive rugs hanging on the walls.

A massy log burned and crackled in the fireplace. Ironside stood in front of it, lifted the back of his sheepskin, and gratefully warmed his saddle-frozen butt.

He saw Shawn glare at him, and said, "I can't abide a cold ass. It wears on a man."

"Cold ass, warm heart, isn't that how the saying goes?" Jacob said.

"Something like that," Patrick said.

The door opened, and a woman glided into the room.

Shawn decided right there and then that he'd found the love of his life.

"I am the Donna Aracela," she said, her voice like rustling silk. "My father will be with you presently. He is still in mourning for my brother, but affairs of his high estate delay him." She smiled and her teeth were very white. "I'm sure you gentlemen understand such things."

Shawn quickly crossed the floor, spurs chiming to the beat of his heels on wood. He bowed elegantly and kissed her hand.

When he straightened, he said, "I am Shawn O'Brien, Donna Aracela." He waved a careless hand. "These are my brothers and our ranch foreman."

"I am pleased to meet all of you." The woman blushed prettily and for a moment her lashes lay on her high cheekbones like black fans. When she looked up, she said, "You have come about the bandit named Joel Whitney."

Ironside reluctantly left the fireplace and stepped closer to Aracela. "Ma'am, we don't want your pa's sheep to move north. That's why we're here."

"Don Manuel does not own the sheep. He levies a tax on the herders for the use of his land, but it is a pittance compared to his other revenues."

Shawn looked around at his brothers, smiling. "Well, don't that beat all, boys. He doesn't own the sheep. But I hope that will not keep you and me from becoming good friends, Donna Aracela."

"If you wish, you may ask my father if you may walk out with me, Mr. O'Brien."

"I sure will, but please call me Shawn."

"I may, once we get to know each other better."

Aracela was tall and slender, dressed in unrelieved Castilian black. Her lace dress was cut low, revealing the upper mounds of her swelling breasts, a simple gold cross on a thin chain hanging between them. Her straight black hair fell over her shoulders like a midnight waterfall. She turned her attention away from Shawn and stared at Jacob. Her eyes were piercing blue, and far from innocent.

"You are the foreman Mr. O'Brien mentioned," she said.

"No," Jacob said, "I'm a brother." He nodded in Ironside's direction. "He's the foreman . . . and my father's friend."

"And your name is?"

"Jacob."

"You have a gift, Jacob."

Aracela's use of his brother's first name burned Shawn and he scowled, making sure Jacob saw it.

"I've been told that I have," Jacob said.

"Yes, for the piano. And for Chopin in particular."

"I guess that's so."

"Will you play for me some time?"

"Of course. I'd be honored."

Donna Aracela smiled. "You have the soul of an artist, yet of the men in this room—no, of the men in this house—you are the most dangerous." Her shiver was almost orgasmic. "It is an exquisite thing to be in your company."

Embarrassed, Jacob was spared the necessity of responding. The door opened and Don Manuel Antonio Ortero stepped inside. Like his daughter, he was dressed in mourning black, his clothing expensive and cut in the tight, severe Spanish style.

He was a gray-haired man of medium height, about the same age as Ironside, but unlike his, Ortero's features revealed little character or intelligence and were relieved from sullenness only by a trace of humor in his faded eyes.

"I am sorry to have kept you waiting, gentlemen, but my business was pressing." He smiled. "I have shares in a diamond mine in South Africa, you see, and it seems that the meddling British stopped production after a dozen native miners were killed in a rock fall. Now every day of their investigation is costing me money." He waved a hand. "But it's all very tiresome and I won't bore you with it. Please, be seated."

Don Manuel stepped to the side of the fireplace and yanked on a cord to summon a servant. When the woman appeared, he said, "Brandy. From the kitchen, not the wine cellar."

The man settled in a chair and steepled his fingers. "Now, what can I do for you gentlemen?"

Not liking this man, Jacob said, "I think you know why we're here."

"Ah, you wish to talk about that devil Joel Whitney, the one who murdered my son."

"Yes," Jacob said. "And we want your promise that you'll do all you can to keep your sheep in the Estancia."

"I own the land, not the sheep, señor."

Shawn said, "Don Manuel, I think what my brother is trying to say is that we will side with you against Whitney if we have your guarantee that the sheep will not move north beyond Lobo Hill."

"As to the sheep," the Mexican said, "I have already told you that they are not mine. Where they go, or do not go, is hardly my concern. But I am honor-bound to avenge my son's death, and I will kill Whitney with my own hand. To this end, I have a score of vaqueros armed and ready, but, of course, any assistance you can give will be welcome and most appreciated."

Frustration gnawing at his guts, Shawn said, "Don Manuel, many of your own people will die. Those folks outside—"

"Mr. O'Brien, people are born and they die. It is a fact of nature. But the land endures forever. I do not wish to sound harsh, but the death of ten peons, or ten thousand, is of little concern to me. I will fight to keep my land, for the land is all that matters. It is eternal, unchanging, and the measure of a man."

Shawn and Jacob exchanged glances, each reading defeat in the other's eyes.

Jacob stood. "Don Manuel, there's a shooting war coming down, and you can die like any other man. What good will the Estancia be to you then?"

The Mexican smiled. "Tell him, Aracela."

The woman had been sitting in a chair with her head bowed. Now, like Jacob, she stood. "I will wed, and I will have sons. They will take the name Ortero and inherit the land." She stared at Jacob. "You have perhaps heard that the peons cross themselves and run from me because they say I am blood eater. It is true that I am blessed with an inner eye that gives me the gift of second sight and much else besides. As you say, there will be war, and much blood. But as to who will live and who will die, that, for the present at least, is veiled to me."

In the next moment, she surprised the hell out of everybody, except her father, whose face didn't change, as though he'd known it was coming. "Jacob, you will give me sons. I can think of no finer sire than a warrior poet."

Taken aback, Jacob said the first thing that entered his mind. "I'm not a poet."

Aracela smiled. "Ah, but you are. The poetry of music runs deep in you."

Shawn rose so suddenly his chair slammed against

the wall. "Before we start discussing the wedding arrangements, let me say one thing to you, Don Manuel. We will not allow sheep north of Lobo Hill. If that means fighting both you and Whitney, then that's just how the deck cuts."

The Mexican looked toward the door. "Ah, good, the brandy is here."

Ironside said, rising, "We'll drink no brandy in this house until we know who our enemies are. Now, my talking is done."

"I am not your enemy," Don Manuel said.

"That remains to be seen." Ironside made for the door and the others followed.

But Aracela intercepted Jacob. She looked up at him, a smile on her lush lips. "You will be my husband, depend on it. I knew that as soon as I set eyes on you."

"Lady," Jacob said, "I'll be no woman's husband. Depend on that."

Ironside and the O'Briens stood outside in a light snowfall, waiting for the hacienda grooms to bring their horses. The black and somber sky scowled from horizon to horizon, and every breath of thin air they took was like drinking ice water. The wind had dropped, and the smoke from the peon shacks rose straight as string.

Donna Aracela followed the men outside, a shawl around her slim shoulders. She stood in the tiled archway of the main door to the house, her unwavering gaze on Jacob, her sharp blue eyes isolating him from the backdrop of the stone-gray day.

The Dromore riders watched as Andre Perez hesitantly approached the woman. The man bowed his head and said, "Lady, may I say this in English so my patrons may hear?"

"You are called?"

"Andre Perez, Lady. Just a poor vaquero from the north."

"Then speak on, Andre."

"Lady, when you hunt with the blood moon, please, I beg of you, spare my children."

Aracela's face did not change. "And why should I grant you this thing?"

"Lady, I am but a lowly vaquero, but perhaps one day I can repay the favor."

"Go," Aracela said. "I grant you this wish and I will remember what you owe."

As Perez bowed again and walked away, Patrick grinned at Shawn. "Do you still plan on walking out with her?"

Shawn shook his head. "Hell, no. I think I'll leave that to Jacob, seeing as how he and Donna Aracela are engaged."

Ironside laughed, but Jacob scowled and said something under his breath that sounded like a blood-curdler of a cuss.

Chapter Twenty-three

Ironside was leading the others out of the village when his horse shied, almost unseating him, spooked by the Mexican who galloped past, bareback on a mustang pony.

Ironside caught a glimpse of the rider's terrified face, and the blood covering the front of his shirt.

The young Mexican with a mop of coal-black hair slid from the mustang's back and began to yell at the top of his lungs, running from shack to shack, waving his hands in the air.

"Andre," Ironside said as he fought to settle his mount, "what the hell is going on?"

Perez swung from the saddle and plunged through the crowd that had gathered around the rider. He grabbed the man by his shirt and tried to shake him into some sort of coherence.

"¿Lo que sucedio?" Perez hollered.

The man babbled away in Spanish for a good three or four minutes before he stopped for a breath.

Perez turned and said, "Three herders were killed

near Rattlesnake Hill this morning just after dawn. Some of their sheep were gunned, the rest scattered to hell and gone."

"Is that man wounded?" Patrick said, urging his horse closer.

"No, patron." Perez let the man drop to the ground. "He's dead." The vaquero kneeled by the body and tore open the herder's shirt. "Three bullet wounds in his chest, so close together I could cover them with the palm of my hand."

Shawn angled a glance at Jacob. "Texans?"

"That kind of shooting?" Jacob said, his face troubled. "You can bet your life on it."

A couple women were wailing, tearing at their hair and clothes, mourning husbands or sons, Shawn O'Brien didn't know which. To Perez he said, "Mount up, Andre." And to his brothers and Ironside, "We'll head down to Rattlesnake and take a look around."

"They'll be long gone," Ironside said.

"I know, but I don't have a better idea. Do you?"

As they rode south, Jacob turned and looked behind him.

Don Manuel, surrounded by vaqueros, was talking to the peons, his body stiff with anger, his face flushed. Donna Aracela silently looked on. She did not make a move to comfort the grieving women. It was as though she'd been chipped from a block of ice.

He was no doubt vowing revenge, for the peasants and for his dead son.

Jacob could clearly see the bad times were coming down fast.

Joel Whitney had opened the ball . . . and now there would be a hundred different kinds of hell to pay.

The volcanic peak of Rattlesnake Hill rose above a rolling flat covered in brush, blue grama, and buffalo grass. A few cottonwoods stood among the piñon and juniper that grew in abundance. The day had grown colder, and the breaths of the five riders smoked in the icy air.

They saw vast herds of sheep, but no herders. The Mexicans had either fled when they got the news of the killings, or were sheltering from the cold and a rising wind that stirred the prairie grass and cut to the bone.

Perez, scouting ahead, appeared at the top of a rise and used his sombrero to wave the others on. Rattlesnake Hill soared behind him. Silhouetted black against the dark sky, its peak was almost lost behind a haze of cloud and the tattered lace curtain of the falling snow.

When the four riders reached the crest, Perez pointed. "Down there by the creek."

"All of them dead?" Shawn asked.

"Yes, patron, but one of them died harder than the others," Perez said. "You will see."

The slope of the rise led down to a flat, then a hundred yards farther, to a narrow stream only about a yard across. He drew rein and pointed to the naked, crucified man.

Some time in the past, the cottonwood had been struck by lightning and had fallen. The trunk and branches were bone white and no longer looked like a tree, more like the skeletal spine and ribs of a great animal.

The herder, a small, thin man with gray in his hair, lay on his back on the trunk, arms over his head. Fencing staples had been hammered into both his palms. Some had hit bone or gristle, and hadn't gone all the way through to the trunk, so a lot more had been used. It looked as though someone had filled the dead man's hands with silver coins. His feet were on the ground, but both his knees had been smashed by bullets.

"My God," Ironside said, his face ashen under his mahogany tan. "He died a terrible death."

Shawn crossed himself. "Jesus, Mary, and Joseph, give him rest."

"Damn it! He's bait!" Jacob roared. He dug his spurs into his horse and the startled animal crashed into Ironside and Patrick, who were side by side. Ironside's mount went down kicking, and Patrick's horse shied wildly to its right.

Rifle bullets split the air between Jacob and Shawn. Another bounced off a rock on the bank of the creek. *Spaaang!* It ricocheted and plowed a furrow across Perez's forehead. The vaquero fell and didn't try to rise again.

Ironside lay flat on his back, winded and clawing for

his gun. Patrick fought to control his crow-hopping horse, the terrified animal bucking him away from the creek. Its iron-shod hooves rang across the frozen ground like hammers on an anvil, a sharp counterpoint to the dull roar of guns.

Jacob had the bushwhackers spotted. "Shawn, follow me." Without waiting for an answer, he kicked his horse into a gallop, his Colt up and ready. Ahead of him, three men crouched behind a rock pile. One rose to his feet, Winchester to his shoulder, and cut loose. Jacob fired, fired again. The man threw up his hands and fell, his rifle spinning away from him.

Behind him, Jacob heard the bang of Shawn's revolver. A man wearing a fur hat and sheepskin coat broke and ran from the rocks. Jacob fired and cut him down. The third bushwhacker rose, making a motion like he was raising his arms in surrender, but Shawn drew rein and shot him. The man grabbed at his left shoulder, spun and fell.

It was all over. Gray gun smoke drifted across the flat, getting tangled in the falling snow. Behind the rock pile a man groaned, then cursed.

When Shawn looked at Jacob, his eyes were admiring, but guarded. "I couldn't have done that."

"Done what?" Jacob fed fresh shells into his Colt.

"Shoot two men while I was on the back of a running horse. Who taught you that, Jacob? Luther Ironside?"

"Nobody taught me," Jacob said. "It's just something a man knows how to do. It can't be taught to him."

"You're hell on wheels with the Colt," Shawn said. "I didn't quite believe it before, but I believe it now."

"I know," Jacob said, without a trace of brag in his voice. "I discovered that I had the skill a long time ago. I don't know where it comes from." He holstered his gun, listening to the wounded gunman curse. "Sounds like the bushwhacker you gunned is still alive, Shawn. Let's go read to him from the book."

The Texan was young, too frightened to act tough, and his wound was devastating. Shawn's bullet had gone all the way through, shattering his shoulder blade into white shards as it exited.

Jacob propped the kid's back against a rock and kneeled beside him so they were at eye level. Ironside, in a thunderous rage, loomed over the gunman. Perez, only slightly wounded, but looking terrible from the blood running down his face, glared at the gunman with a killing light in his eyes.

"How did you know we'd be here?" Shawn said.

"I don't know you," the Texan said. "I didn't know you'd be here. I thought you was greasers."

"Hell, boy," Ironside said. "Do I look like a Mexican to you?"

"It's snowing," the kid said. "It was hard to see."

"So you shot at us, and didn't even know who we were?"

The young Texan had no answer for that. Grimacing, he said, "I need a doctor."

"What's your name, son?" Jacob said, although he and the kid were about the same age.

"Ted White. Up from Tarrant County, Texas."

Jacob pointed with his chin. "And them?"

"The one in the fur hat is, or was, Deck Rawlins. We called the other one Heap. I never heard his real name."

"You killed the herders?" Shawn said.

"Yeah."

"And the man nailed to the tree?"

"Yeah. We figured he'd draw in more greasers. We stashed our horses in a canyon back there and laid up for them. Then you boys showed up."

"Your mistake," Jacob said.

"Who are you taking orders from, Ted?" Patrick asked. "Is it Joel Whitney?"

"Yeah, him and Clay Stanley."

Jacob jerked a thumb over his shoulder in the direction of the creek. "That's a hell of a way to kill a man. Whose idea was it? Whitney's?"

"No, Deck came up with it, and we went along with him." The kid looked at the hostile faces surrounding him. "Hell, what are you boys getting so worked up about? He's only a greaser sheepherder like the rest."

Jacob nodded. "Yeah, you're right. That's all he was, and now it's all he'll ever be."

"Get me to a doctor," White said. "I'm hurtin' real bad."

"I bet the sheepherder hurt real bad too, huh?" Jacob said.

"You're a murderer, Ted." Shawn's scowl disappeared, replaced by a look of slight sympathy. "We're going to hang you."

The Texan was shocked, incredulous. His eyes widened. "For killing greasers? You can't do that. You ain't the law."

"Yes, for that. And for taking the wrong side against Dromore, our home ranch."

"Damn you, I never heard of Dromore," White said.

"Nevertheless, it exists. And when you signed on with Joel Whitney you declared war on Dromore and all who are a part of it."

It was Shawn who kneeled next to him, but it was his father's voice Jacob heard, and his father's face he saw. He expected to hear a challenge from Patrick or Ironside, pleading for the Texan's life. But White had admitted his crimes and the brutal crucifixion of the Mexican sheepherder allowed him little leeway.

Ironside's face was grim, as was Patrick's, but Jacob saw no hint of mercy in their eyes. He rose to his feet, drew his Colt, and shot White in the middle of his forehead.

Shawn, his face suddenly splashed by the Texan's blood, brain, and bone, sprang to his feet. "Why the hell did you do that?" he yelled.

As he always did, Jacob replaced the spent round in his revolver.

"Because I've seen enough of hanging, and so have you. He's dead and there's an end to it."

"Damn it, Jacob"—Shawn's handsome face flushed— "he died too easy."

"No man dies too easy," Jacob said. "Even in bed, with the priest at his side saying the words, he doesn't die too easy."

"Shawn, let it go," Patrick said. "I've little appetite for hanging a man. How many times over the years have we seen men kicking at the end of ropes with all that was inside them running down their legs?"

It was left to Ironside. As he'd done so often when the brothers were boys, he put a comforting arm around Shawn's shoulders. "Jacob did the right thing. Sometimes a man has to shape up to what he thinks is best."

Shawn nodded, but said nothing. Finally he looked down at the dead Texan, then at the two others lying sprawled on the ground, snow already gathering on their bodies. "We'll put them on their horses and take them back to Estancia. It might convince Whitney that his hired guns can't get away with murder."

Patrick nodded to the crucified man and the bodies of the two other Mexicans. "What about them?"

"We'll take them, too. It's kind of fitting that their last journey is beside the men who murdered them."

"Luther, help me free the man from the tree," Patrick said.

"Sure," Ironside said, "but it sure as hell ain't gonna be easy."

Chapter Twenty-four

The afternoon was so dark it was difficult to determine when the day ended and the night began. But when the O'Briens' melancholy procession rode into Estancia, lamps already burned in the hotel and saloon. A lantern on the front wall of the general store cast a shifting circle of orange light on the snow-streaked street. The air snapped of the hoarfrost glistening on roofs and lacing every window in town.

There was no law in Estancia, but there was an undertaker who prospered. Godwin J. Kendrick had the instincts of a buzzard. It was said he could smell death at a ten-mile distance. True or not, he was the first to greet the O'Briens when they brought the bodies into town.

Kendrick wore a black top hat, a claw-tailed coat of the same color, and a professional expression of the deepest despondency.

Ironside pegged him at once. "We've got business for you."

The undertaker did a little hand wringing, then

said, "And who are the recently departed?" His eyes roved over the bodies hanging head down over the horses. "Oh dear. So many of them."

"Three Texans, three Mexican herders," Ironside said. "The Mexicans we'll take back to their village."

Kendrick had a strange walk. Listing to one side, he hopped around like a seedy black crow with a broken wing, and looked up at Ironside. "I do a real nice embalming, and extend full viewing privileges to loved ones. In this kind of weather, I can display the deceased for three days if that's what the grieving families desire. I also provide, at cost mind you, a planed pine coffin with a brass nameplate and chocolate cake and ice cream to refresh the mourners. All this for just ten dollars a head." He smiled like an animated cadaver. "I could say ten dollars a skull, a little undertaker's joke, you understand."

"Take their horses and traps, sell them for what you can get, and bury the Texans decent," Ironside said, ignoring the man's sales pitch. "They don't need cake and ice cream. There won't be any mourners."

"Trouble," Patrick said, his voice edged. Ironside turned and looked at him, then followed the younger man's eyes to the hotel.

Clay Stanley stood on the porch, flanked by Charlie Packett and a tall, loose-geared man the O'Briens had never seen before.

Stanley was not wearing a coat, the Russians in his shoulder holsters butt-forward and significant. Packett's coat was swept back, clearing his gun. The third man slanted a Greener shotgun across his chest, but he seemed relaxed, as though he knew he wasn't about to get into a shooting scrape any time soon.

"'Evenin', Jacob," Stanley said.

"Clay," Jacob acknowledged.

"You've been out riding, huh?" Stanley said. "All of you look half froze."

Jacob moved in the saddle, the cold leather creaking. "Frozen some."

"What you got there, Jacob?"

"Three dead Texans and the same number of dead Mexicans. I reckon you'll know the Texans, Clay."

"Mind if I take a look?"

"Go right ahead."

Godwin Kendrick, his lank, pale, shoulder-length hair under his top hat tossing in the wind, had enlisted the help of his assistant, a small, fat man with a jolly face, reminding Patrick of Mr. Dickens' old Fezziwig. The two undertakers had laid the Mexicans side by side on the street, and were leading away the horses with the dead Texans.

"Hold on there, bone planters," Stanley said. "I want to take a look."

He examined the bodies closely, even getting Kendrick to help turn them over. Finally, his jaw knotted, he said, "All right, take them away."

The snow flurried again, borne on the coldest of wind. Stanley, shivering, stepped back to the porch. "All their wounds are in front, Jacob."

"I reckon so, Clay. Those boys killed the Mexicans,

and then tried to bushwhack us. Their day went downhill pretty fast after that."

"Seems like you boys have taken sides," Stanley said.

Shawn could be hot-tempered. "Sure as hell, I'm not going to discuss taking sides sitting a horse out here in the cold. Are you planning to skin those irons, Stanley, or will you give us the road?"

"This is not the place or the time for gunplay, Mr. O'Brien." Stanley made a little bow. "The road is yours."

Shawn turned in the saddle. "Luther, tell the undertaker to put the Mexicans somewhere until tomorrow. Hell, we can't leave them lying in the street."

Ironside nodded and rode toward Kendrick's place.

"Andre, you and me will put up the horses and feed them a bait of oats." Patrick looked at Ironside's retreating back. "I guess Luther can fend for himself."

"*Sí*, patron." Perez swung out of the saddle, as did the others. Jacob handed the reins to the vaquero and was turning away—when Clay Stanley drew and fired.

The man was fast, blindingly fast. He'd shot both Russians dry by the time Jacob's hand dropped to his gun. Stanley had triggered the big, bucking .44s so rapidly it sounded like he'd fired only one shot from each.

Jacob had time to take only one wild glimpse at the Texan, enough to realize the man was shooting off to his left, away from him and the others.

Jacob turned in the direction of the shots, Colt in hand, and saw two coyotes writhing in death about twenty-five yards from the hotel. Both had been shot many times, their ragged winter coats splashed scarlet with blood.

The smoking Russians in his hands, Stanley smiled at Jacob. "I didn't mean to scare you."

Ironside arrived at a gallop, a revolver in his right fist. He drew rein so violently his horse's rump slammed into the frozen earth. Glancing at Jacob and the others, he saw that everyone was unhurt. He glared at Stanley. "What the hell were you doing, boy?"

"Shooting at coyotes," the gunman said. He nodded. "Over there. The smell of the bodies must've brought them in close."

Ironside kneed his trembling horse forward and looked at the torn-up animals. After a while, he turned in the saddle and called out to Stanley, "Hell, you don't miss much, do you?"

"Not as a general rule," the Texan said. Beside him, Packet grinned, enjoying the show. Jacob's eyes clashed with Stanley's. A single shot at their feet would have sent the coyotes scampering, but the man had chosen to gun them. Why? The answer was that he'd sent a message Jacob O'Brien read clear: *Don't mess with me, Jacob, because I'm a lot faster than you.*

A sudden sickness in his belly, Jacob realized that Stanley could be right.

Chapter Twenty-five

"Strange kind of range war this, isn't it?" Clay Stanley said.

Shawn O'Brien, firelight reflecting on his face, said nothing.

"I mean, here we are, sworn enemies, yet we sit in the hotel parlor drinking brandy and listening to Chopin like we were old friends."

"We're not your enemy, Clay," Ironside said. "At least not yet we ain't."

He sat on an easy chair, facing the fire, Stanley and Shawn on either side of him. All three men held brandy snifters and smoked Havana cigars, the aroma of both heavy in the warm room.

Jacob, to his joy, had found the parlor's upright piano was in tune, and his long fingers moved over the keys coaxing Chopin's genius from ebony and ivory. Befitting the weather, he played the composer's stormy *Polonaise in F-sharp minor*, a piece that also fitted his present, unsettled mood.

"The Mexicans must get off Whitney land," Stanley said. "That's the beginning and end of it."

Shawn had been staring into the log fire. He shifted his attention to the Texan. "I've got no quarrel with what you say, so long as they don't drive their sheep north of Lobo Hill."

"I still can't guarantee that won't happen," Stanley said.

"I know, and that's why we're on opposite sides," Shawn said.

"Even if Don Manuel looks like he's winning, the herders won't stay put in the middle of a range war. They'll get the hell out of there."

"I know."

"Then you can't win either way."

"There is a way to finish it quickly," Shawn said. "It's a risk, but it would end the threat to Dromore."

Stanley's interest quickened. "What's your plan, O'Brien?"

Shawn smiled. "You don't really think I'd tell you, do you?"

Easing back in his chair, the Texan smiled. "No, I guess you wouldn't."

Jacob played the melancholy middle section of the Polonaise while Patrick and Perez sat at a table arguing over a game of checkers. Judging by the vaquero's groans and string of Spanish curses, Shawn reckoned he was getting a drubbing. But then, Patrick had read books on how to play checkers—and on just about everything else.

Now and then drifts of smoke gusted from the

fireplace as the wind explored the chimney. The panes of the parlor windows were etched in frost and there were no sounds from outside.

Shawn rose, poured brandy into Stanley's glass, refilled his own, and sat back down. "Who ordered the murder of the herders?"

Stanley seemed surprised. "You think it was me?"

"Ted White said he took orders from you and Whitney."

"I didn't give that order. Killing sheepherders is not my style. But I did tell White to scare the Mexicans off the land, any way he knew how."

Stanley was quiet for a while. "But if it comes to that, and there's no other way, I'll kill a Mexican herder as fast I'd kill any other man."

"There may be no other way," Shawn said.

"Then that's how the pickle squirts."

"I planned to hang White for murder."

"And what stopped you?"

"Jacob shot him. He said he didn't hold with hanging."

"What are you telling me, O'Brien?" Stanley still sat at ease, smiling, but he had tenseness in him nonetheless.

"That I'll hang any man I find killing herders."

Stanley recognized the implied threat, but felt no need for belligerent talk. He knew how hard he was to kill, let alone hang, and Shawn O'Brien was certainly aware of it. "If the Mexicans move their herds north, you'll slaughter them. There's no difference between you and me, O'Brien."

"There's a big difference," Shawn said. "You fight for wages. I fight to save my land."

"And that puts you in the right?"

"Yes, it does. If it's for Dromore, then there can be no wrong to it."

The wind, coming hard off the flat lands, talked around the building, and if a far-seeing man had stepped outside, he'd have seen more snow clouds building above the Manzano Mountains.

Stanley stood and tapped ash from his cigar into the fireplace. "Joel Whitney will be here tomorrow or the day after with more Texan guns. I say we call a truce until then."

"Sets fine by me." Shawn glanced at Packett. "If there's no grandstand plays on your side."

"There won't be. At least, until Whitney arrives." Stanley studied the glowing end of his cigar at arm's length, as though it was of immense interest to him. "Ted White was trash and so were the other two."

"You'll get no argument with me on that score," Shawn said.

"You'd have been right to hang him. I saw the hands on one of the dead herders."

"They crucified him," Shawn said. "They used fence staples."

Stanley nodded. "Well, none of them Texas boys are a great loss. They were as slow on the draw and shoot as molasses in winter."

* * *

By midnight, most everyone had turned in. Only Shawn, Jacob, and Luther Ironside sat around the dying embers of the fire.

"So there you have it," Shawn said. "I don't see any other way."

"As you say, Shawn, it's a way," Ironside said. "But it's a tall order. How many of us will be left standing when the smoke clears?"

"I guess that depends on how we handle it." Shawn looked at his brother. "Jacob?"

"I'll go along with it, for now. I say we hold fast for a few days and see how things shake out."

"Luther, do you feel the same?" Shawn said.

"Clay Stanley says Whitney will be here tomorrow or the day after. We can wait that long. Hell, we have to wait that long."

Shawn was silent for a while, thinking. "All right, we play it your way. But if it goes belly-up all of a sudden, we act. We kill Whitney and Don Manuel and it's all over."

Jacob smiled. "Maybe we should get us a Gatling gun and shoot all the woolies. That would solve our problem."

Shawn shook his head. "I wish to hell it was that easy."

Chapter Twenty-six

From the dining room window, Donna Aracela saw the O'Brien brothers ride into the village, three bodies draped over the saddles of the horses they led.

She dabbed the corners of her mouth with a napkin. "Look outside, Father. It appears we will have more bad news."

Don Manuel glanced out the window and swore. Throwing down his napkin, he jumped to his feet, bumping the table with such force the coffeepot toppled and a brown stain spread across the white tablecloth. "It's the dead men, by God. The handiwork of the devil Whitney arrives on my doorstep."

From the window, Aracela watched Jacob O'Brien intently, a hard man bred from a hard land that winnowed out the weak and nurtured the strong. His shoulders were wide, his gloved hands large and capable, and the great beak of a nose that dominated his face spoke of determination and power of will.

She smiled. Truly, he was a man with whom to

breed, a man who would give her a fine son. Later, after they'd coupled and his duty was done, she would dispose of him.

The woman threw her mud-stained cloak over her russet silk morning dress and stepped outside. She made a face. The snow still fell. Lord above, would it never end?

Chapter Twenty-seven

Jacob O'Brien was more convinced than ever that the village surrounding the Hacienda Ortero was an annex of hell.

Women wailed and cried over the bodies of the three dead herders, all from the village.

Andre Perez was visibly upset. The vaquero stared at the hacienda, tolling his beads, his lips moving in silent prayer. Ironside noted the man's deep distress. Now that the rented packhorses were free of their dead, he ordered Perez to return them to Estancia.

Perez, after casting one last, frightened look at the hacienda, gladly obeyed.

Ironside frowned in thought. He'd known Andre Perez for a long time and the vaquero had sand. He was a top hand, fast with the iron, and feared no man. But something around the hacienda scared him badly. Ironside, for the life of him, couldn't figure what it was.

"Thank you, Mr. Ironside, for returning our dead. It is a sad day for all of us." Donna Aracela stood at

Ironside's left stirrup, looking up at him, her lush mouth parted in a smile.

Enchanted by her breathtaking beauty, Ironside touched his hat. "God bless you, ma'am, your concern for the dead men does you credit. But you must go inside. You'll catch your death of cold out here."

"I will, later. First I wish to speak with Jacob." She turned her head. "Ah, he and his brothers are talking with my father." Aracela directed her attention back to Ironside. "Please, when he is free, ask him to visit me at the hacienda."

Ironside nodded. "I sure will, ma'am. Now get yourself inside."

He watched the woman walk away, tall, stately, with the kind of body that keeps a thinking man awake of nights. Ironside nodded. She was a fine lady, no doubt about that.

"You avenged the deaths of my villagers," Don Manuel said, "and for that I am grateful. But, like the devil Whitney and his mercenaries, I want you off the Estancia." Flanked by vaqueros, the Mexican stood bareheaded in the snow, a woolen military cloak slung over his shoulders. "You have Dromore, Mr. O'Brien, and now you must go back to it."

"I will," Shawn said, "if the sheep stay well away from our range."

Don Manuel looked around him, saw the man he wanted, and called him over. The peon was nervous, his gaze constantly shifting from his patron to the hard-eyed vaqueros. The don said something to the man in quick Spanish and Shawn caught only a few words of it.

Finally Don Manuel looked at Shawn again. "This man says the sheepherders are scared, and, indeed, there is much talk of moving north onto your grazing lands."

"Have any sheep passed Lobo Hill?" Shawn said.

Don Manuel spoke to the peon again, then again to Shawn. "He says not yet, but if another herder is killed that will change very quickly."

Shawn was about to make war talk to the peon, but realized it was useless. It would be like threatening the north wind not to bring the winter snows.

Don Manuel saw his confusion and said, "I will rid the Estancia of the Whitney infestation very quickly. Once the land is free of him, the herders will stay, and those that have already crossed into Dromore will return."

"I can't let that happen, Don Manuel," Shawn said. "I won't allow a single sheep to set foot on our range."

The Mexican let out a theatrical sigh. "Then I can do no more for you. I'm sorry, Mr. O'Brien, but you will be gone from the Estancia by this time tomorrow. If you still remain, my men will consider you an enemy." He waved hand toward a group of weeping women. "Now go, and let us bury our dead."

Shawn knew he was being pushed, but let it go. To put Don Manuel on guard could ruin his plans. He swallowed his pride and said only, "I'll leave your people to their grief."

But Don Manuel had already walked away, as though he hadn't the slightest interest in what Shawn O'Brien had to say.

"Luther told me you wanted to see me, Donna Aracela," Jacob said.

The woman smiled. Her hair was piled on top of her head, held in place by a tortoiseshell comb. Jacob figured if she was not the prettiest gal in the West, she came almighty close.

"I'm afraid you visit the Hacienda Ortero at a sad time," Aracela said. "There is much to be mourned."

"Well, it wasn't a hug-the-kinfolk kind of visit," Jacob said. "We brought back the three men who were killed by Whitney's riders."

"You haven't told me when I can hear you play."

"I don't know. Soon, maybe."

"How very vague, Jacob."

"Maybe it's because I'm living in parlous times."

"But there is nothing parlous between us, is there?"

"No. Unless we end up on opposite sides."

"Look out there, Jacob. My father is talking with your brother. Perhaps they can work things out."

"I sure hope so."

Aracela waved to a silver jug and goblets on the parlor table. "Wine?"

"Too early in the morning for me," Jacob said.

"Do you mind if I do?"

"No, please go ahead."

The wine poured bloodred into Aracela's goblet. She drank, and then said, "Have you thought more about our wedding day?"

Jacob smiled. "I've already told you, I'm not the marrying kind."

She laid her glass on the table and stepped close to him. As she pressed her body against his, her arms encircled his neck. Her searching lips hungrily found his.

He surrendered to the pleasure the woman brought him, the feel of her body so close, her grinding hips, and the firmness of her breasts. His manhood swelling, he pushed hard against her, but Aracela smiled against his mouth and stepped back.

"What's wrong?" Jacob said, his voice husky with desire.

"Not like this," she said. "After we marry, you'll bed me and I'll make you bless the day you were born. I want a son from you, Jacob, a son."

"Hell, I can give you a son without us getting hitched."

"No!" Aracela's eyes blazed. "I don't want a bastard. A bastard cannot become master of the Hacienda Ortero."

"Hell, then why me?" Jacob said.

"Because you are a man. Mucho hombre!"

She stepped toward him, her eyes aglow, but Jacob held up a hand. "No, not again. I'm still recovering from the last time." He managed a weak smile. "I was told men died after kissing you. Now I know what that means, because I'm dying a hundred different kinds of death right now."

Aracela drank again. A thin trickle of wine ran from the corner of her bruised mouth like blood. "You will come to me again, Jacob. I will send for you and we will talk of our wedding day."

She laid the goblet down, turned, and swept from the room.

Jacob's head was reeling, as though he'd drained Aracela's silver wine jug to the last, scarlet drop.

Outside, his brothers and Ironside waited for him at the far end of the village. Shawn's face was tight, the weather lines showing deep. Ironside was solemn, but Patrick grinned from ear to ear when Jacob rode up to him.

"Ah, brother, and how is *La Belle Dame Sans Merci*?"

"Huh?" Jacob said, his eyes unfocussed.

"Then you haven't read the poem by John Keats, about the knight who falls in love with a fairy princess who loves him and leaves him."

"Hell, are you taking about Donna Aracela?"

"No brother, I'm talking about you." Patrick's grin grew. "'O what can ail thee knight at arms, alone and palely loitering? The sedge has wither'd from the lake, and no birds sing.'"

"I'd say he's pale because Donna Aracela is still determined to marry him," Shawn said.

Jacob nodded. "Yeah, something like that." He

shook his head, trying to clear his brain. "I swear, it's like the woman cast a spell on me."

"I've got a pretty good idea what she cast a spell on," Shawn said. "Get your mind above your belt buckle and back on the job, Jacob. Unless I'm very much mistaken, we'll soon have troubles coming at us from every direction."

Chapter Twenty-eight

Shawn O'Brien stared across the snow and wind-swept plain east of Lobo Hill. "Not a wooly in sight. They aren't moving north, at least not yet."

"I reckon that'll change when Joel Whitney gets here," Ironside brushed snow from his mustache with the back of his gloved hand. "He'll scare them herders into a run."

The land around the Dromore riders lay white under a black sky, but it was more frost than snow, and the ground underneath was iron hard. Above them a red-tailed hawk quartered the sky, its wings motionless as it sailed the air currents.

Andre Perez, a far-sighted man, stood in his stirrups, his eyes searching into the distance.

"What do you see, Andre?" Patrick looked where Perez looked, but saw nothing, only the blustering snow.

"I thought I saw something move in the draw," Perez said.

"An antelope, maybe?" Patrick said.

The vaquero shook his head. "A rider, I think."

Jacob slid the Winchester from the boot under his left knee. He said to Ironside, "Apache?"

"I doubt it." Ironside said. "Only white men are crazy enough to ride out in this kind of weather. It's more likely Clay Stanley decided to break his truce."

"I'll go take a look-see," Jacob said.

Shawn kneed his mount forward. "I'll come with you." He turned to the others. "If you see us split-ass away from there, come a-shooting."

Jacob and Shawn rode toward the draw at a walk, snow stinging into their faces. "Hell," Shawn said, "I can't see a damn thing."

"Well, it isn't a bushwhacker," Jacob said.

"How come?"

"Because he'd be shooting by now."

Jacob reined to his left and rode up on the draw at its widest point. Piñon, juniper, and a few cotton-woods grew on the sand and shingle slope. Ice puddles were scattered along the bottom. He swung out of the saddle and stepped to the top of the slope, his rifle up and ready.

"See anything?" Shawn called out above the howl of the wind. He sat his horse about twenty yards away near a mesquite thicket, a Colt in his hand.

"Nothing," Jacob yelled back.

Snow flurried through the draw and the wind bit savagely. Jacob's face was raw from cold and the fingers in his gloves were stiff. He made his way down the slope, digging in his heels to avoid sliding, doubt accompanying each tentative step.

After what seemed like an eternity, Jacob reached

the bottom of the draw. Despite the snow, hoofprints were still visible in the sand, heading east. He followed the tracks for fifty yards, but then lost them. The rider had left the draw at that point and disappeared into the darkness of the day.

Shawn stood on the top of the slope. "What do you reckon?"

"I reckon we're being watched," Jacob said.

"Stanley?"

"Could be."

Shawn holstered his gun. "Let's go ask him."

"Suits me," Jacob said. "I've had enough of snow and ice for one day."

None of the horses in the hotel barn had been ridden recently. Jacob acknowledged that fact, then said, "Well, we know it wasn't one of Stanley's men."

"Then it could only be Don Manuel," Shawn said.

"Why? He'd just spoken with us. And he knew where we were headed. He didn't need to spy on us."

Shawn shook his head. "Then it's a mystery."

"Yeah," Jacob said, "but one we could do without."

The O'Briens walked into the hotel parlor, bringing cold air with them. Fat flakes of snow fell from their coats and boots.

Clay Stanley was taking his ease by the fire, a book in his hands. He looked up, smiled, and laid the book on the side table beside his chair. "You boys delivered the dead Mexicans, huh?"

"Your men did the killing, Clay," Jacob said. "It should've been your job."

The Texan shrugged. "It was none of my doing."

"Your boss arrived yet, Stanley?" Shawn said.

"No. Not yet."

"Then why are you wearing your guns?"

"Because I feel undressed without them." He looked pointedly at Shawn's open coat. "You're wearing yours."

"Yeah, for killing varmints," Shawn said, the challenge in his voice easy to hear.

But Stanley, unruffled, took it in stride. "Plenty of those around the Estancia." Patrick picked up the Texan's book from the table and glanced at the spine. "*Jane Eyre.* Are you keen on Charlotte Brontë?"

"Hell, I don't know. Somebody left the book in my room. It's about this little gal who—"

"I know what it's about," Patrick said.

"Them English gals are mighty strange," Stanley said.

"Seems like all the gals we've met recently are that way," Shawn said, his eyes angling to Jacob.

His brother smiled and said nothing.

Just before midnight, Joel Whitney led a column of twenty riders and six mule wagons into Estancia.

After he palmed a clear circle in the frosted pane, Jacob watched from his bedroom window. Men, horses, and wagons were covered in snow and moved through the darkness like gray ghosts. A small man wearing an ankle-length fur coat dismounted and shouted orders, his breath steaming in the crystalline air.

His men dismounted, then four of them gathered

up the horses and headed for the barn. The rest, led by the small man—who could only be Joel Whitney—crowded into the hotel, and Jacob heard the clump of booted feet in the lobby below.

He dressed quickly, strapped on his gun, and stepped to Shawn's room.

His brother was already awake and armed. "Get the others up, We'll go down to the parlor and see what's shaking."

A few minutes later, the O'Briens, Ironside, and Perez stepped into the parlor where Whitney was arguing with the owner, a handsome, portly woman who called herself Mrs. Hazel. Behind her, the desk clerk wrung his hands and looked scared.

"But there's a saloon just across the way, Mr. Whitney," the woman said. "I'm sure you can wake the owner, Mr. Simpson. He's such a nice man."

"You serve booze here, am I right?" Whitney said.

"Yes, but—"

"Then bring all the bottles you have in here. My men need a drink and they need it now."

He turned away from Mrs. Hazel, but swung back on her. "And rooms. I need rooms for myself and twenty-six men."

"But this is a small hotel." The woman's face was frantic. "I have only twelve rooms, and all but one is occupied."

"How many rooms do my men already have?" Whitney had the eyes of a carrion-eater.

"Three. But—"

"Then throw the others out, and you'll have nine rooms available."

"But I can't throw my guests out in the snow," Mrs. Hazel said.

"Oh dear me, no," the clerk said, wringing his hands some more. "That just isn't done."

"All right, if you don't want to do it, I will," Whitney said.

"Then I guess you'd better start with me," Jacob stood easy, his right thumb hooked into his gun belt near his holstered Colt. His eyes were colder than the night outside.

Sudden anger flared in Whitney's face. "Who the hell are you?"

"I'm one of the guests you plan to throw out in the snow. I'd take being rousted from my room real hard."

It was a measure of Whitney's arrogance that he didn't recognize the warning signs that the tall, hatchet-faced man was ready and had no backup in him.

But Clay Stanley knew better.

He watched the Dromore men spread out on either side of Jacob and noted the whispering uncertainty of the hired guns. The parlor was small and crowded with furniture. In a close-range drawfight with tough men who knew how to shoot, the concussion of the revolvers would extinguish the oil lamps and fill the room with smoke. Men would drop in the darkness, and it didn't take a mastermind to figure out that far too many of them would be Texans.

Stanley's words dropped like rocks into the tense silence and ended it. "Mr. Whitney, these men are my friends."

Every man present knew the next move was Whitney's. Despite his growing irritation, the little man realized he'd run out of room on the dance floor. It was not the place or the time to push a gunfight.

"All right," he said to Mrs. Hazel, "since these men are friends of Mr. Stanley, leave them be, but clear out the rest of the rooms. My boys will double up. They won't be here long."

Mrs. Hazel was horrified. "But there's old Widow Allison, who can barely walk, and old Mr. Robson who has the rheumatisms, and—"

"I don't give a damn. Get them out of here." Whitney glared at the woman. "If you're so all-fired worried about the old people, take them into your room." He pointed at a couple of his men. "You two, see that the rooms are cleared."

The grinning gunmen walked to the door, Mrs. Hazel following after them, clucking like a distressed hen.

"And don't forget the whiskey," Whitney called out to her retreating back.

The desk clerk continued wringing his hands and said, "I'll bring the refreshments right away, gentlemen."

"Good," Whitney said. "Now get the hell out of here." He waved a dismissive hand at Jacob. "And that goes for you, too."

Outside the snow lay thick on the canvas covers of Joel Whitney's wagons and a rambunctious wind tossed icy flakes at the mules and howled its delight.

Chapter Twenty-nine

Shadows flickered in the chapel of the Hacienda Ortero as Donna Aracela lit a second candle and placed it on the altar, to the right of the tabernacle where the village priest kept the consecrated hosts. The candle flame cast light on the nearby image of Our Lady of Montserrat. The Black Madonna's statue was an exact copy of the one that stood in the Santa Maria monastery in Catalonia, and Don Manuel had brought an artist all the way from Spain to carve it.

Donna Aracela, her hair covered by a mantilla of fine black lace, left the altar and kneeled in a pew. She let her rosary beads count through her fingers, her scarlet lips moving in prayer.

A sleek wind rapped the chapel's arched wooden doors, demanding entry. Intrusive gusts made the flames of the altar candles dance and stirred the tapestries on the walls. The air smelled of incense and smoke, and of Donna Aracela's perfume.

Midnight came and went, then the chapel doors

opened, letting in a blast of icy air and snow. The man who stepped inside had trouble pushing the doors shut against the wind, but he finally slammed them home and shoved a wooden bolt into place. His spurs ringing on the flagstone floor, he walked toward the altar, then kneeled beside the woman.

She turned her head and looked at the vaquero. "Well?"

"I have bad news."

"Then you killed no one."

"I watched them for a while, but the weather was so bad I could not risk a shot."

"I want the man with the handsome face dead first, Otilio. He does not like me and could be a problem."

"I won't fail you next time, Donna Aracela."

"See that you don't. I expect much of you, Otilio, now and in the future."

The young vaquero's face was earnest. "I am yours to command. I love you, more than life itself." He suddenly looked almost shy. "You promised me . . ."

"But only if you succeeded."

"I tried. I really did try. It was the weather that spoiled my aim."

Aracela smiled. "Otilio, I can deny you nothing. But tonight, only a taste. When the handsome one is dead, and you perform my other tasks, you will have more." She smiled. When the time came, Otilio would be easy to kill.

The Black Madonna held her baby son close, and looked down with painted eyes at Donna Aracela.

* * *

She was restless, unable to sleep. She rose, stepped to the bedroom window, and drew back the curtain. The village slept under a mantle of snow, blue smoke from the wood fires hazing the air.

She needed Jacob O'Brien in her bed, to breed with her and satisfy her lust.

Through a break in the clouds Donna Aracela caught a brief glimpse of a haloed moon. She lifted her head and stared at it, trying to draw from its power, but the clouds drew together and the moon was gone.

She knew she'd need all of her strength for what was to come. The killings she planned were necessary, and they'd be lost in the greater killing of the coming range war. Well, all but one, but even then, no suspicion would fall on her.

Donna Aracela ran her hands over her breasts, enjoying the way the firm globes filled her palms. They were breasts made for the pleasure of a man and to suckle a boy child. In the fullness of time, they would be used for both.

Down in the village, a dog sniffed around a dung heap, then walked, head hanging, into darkness, its slatted ribs visible even in the night gloom.

"Poor thing," Donna Aracela whispered aloud.

She wondered where Jacob was right then, at that very minute. Asleep probably, perhaps dreaming of her.

"Poor thing," Aracela said again. She smiled, showing her teeth.

Chapter Thirty

Shawn O'Brien stepped in front of Jacob and, as Clay Stanley had done earlier, defused a possibly explosive situation. "When we leave, we'd like to think it was our idea. In the meantime, Whitney, we need to talk."

The Texas gunmen had found chairs or were sitting against the parlor walls. All of them looked tough and capable, and at least three seemed like they'd been through hell and back. They had careful eyes and an air of quiet confidence combined with an implied threat of sudden violence—the unmistakable hallmarks of a named gunfighter.

Whitney sat in a chair by the fire. He glanced at Shawn irritably. "Mister, right now all I want is a drink and a soft bed. Talk to me in the morning."

"We need to talk right now," Shawn said.

Whitney turned his head and stared a question at Clay Stanley, who sat opposite him.

"What he has to say won't take long, boss," he said.

The desk clerk hustled in with bottles and glasses,

and the Texans cheered, then clustered around him. One of the gunmen handed Whitney a full glass and the little man held it to the firelight, as though enjoying the whiskey's amber glow. Without looking at Shawn, he said, "Speak."

Nettled, Shawn said, "I'll make it short and to the point, Whitney. I don't want to see any sheep north of Lobo Hill."

The little man's eyes moved in Shawn's direction. "What the hell are you talking about?"

"When you move the Mexican herders off the Estancia they'll look for new grass," Shawn said. "And the only place they'll find it is north, onto Dromore range. I won't let that happen."

Clay Stanley leaned forward in his chair. "O'Brien's father owns Dromore, a ranch up on the Glorieta Mesa high country."

Whitney sipped his whiskey, then his nostrils thinned, as though the air had suddenly gone bad. "How is it the farther west of the Mississippi I go, the stupider the people become?" He stared at Shawn. "Answer me that, huh."

It didn't take much to push Jacob too far, and he angrily took a step forward, his fingers spread as though he wanted to throttle the little man. Shawn's restraining arm stopped him, but even so, some of the Texans moved whiskey glasses to their left hand.

As though he'd noticed nothing, Whitney said, "I have six supply wagons outside, and, starting tomorrow my men will be out in the field with orders to shoot trespassers wherever and whenever they find them. And they'll remain out until every last greaser is accounted for, and that includes Don Manuel Ortero. I want him out of the valley." He stared hard at Shawn. "Don't you realize that sheep need herders? Without them, they'll stay where they are and later I'll round them up at my leisure." He shrugged and his smile was thin as a razor. "Or kill them if I can't find a market for mutton."

Stanley rose and faced Shawn. "See, O'Brien, your worries are all over. Listen to Mr. Whitney. There'll be no woolies on Dromore range."

"How many Mexicans will die to make that a reality?" Shawn said.

"Hell, O'Brien," Stanley said. "I thought you were worried about sheep. Now you're all a-fluster about Mexicans." To general laughter, he added, "Well, greasers or woolies? What's it to be?"

"The law . . ." Shawn began, and then let the words die in his mouth, knowing how lame he'd sound. Joel Whitney was the law in the Estancia, just as Shawn's father was the law in Dromore. Unbidden, a question forced itself, fully formed, into his mind. *Would the colonel kill the Mexican herders to save his ranch?* The answer to that was obvious: He would, and without a moment's hesitation.

Whitney, with the instincts of a predator, sensed Shawn's confusion. He jumped, rather than rose, to his feet. "This grows tiresome." He looked at his men. "Clear the bottles off the table, gentlemen. I have a map of the valley and we'll discuss our strategy, including the destruction of Manuel Ortero's hacienda."

Clay Stanley and the rest of the Texans crowded around the table. Shawn and the others were left to stand around.

But Jacob was still on the prod. He leaned over and whispered into Shawn's ear, "I can drop Whitney, Clay, The Memphis Kid, and two others. I'd say that would just about end it."

Shawn was tempted. He looked around him. Perez was always ready, and so was Ironside. Patrick would draw when the firing started and he could be depended on to get his work in.

But he saw that Clay Stanley wasn't paying attention to Whitney. As Whitney made circles on the map with the flat of his hand, the Texan's eyes were on Jacob, knowing he'd be the fastest with the iron.

The risk was too great and Shawn dismissed the idea. "Let's call it a night. We'll talk about things at breakfast."

"You go on ahead," Jacob said. "I think I'll sit by the fire and have a nightcap."

"Don't try to take 'em on by yourself," Shawn said.

Jacob gave him a look. "I'm not that crazy. But by settin' here and minding my own business, I can irritate the hell out of Whitney."

The morning dawned cold, but the snow had stopped and the sky was clear. To the west of Estancia, the Manzano Mountains stood lilac against a blue backdrop, their peaks sharply etched as cut steel. Despite the brightness of the morning, winter still held the land in its grip. The trees were encased in crystal, the hard ground glittered white as far as the eye could see, and Jack Frost busily painted every window with his icy palette and brush.

Dressed in coats, scarves, and chaps, Jacob and Shawn sat in rockers on the hotel porch, cups of smoking coffee in their hands.

"I asked Whitney a question last night." Jacob laid his cup by his right boot and carefully built a cigarette. "I surely did."

Shawn stared at him, his irritation flaring. "Damn it, Jacob, you don't say that! You don't say, 'I asked Whitney a question last night,' then leave it hanging."

Unfazed, Jacob took time to light his cigarette. "Says I, 'Whitney, why did you give the order to kill them Meskins down by Rattlesnake Hill? Jumpin' the gun, weren't you?' Says he, 'What Meskins?' Says I, 'Well, we was riding—'"

"For God's sake, Jacob, spit it out and I'll read it," Shawn said.

"Why is it so all-fired important?" Jacob said. "I wish I'd never mentioned the damned thing."

"What did he say?"

"He said he never ordered Ted White an' them to kill any Mexicans. He said he wanted his campaign to come as a surprise, but now the greasers will be watching for him. That's what he said, and he seemed mad enough to kick a hog barefoot."

"You believed him?" Shawn said.

"Yeah, I did. Whitney doesn't come across to me as a lying man, at least when he talks about killing."

Shawn was quiet for a long time, so long that Jacob leaned over and said, "Hey, your coffee's getting cold."

Like a man surfacing from a snooze, Shawn said, "I was thinking."

"About what?"

Shawn turned his head and looked at his brother. "Do you know what evil is?"

"I've heard of it. Remember Rusty, the sodbuster's dog that used to chase us when we were kids? Now, he was evil."

"I'm talking a greater evil than that, Jacob."

"Shawn, I'm not catching your drift."

"Maybe I'm just imagining things."

"Imagining what?"

"That somebody is trying to destroy us. Don Manuel, Whitney, me, you, all of us."

"Give me a name and I'll gun down the son of a bitch," Jacob said.

"It may come to that, Jacob, but later, when I think this thing through."

"Well, don't study on it too long, or we could all wind up dead."

The morning did not live up to its bright promise. By noon, the dove-gray sky was overlaid with black clouds looking like gigantic Pacific rollers, threatening to crash onto land and send up cascades of foam that would fall back to earth as snow. The air snapped with cold and in Estancia raw-cheeked people hurried on errands, their muffled mouths fuming like steam engines.

Joel Whitney and his men pulled out of town at one in the afternoon. All five Dromore riders stood on the hotel porch watching them go.

Whitney had made no secret of the fact that he was anxious to get the job done and open the valley for settlement. He needed to recoup his investment, satisfy his investors, and, above all, return to Boston and civilization.

According to what Jacob had heard, the little man was splitting his Texans into three columns, each with two supply wagons. They'd drive from west to east across the Estancia and dispose of any herders they encountered. After that, they would mount an attack on the Hacienda Ortero and tie up that piece of unfinished business. Whitney believed the entire campaign would take no more than two weeks, maybe less. He didn't want to draw it out, not when he was paying gun wages to Texans who didn't come cheap.

As Shawn watched the Whitney riders leave, he said to Ironside, "Luther, would my father kill the herders?"

After a moment's hesitation, Ironside said, "The colonel is a hard, unforgiving man."

"Would he kill the herders?" Shawn asked again.

This time Ironside didn't hesitate. "If they drove sheep onto Dromore range, yes he would."

Shawn dropped his head. "Well, I've studied on it, and I can't step aside and see men killed for no other reason than that they stand on another man's ground." He looked at Patrick, then Jacob. "I want to help them, but I need you to tell me if I'd be doing right or wrong."

"A man has to do what he feels is right," Jacob said. "Clear his conscience that way."

"Hell, any man with a clear conscience has a bad memory," Ironside said. "Shawn, do what you think is best. Don't do something that goes against your grain because you think that's the way the colonel would play it."

"And the rest of you?" Shawn said.

"I ride with you, patron," Perez said.

"I've made the colonel mad enough as it is," Ironside said. "But I'll go for broke and stick with you, Shawn."

"Patrick?" Shawn said.

"There's been enough killing already," Patrick said. "I'll stick."

"And what do you think, Jacob," Shawn said.

"I think I want to know how you'll play it," Jacob said.

"I'll warn the herders, get them to hide in the hills. Maybe they can arm and give a good account of themselves."

"Mexican peons won't give a good account of themselves against Texas gunfighters," Jacob said. "That just isn't going to happen."

"Then what do you suggest we do?" Shawn said.

"Leave here, head north, and stop the woolies drifting onto Dromore range, like the colonel wanted."

"We'd have to kill sheepherders, Jacob. You know that."

"Damn it, Shawn, what I know is that we'll have thousands of woolies poisoning our grass if we don't."

Ironside took off his hat and busied himself with the beaded band, as though it had suddenly become of greatest interest to him. "Jacob," he said, without looking up, "I don't hold with gunning sheepherders."

"You have to choose your own trail, Luther," Jacob said.

"I told Shawn I'd stick with him," Patrick said. "I'm not going back on my word."

Jacob's eyes read Perez's face. The young vaquero was tormented by split loyalty and wouldn't meet his eyes.

"Shawn, you, Patrick, and Luther go warn the herders. Andre can ride with me," Jacob said.

"That set all right with you, Andre?" Shawn said.

"*Sí*, patron."

"Then that's how we'll play it," Shawn said. "Jacob, no more killing if you can avoid it, huh?"

"I don't kill for pleasure," Jacob said.

"I didn't mean to imply that," Shawn said. "I just meant . . . ah, the hell with it. Just be careful, Jacob. And you too, Andre."

Jacob looked around him and smiled. "All the speechifying done? Good. Now let's ride."

Chapter Thirty-one

The Whitney mercenaries were either stupidly overconfident or just stupid. Don Manuel Antonio Ortero could not decide which.

He sat atop a beautiful palomino stud among the foothills of Duran Mesa, a brass ship's telescope to his eye. Snow was falling, but it was too early to make camp. The Texans had already built a fire in the lee of one of their two wagons, and were passing bottles from hand to hand, slapping each other on the back, roaring with laughter.

About what? Don Manuel wondered.

He spotted one source of their amusement. One of the men lay on top of a bucking woman under a wagon, while another watched and rhythmically slapped his knee, keeping time as he offered words of drunken encouragement.

Don Manuel smiled. So they had brought a whore along. He made his decision. The mercenaries were both overconfident and stupid.

A cheer went up from the camp as a tall, loose-geared man approached the campfire, carrying a heavy burlap sack. He tossed the sack on the ground, then grinned as he grabbed the bottom and tumbled three round cannonballs onto the ground.

Don Manuel leaned forward in the saddle and used two hands to steady the spyglass. Not cannonballs— human heads. Mexican heads.

A Texan grabbed two of the heads by the hair and placed them on the ground, about twenty-five yards from the camp. The third head, he laid between them. Joined by his companions, he stepped back to admire his handiwork. A few men shot revolvers into the air, and one even danced a little jig.

Don Manuel's smile was grim. Ah, it was such fun. *A Festival de los Muertos,* to be sure.

He felt no sadness for the peons. There were plenty of them. But they'd been hunted and murdered on his land without his permission, and Don Manuel took that as an affront to his honor.

Before, killing the gringo trespassers in freezing weather shaped up to be a chore. Now it would be a pleasure.

Don Manuel took the telescope from his eyes and swung his stud back to the men who were waiting behind him. They'd dismounted and stood by their horses, each man with a rifle in his hands.

"Otilio," he said, "a word."

The handsome vaquero stepped forward, leading his horse as snow swirled around him. His eyes were black as coals in the glacial gloom.

"Your eyes are young, Otilio," Don Manuel said.

"You see how the interlopers parked their wagons one behind the other to form a barrier against the wind?"

"*Sí*, patron."

"You will take half the men and swing wide around the camp. When I start my attack, you will charge the gringos from that direction. They suspect nothing, so stay out of sight by keeping the wagons between you and them for as long as you can. When you are among them, kill without mercy." Don Manuel reached down from the saddle, placed a hand on the vaquero's shoulder, and looked into his eyes. "Is all this clear to you, Otilio?"

The man nodded. "*Sí*, patron."

"Then get it done."

After Otilio and ten vaqueros rode out, Don Manuel signaled his remaining vaqueros to mount up. He drew his Colt as his men formed a skirmish line on each side of him. In the distance the Texan's camp was lost behind the wind-tossed snow, but the fire glowed like a ruby caught in a white curtain.

"Are you ready, my children?" Don Manuel called out.

A chorus of voices answered. "*Sí*, patron."

Don Manuel dug the rowels of his Spanish spurs into the palomino's flanks and led the charge across the hard, winter-browned grassland.

The Texans were taken completely by surprise. When the hard-charging vaqueros rode into the camp, several fell in the first volley.

But the hired guns were first-rate fighting men, and they recovered quickly. Three of them made a stand with the two wagon drivers, their guns hammering steadily as they backed toward the horse line. Half of Don Manuel's vaqueros sprawled on the ground, and a couple more fought to disentangle themselves from their downed, kicking horses.

For a moment the chaotic, smoke-streaked battle hung in doubt, then Otilio's horsemen crashed onto the scene, their rifles firing. Two of the Texans fell, and then a muleskinner was cut down. The two men who were left standing raised their arms in surrender.

Don Manuel, who up until then hadn't fired a shot, gunned them both.

When the bullet crashed into his chest, Don Manuel swayed in the saddle and looked around him, his eyes searching to find the man he knew had killed him.

Ten yards away, hazy behind snow and smoke, Otilio lowered a rifle from his shoulder, his eyes fixed on the don.

The old man saw a slight smile on the vaquero's lips, before he fell slowly from the saddle. He groaned when his small body hit the ground, a puzzled expression on his suddenly pale face.

Otilio rode toward the old man, but drew rein when a woman rolled from under the wagon. With her skirts hiked up, she ran at him, the pepperbox revolver in her hand spitting fire in the murk. He worked his Winchester with one hand, pushing it out in front of him. He shot the woman between her huge breasts and she tumbled to earth in a flurry of white petticoats, like a puppet whose strings had just been cut.

Without another glance at the woman, Otilio sought Don Manuel again. Finding him, he cursed under his breath. Two vaqueros kneeled beside the old man. One looked up at him and yelled, "He's still alive!"

Fear spiking at his belly, Otilio walked his horse to the vaqueros. "What happened?"

"One of the gringos shot him. The patron is badly wounded, but he is still breathing."

Otilio gritted his teeth. Of all the bad luck—a center chest shot should have dispatched Don Manuel quickly, but the old man was tough as a sow's snout.

A vaquero, bleeding from a flesh wound on his left cheek, stepped to Otilio. "We lost eight men, and three are wounded, Otilio. Two of those won't live out the night."

Otilio totaled up the butcher's bill. Excluding Don Manuel, ten of the hacienda's men were dead or dying. It had been a great victory. Eight Texans were killed, but only six of them were *pistoleros,* the men who mattered. Another great victory like this one and the Hacienda Ortero would cease to exist.

"Carry Don Manuel into one of the wagons and our dead and wounded into the other," Otilio said. "We will return to the hacienda."

"Our women will wail tonight." A vaquero shook his head. "So many dead."

Otilio said nothing, his mind on more important matters. Surely a bumpy ride in a wagon would kill the old man. He crossed himself and prayed that it would be the case.

"He still lives, Otilio," Aracela said. "It seems you have failed me a second time."

"No man can survive a bullet in the middle of the chest."

"My father did."

"He has the luck of the devil," Otilio said.

They stood in the shadowed hallway outside her father's bedroom door. The hacienda was quiet as death, except for the soft sobs of the servant women who'd gathered in the kitchen to drink wine and grieve for their patron.

"Leave me, Otilio," Aracela said.

"Has he talked?"

"Yes, he asked for his priest."

"He might say what happened. A man tells much to his confessor."

"I haven't sent for the priest. Not yet." She stepped to the door, then turned. "How many enemies did you kill, Otilio?"

The man was taken aback. "None. I had another, more urgent task to carry out."

Aracela's face hardened. "You disappoint me, in

so many ways. Now, get out of my sight." She hesitated, then added, "But stay close."

She waited until Otilio left, then opened the bedroom door and slipped inside with no more sound than an errant breeze. Her father lay in a bed of snowy silk, his gray head propped up on a feather pillow. Aracela looked down at him , her eyes unfeeling and calculating.

Earlier the doctor had said the bullet in Don Miguel's chest was too deep to remove. He'd added a medical man's hollow platitude, "It's now in the hands of God."

Aracela smiled. Don Manuel's fate was not in the hands of God, but in her own hands. She'd already banished the servants from the bedroom, because there was always the possibility he'd rave in his fever. She touched his forehead lightly. He was burning. The fever would kill him . . . eventually.

But suppose that prattling prelate Father Diego heard the news and forced his way into the bedroom? What then?

"Aracela . . . is that you, my child?"

The tremulous whisper from the bed startled her, but she recovered quickly. "Yes, Father, I am here."

Don Manuel's lips were dry and cracked from the prairie cold, and his black eyes burned in shadowed sockets. "I won a fine victory today."

Aracela didn't try to keep the contempt out of her voice. "You lost half your vaqueros. It was hardly a fine victory."

As though he hadn't heard, he said in a paper-thin voice, "Otilio, who was a son to me, tried to kill me."

She nodded. "I know."

"But I will live to see him hang." Don Manuel then proved he'd been listening to his daughter's earlier criticism. "I needed more men, Aracela. I will hire more guns, many more." He tried to raise his head from the pillow, but the effort was too much for him, and he sank back again. "Aracela, you must get me well again. Next time I will finish Joel Whitney and his mercenaries once and for all."

She smiled again. "You will cost us all we own, this hacienda, the Estancia, everything. There won't be a next time, old man, at least not for you."

"Aracela . . . why do you speak to me this way?" There were flecks of blood on his lips, and his face was ashen, the death shadows deepening.

"Because I want you to die. Your time is long over, and it's time for you to step aside."

Don Manuel looked frightened. "Send for my doctor, and the priest. And tell the servants I need them here."

"I will send for them all, *mi padre*"—Aracela smiled at her father—"once you are dead." She moved quickly. It was an easy matter to yank the pillow from under her father's head and shove its feathery softness into his face.

He struggled, but his wound had weakened him. Aracela pushed harder, her face twisted in concentration as she smothered the old man. She felt his struggles weaken and pressed harder, growling like a she-wolf. But Don Manuel still fought for his life. His feeble struggles wormed him across the bed, and he managed to get his feet on the floor. But there it ended. He suddenly went limp and death rattled in his throat.

Aracela lifted the pillow and stared down at her father's face. His lips were blue, his eyes wide and staring. His features wore an expression of horror, as though, in his last moments, he couldn't believe the way of his dying.

The pillow in her hands, Aracela threw back her head, lips parted, her breath hissing between her teeth. She felt warm all over, like the afterglow of sex, only better. Much better. How wonderful it felt to kill. Suddenly she felt more alive than she'd ever been in her life.

Panting, her breasts heaving, she needed a man that very minute, to share her heat. She stepped to the door and whispered into the dark hallway, "Otilio, come."

The man stepped inside, an uncertain smile on his lips.

"Lock the door."

"Is he dead? Otilio said.

"He's already making his excuses to the devil." Aracela smiled.

Otilio turned the key in the lock and heard the woman say, "Do you still want me, Otilio?"

Unable to speak, the vaquero nodded.

Chapter Thirty-two

Luther Ironside was three miles north of the salt lakes and had begun a loop back to the west when he heard what sounded like distant gunfire. He drew rein on his tired horse, and lifted his nose to read the wind, but it told him nothing.

In the high, lonesome country, imagination can play tricks on a man, and Ironside was willing to let it go. "Hearing things," he said aloud, as is the habit of men who ride forsaken trails. Yet, as the snow settled on his hat and shoulders, he realized he was denying the obvious. Yes, it had been guns firing, miles to the south.

All the Dromore riders were to the north, so they were not involved. It was raiding Apaches, then. Ironside shook his head. He reckoned that possibility at one chance in a hundred. Much more likely he'd heard a clash between Whitney's Texans and Don Manuel's vaqueros. Or had it been an attack on sheepherders?

He, Shawn, and Patrick had decided to split up.

Shawn said they'd cover more ground that way and warn more herders about Whitney's planned attack.

Ironside had scouted his part of the Estancia all day and hadn't seen another living thing, let alone a Mexican herder. Cold, hungry, and wishing for coffee, sitting his horse in the middle of endless miles of open range, his opinion of Shawn's plan was mighty low.

The firing had come from the south. Duran Mesa was in that direction. If nothing else, it might provide some kind of shelter for the night. Ironside made up his mind. He swung out of the saddle, the late afternoon light fading around him, and walked his mount in the direction of the mesa. It is the nature of things that men are more enduring than horses. Ironside spared his weary gray because if the horse foundered in that wilderness he was a dead man.

He walked across cold, aloof brush flats for an hour, wind and snow dogging his every step. By the time Duran Mesa came in sight through the crowding gloom of the waning day, he was pretty much used up, and his horse was in no better shape.

The cold had played hob with Ironside's rheumatisms. His hips hurt and his knees hurt worse. The misty breath of frost cut into his lungs, and when he glanced at the sky it looked like an iron helm about to settle onto the hoary head of earth.

Everywhere he looked, the shadowed land glittered with ice, the sheen of death.

Ironside didn't stumble onto the battlefield by

accident. The gray gave him plenty of notice. The big horse lifted its head and whinnied, jerking back, its front hooves lifting off the ground. Ironside stopped, and his eyes searched into the distance. At first he thought the black shapes on the ground were upthrust eruptions of the cap rock, but as he got closer he realized they were bodies.

One cautious step at a time, Ironside led his uneasy horse forward. A prudent man, he slid his rifle from the boot and levered a round into the chamber. But there was no need for a Winchester. The patch of prairie was drenched with the blood of the dead, not the living.

The bodies were stiff, in the postures they'd taken as they died; forever frozen in place like the corpses of Civil War soldiers in a Mathew Brady photograph. Each face was covered in a mask of ice, and a few had rigid fingers curled around the handles of guns that were no longer there.

Ironside pieced it together. Judging by the horse tracks, the Texans had been surprised by a mounted force and wiped out to a man. At the end, the hired guns had made a desperate stand with two muleskinners and had been shot down. Judging by bloodstains on the grass, the fight had taken a heavy toll of both sides.

The gray's hoof clinked on a whiskey bottle as Ironside led it toward the body of the woman. After getting shot in the chest she'd collapsed in a heap and died where she fell. Unlike the men, the woman's face was not grotesque in death. All the lines etched by years of hard living had disappeared and had again given her the face of a young girl. Thinking about it, he figured he was witnessing one of God's tender mercies. He'd got her set up right before He called her home.

Ironside smiled and looked down at the woman. "Well, Rosie, that's what I hope He did, anyway."

Ironside took one last look around through snow and a gray cobweb of mist. The wagons and the horses were gone. The Texans had been stripped of their guns, and a couple of their hand-stitched boots.

Joel Whitney had suffered a defeat here, but he would be unaware of it for a time to come.

Ironside led his horse toward Duran Mesa, but stopped after he stumbled over a small mound of dirt. It looked like a shallow hole had been chiseled out of the hard ground. He cleared a patch with the side of his boot and saw what looked like the top of a human head. He kneeled and dug out more dirt with his gloved hands. A face emerged, then another. Finally he uncovered three human heads, all of them Mexicans. Here were some of the herders he'd been supposed to warn.

Shivering from cold, he hoped, rather than fear, he buried the heads again. The Texans had collected three trophies. The fact that the victors of the battle had taken time to bury the heads suggested other Mexicans—and that could mean only Don Manuel and his vaqueros.

The old man was not going down without a fight, and that could be good news for Dromore. The herders would stay put if their patron kept a grip on his valley.

Luther Ironside camped that night in a stand of mixed juniper and piñon that backed up to a rock wall in the shadow of the mesa. Despite the snow, he found firewood enough to build a fire. He cooked a meal of bacon broiled on a stick, and a hunk of sourdough bread. Mrs. Hazel had packed a small pot and he melted snow for coffee that he laced liberally with Old Crow.

He smoked a cigar and looked out into the wind-tossed night, figuring his next move. His options were limited. He could look for Shawn and Patrick or head north and hook up with Jacob. Neither alternative appealed to him. The war was on in earnest, and he might be better off returning to Estancia, where he could keep in touch with the situation. Certainly it was better than wandering all over the wilderness searching for Mexican herders who were either dead or had skedaddled.

That Estancia promised a soft bed and hot meals didn't enter into Ironside's thinking. At least that's what he told himself.

Chapter Thirty-three

The body of Don Manuel Antonio Ortero was carried to the hacienda chapel, where he lay in state. His body was covered with the banner of his Spanish ancestors and four huge wax candles burned at each corner of his bier.

Great was the grief of the village women. The don had sired children with most of them, and some were already mourning dead vaqueros. The chapel pews were filled with kneeling, black-clad peons, their rosaries clicking against the polished oak of the pew in front.

Donna Aracela, the new mistress of the Hacienda Ortero and all the lands pertaining thereto, sat in her reserved box as befitted her rank. She wept bitterly, her sable garments as somber as those of the peasant women. So moved was Father Diego by her tears that he sat beside her, put his arm around her, and assured her Don Manuel was already in Heaven, drinking deeply from the cup of salvation.

Aracela smiled gratefully, dabbing a scrap of lace handkerchief to her red eyes. "God bless you, Padre."

Father Diego, touched deeply, declared that she was the most dutiful daughter a man could ever wish for, and surely she was her father's choice, and God's, to become the new patron of the Hacienda Ortero.

Finally, the elderly priest, a sensitive man, left her to mourn alone in an odor of sanctity.

Aracela was most grateful. How to get in touch with that son of a bitch Joel Whitney was preying on her mind, and she needed time to think.

The chapel smelled of damp peasants and the wax candles that cast shifting shadows over her father's body. She wriggled uncomfortably in her pew. The kneeling was hard on her knees. It was still snowing outside and icy drafts sharked at her from every nook and cranny of the old building. It was freezing cold, and she badly wanted one of her furs, but that would not be seemly.

She sighed. It sounded like a sigh of great sadness and she hoped it would impress the peons.

Now, about Whitney.

When he heard about the deaths of so many of his men, and of the loss of his wagons and mules, she thought he might return to Estancia sooner than he'd planned, looking to replace his dead gun hands. Just in case, she'd station Otilio—he was a useless *bastardo* anyway—in the town with instructions to tell her if and when the man arrived.

If everything went as she hoped—an invitation to dinner, a quiet seduction perhaps, and an offer of an alliance—she would help the gringo rid the Estancia of sheep and sheepherders for a percentage of the profits to be made by opening the valley up to settlers . . . and, with luck, the railroad.

When all was settled, Mr. Whitney would meet with a terrible accident and, as his partner, all of his money would fall to her.

It was a wonderful plan, and Aracela smiled into her handkerchief. How nicely things had fallen into place. She hadn't appreciated it at the time, but the death of her brother at Whitney's hands had been a blessing. The gringo had removed a major obstacle in her path, and then Otilio had helped her remove the other.

Aracela heard the priest's droning voice and her heart sank. He was beginning a mass for the dead, the first of many, no doubt.

Aiiii, more hours of crushing boredom.

With the priest's jabbering in her ear, Aracela let her thoughts drift to Jacob O'Brien. She no longer needed the man. She was now patron of the hacienda and the need for a son had suddenly become less urgent. Why share her power with anyone, including an heir? Besides, murder was so much easier than marriage.

Donna Aracela stared at her father's body, making sure everyone in the chapel saw her tear-reddened eyes and mournful expression. She felt a little thrill of delight. Everything was planned and promised to go well. Her gaze fixed on her father's gray face and she thought, *Why the hell didn't I kill you a lot sooner?*

Chapter Thirty-four

Joel Whitney was in a foul mood. He and his men had scouted the entire day and found plenty of sheep, but no herders. Charlie Packett, the one they called the Memphis Kid, had been riding wide of the main column and had shot an old man and a boy, who turned out to be a couple of raggedy-assed Apaches. After a day in the saddle and nothing to show for it, Whitney was cold, frustrated, and had a raging toothache.

He and his men were camped in a narrow, treed valley about a mile west of Rattlesnake Draw. Around him stretched a wild, inhospitable land that offered nothing.

Whitney looked sourly at Clay Stanley, who sat beside him near the fire. "Does the snow ever stop in this damned country?"

"Sure boss. Just as soon as spring gets here." Stanley smiled. "How's the tooth?"

Whitney seemed less than amused. "Bad. Damn thing hurts all the way to my back pocket."

"The Kid says maybe he can get it out with his knife," Stanley said.

Whitney was horrified. "In a pig's eye, he will. Hell, he can't even tell the difference between a Mex and an Apache. He'd cut out the wrong damned tooth."

Stanley shrugged. "He offered, was all."

"Is there a dentist in that godforsaken town? What's it called?"

"Estancia."

"Hell, yes, that's the name." Whitney pulled his fur coat closer around him. "What a damned dung heap."

"I heard tell there's a mule doctor there does teeth pullin'," Stanley said. "He does regular doctoring as well, or so Mrs. Hazel told me."

"I'll have to go back there and get it done. This goddamned tooth is killing me."

"I'll send the Kid with you. You might run into herders and he can take care of them."

Whitney looked at the man, his pinched face reflecting firelight. "You don't suppose we've run 'em all off already?"

"I doubt it," Stanley said. "They wouldn't leave their herds behind."

"Then they're hiding out someplace, maybe at the Ortero hacienda," Whitney said.

"Well, we'll take care of that problem later," Stanley said.

A man handed Whitney a cup of coffee and a salt pork sandwich. The little man bit down, then jumped to his feet, threw the sandwich away, and slapped his hand to his jaw. "Damned tooth," he yelled. "Hell, I can't stand this any longer." He glared at Stanley, as though he blamed the Texan for his suffering. "Tell the Kid to saddle up, we're leaving now."

Stanley said, "Shouldn't you wait until first light, boss?"

"Hell, no! All we have between Estancia and us is miles of flat. We can't get lost, and anyhow, this rotten tooth won't wait."

Ten minutes later Whitney and Packett rode out into darkness, snow, and a slicing wind. Huddled in the saddle, nursing his misery, Whitney hoped they'd ride up on some herders so that they could shoot them down and make them pay for the pain they were causing him. Serve them right.

A mile later, walking their horses through what shaped up to a fair blizzard, Whitney turned to the Kid. Opening his mouth just wide enough to clear his words, he said, "We aren't lost, are we?"

"Not if we're heading west, we ain't," Packett said.

"Are we heading west?"

"Hell if I know."

After wandering in circles most of the night, Whitney and Packett led their exhausted horses into Estancia just after daybreak.

Mrs. Hazel was not glad to see them.

"I have no rooms available," she said. The memory of having to share her quarters with two ousted guests, one of them an old lady who couldn't control her bladder, still rankled.

Whitney was tired, irritable, and in pain. The Memphis Kid was merely tired and irritable, and in him, that was a dangerous thing. He pulled his Colt, pressed the muzzle against the woman's temple, and thumbed back the hammer. "Lady, two rooms or I'll scatter your brains."

Mrs. Hazel could be belligerent at times, but what she read in the Kid's eyes scared her. She pushed the register in front of Whitney. Then, trying to salvage some shred of dignity, she said sternly, "Any trouble like there was the last time and you'll have to leave."

Whitney signed the register, ignoring her threat. "Where is the mule doctor?"

"Over to the saloon, where he usually is," Mrs. Hazel said.

"At this time of the morning?" Whitney asked

"You'll find him there any time of the morning, and any time of the afternoon and night."

"I've got a tooth needs pulled," Whitney said. "Damn thing is killing me."

"Findlay McLean is not the man for that, Mr. Whitney," Mrs. Hazel said. "He's not even a very good mule doctor, and I've never known him to pull teeth."

Neither Whitney nor Packett paid any attention to the young vaquero filling a cup from the pot simmering on the potbellied stove. When he heard Whitney's name, he stared hard at the man for a moment, then rushed upstairs.

"Is there anyone else?" Whitney's voice rose in a growing note of alarm. His tooth throbbed, and he felt that his whole lower jaw was on fire.

"Yes, Joe Tuthill. He'll pull it for a dollar."

"Is he a dentist?"

"No, he's the town blacksmith."

Whitney felt like a man taking the last step onto a gallows platform. He looked at Packett, expecting to see at least a glimmer of sympathy, but the man held a cup of coffee to his mouth, trying to hide a grin.

His voice hollow, like a man talking inside a tomb, Whitney said, "Can you get him over here? I'm damned if I'm going to sit on an anvil to get a tooth pulled."

Mrs. Hazel nodded. "I'll send my son." Her face showed concern, and Whitney thought it was for him. But that illusion vanished when the woman said, "Perhaps you should sit on the porch, Mr. Whitney." She smiled. "It's the blood, you know. I don't want it staining my new rugs."

Mrs. Hazel's son, a sullen youth with an overbite, brought bad news. The blacksmith's wife said her husband was out in the Manzano Mountains making emergency repairs to a freight wagon with a broken axle and she didn't know when he'd be back. She further added, "If there's whiskey on that wagon, he won't be back for days."

The Memphis Kid ate breakfast, and then sought his bed, leaving Whitney to suffer alone in the hotel parlor. Mrs. Hazel, who had a fairly kind heart, brought him brandy and a bill, and Whitney was quite tipsy when the blacksmith showed up a little after noon.

As befitted his profession, Joe Tuthill was a

muscular man of medium height with a black beard that spread across the chest of his leather apron. He had tools wrapped in a burlap sack and these he clanked onto the parlor table, much to Mrs. Hazel's annoyance.

"Plenty of Apache sign out there by Red Canyon, Mrs. Hazel," he said, disregarding the woman's irritation. "I heard they attacked a stage station a couple days ago and stole a mule."

"Heaven help us, Mr. Tuthill. Will they come here?"

The blacksmith smiled, revealing better teeth than Whitney's. "Bless your heart, no. The army has them on the run and the talk is they're already headed west into the Sierra Lucero country. And if they did come this way, I reckon we're ready for 'em."

Tuthill looked at Whitney, who sat hunched and miserable. In his fur coat, the little man looked like a sick mouse. "Is this the patient?"

"Of course I'm the patient," Whitney said. "Damn it, don't I look like a man with a toothache?"

"Open wide." Tuthill peered into Whitney's mouth, but the day was gloomy and the parlor dark. "Mrs. Hazel, could you bring a lamp closer?" The woman did, and the blacksmith looked again. "Ah, yes, I see it. 'Tis way at the back and black as the bottom of a dry well." He gave Whitney a sympathetic glance. "It has to come out."

For his part, Whitney had reached the end of tether and his anger flared. "Damn it, man, I know it has to come out. Now, yank the tooth!"

"Brandy first," Tuthill said. He picked up the bottle

from the table beside the little man's chair and filled a glass. Whitney reached out a hand, but the blacksmith ignored him, drained the glass, and shuddered. "All right, let's get to it."

Tuthill unrolled the burlap sack and one by one selected a pair of iron tongs, only to reject them. To Whitney the tools looked like artifacts forged by the devil, great metal pincers designed to tear a man to pieces. His terrified eyes as round as coins, he watched the blacksmith work the handles of a small pair of black tongs, their gleaming metal edges snapping together like fangs.

"These will do nicely," Tuthill said, the tongs grasped firmly in his hairy fist. "Open up, Mr. Whitney."

Appalled, Whitney made a barrier of his hands, but the blacksmith pushed them aside. "If you please, Mr. Whitney, open your mouth."

Whitney rapidly shook his head, his mouth clenched shut. His eyes looked as though they were going to pop right out of his head.

Tuthill turned and looked at Mrs. Hazel. "Some patients are more difficult than others."

The woman nodded. "Isn't it always the way of things, Mr. Tuthill?"

The blacksmith sighed. "Ah well, Mrs. Hazel, sometimes we must be cruel to be kind."

He grabbed Whitney's lower jaw in a horny hand as strong as a vise and forced the little man's mouth open. The tongs clanked against Whitney's front teeth, opened, then crushed the malignant molar in their steel jaws.

Whitney tried to scream, but all he could do was kick his feet and strangle out an agonized, "*Aaaargh!*" He felt the tooth tear free of bone and gum and when he opened his eyes he saw Tuthill holding it aloft in the tongs like a headhunter's trophy.

"A tough one indeed, Mrs. Hazel," he said.

"Isn't that always the way of it, Mr. Tuthill?"

Whitney, frantic, his mouth full of blood, spat on Mrs. Hazel's new rug and made a dive for the brandy. His hands trembling, he two-fisted the bottle to his mouth and drank deeply, his prominent Adam's apple bobbing.

Tuthill dropped the tongs into the sack and held up the molar for Whitney to see. "Do you mind if I keep this? It's for a souvenir, like."

"Youth a thamned buther," Whitney said, aware that he'd lost a chunk of tongue with the tooth.

"That will be a dollar, Mr. Whitney," Tuthill said, unfazed.

The little man reached into the pocket of his coat and produced a coin. "Here, thake your thamned bloth monthey," he said, blood trickling from the corner of his mouth onto his chin.

The blacksmith accepted the dollar and rolled his tools in the sack. "A very difficult patient, Mrs. Hazel."

"Yours is a thankless job, Mr. Tuthill." l said.

The blacksmith nodded. "One learns to accept it, Mrs. Hazel, but it does hurt."

Whitney crouched in his chair and suffered in silence. He badly wanted to kill Mr. Tuthill. And Mrs. Hazel.

Chapter Thirty-five

Luther Ironside was glad to see the lights of Estancia. The afternoon had been so dark that as it shaded into evening, there was little discernable difference. Snow, driven by a determined wind, danced around man and horse, and Ironside's breath smoked in the raw air.

He swung out of the saddle and walked stiffly into the hotel, feeling his years. The desk clerk saw a wind-weathered man wearing a blanket-lined canvas coat, chaps, and a wide-brimmed hat. Unhappily, he remembered him as one of the ruffians who'd recently been frequenting his place of business.

"Room," Ironside said, his jaw stiff from the cold.

"I'll see if we have one available," the clerk said.

"What's your name, son?" Ironside asked. The man was taken aback, as though no one had ever asked him that question before. "It's Wilfred, sir. Wilfred Spooner."

"Well, Wilfred Spooner," Ironside said, "look real

hard because I need a room. I'm getting too damned old to spend another night sleeping on rock."

Spooner took a key from a hook. "You're lucky, sir. We have one available."

"Oh, it's you again, Mr. . . . ah . . ."

"Ironside, ma'am."

"Yes indeed," Mrs. Hazel said. "Mr. Ironside as ever was." She smiled. "I remember your face because you're such a handsome, well set-up man, but names often escape me nowadays."

Ironside smiled. "And you, dear lady, are such a sweet distraction a man might easily forget his own name."

Mrs. Hazel blushed prettily. "Sir, you are so gallant."

Ironside made a little bow. "My gallantry is no more than your due, ma'am."

Deciding that his courtliness had reached its limits, Ironside said, "Is there anyone else in the hotel I should know about?"

"Only my regular guests and"—she made a face—"Mr. Whitney. Oh, and that nasty boy, Mr. Packett."

Ironside was puzzled. *Why are Whitney and one of his Texas guns here?* "Is he sick? Whitney, I mean."

"Oh no. He had a tooth pulled earlier today, poor thing," Mrs. Hazel said, though she seemed less than sympathetic. "He's in the parlor if you wish to speak with him."

"Yeah, I'll do that," Ironside said.

"Can I bring you something?" Mrs. Hazel said.

"A whiskey, and something to eat, if you can manage it."

"Why, of course, Mr. Ironside. I have a chicken stew in the pot and a batch of my freshly made buttermilk biscuits."

"It sounds just fine, Mrs. Hazel." Ironside bowed again. "And now, dear lady, if you will excuse me."

He entered the parlor. Joel Whitney was sitting in a chair by the fire. The right side of his jaw was swollen, and he stared up at Ironside without interest. Charlie Packett rose from his own chair, not out of respect for the older man, but making room to clear his gun.

Ironside looked down at Whitney. "How are you doing? I'm sorry to see you laid so low."

"Like you care," Whitney said.

Ironside stepped to the chair recently vacated by Packett. "I guess you're tired of sitting, huh?" he said to the young gunman. He settled into the chair and accepted a glass of whiskey from Mrs. Hazel. Behind him Packett, caught flat-footed, stepped away, his eyes angry.

"Got bad news for you, Whitney," Ironside said.

The little man stared at him, but said nothing.

Ironside took time to light a cigar, waiting for Whitney to snap.

Finally the man did. "What bad news?"

"You're talking funny," Ironside said.

"Damned blacksmith pulled my tooth and took a chunk of my tongue." Whitney said again, "What bad news?"

Ironside tried his whiskey. "Good. Puts heat back into a man."

"Damn it, what bad news?"

"Answer the boss," Packett said.

"All right, I'll spill it," Ironside said. "Yesterday, about this time, I found eight of your men dead just north of the salt lakes. Your wagons, horses, and mules were gone. Found a whore who'd been killed with them, but I don't suppose you're interested in her."

For a few moments Whitney was too shocked to talk, and even the Memphis Kid looked like he'd just been punched in the gut.

Ironside smiled without humor. "The good news is that I also came across the heads of three Mexican herders, so your boys had been doing their job well before they were wiped out."

Whitney struggled to keep his voice level. "How did it happen?"

"Well, it looked to me like they'd been surprised by a superior force," Ironside said. "And in this neck of the woods, the only man who can muster a force that size is Don Manuel Ortero."

Mrs. Hazel brought Ironside his food on a tray and placed it carefully on his lap.

"Thank you, dear lady. This cold weather does give a man an appetite."

Whitney sat in brooding silence for several long minutes, staring into the fire. Suddenly he jerked upright and slammed his hand into the leather arm of the chair. "Packett, we're going out again. We'll round up the men and burn Ortero's hacienda to the ground."

"Judging by what I saw yesterday, you'll have a fight on your hands, Whitney."

The little man rose to his feet. "You stay out of this. It's got nothing to do with you."

Speaking around a mouthful of biscuit, Ironside said, "What about the sheep?"

Whitney glared at him. "What the hell are you talking about?"

Ironside smiled. "Speaking for Dromore, we still don't want woolies on our range. If the herders think Ortero is no longer protecting them, they might pull out and head north. If that happens we'd come after you, Whitney. I reckon you'd find that trying to burn Dromore to the ground ain't a cakewalk."

"We'll destroy Ortero, then kill every damned sheep-herder and wooly in the Estancia Valley." Whitney sneered at Ironside. "Now you can enjoy your stew."

Ironside nodded. "I was just sayin'."

Packett said, "Boss, it's snowing outside. Are you sure you want to do more night riding?"

"Are you showing yellow on me, Kid?" Whitney asked.

"I don't show yellow to any man," Packett said.

"Then shut your trap and saddle the horses."

"You do what your boss tells you, son," Ironside said, staring at the gnawed chicken leg in his hand. "If you don't he might paddle your butt."

Packett's anger flared, but he never got the chance to give it voice. Mrs. Hazel stepped into the room with a cream-colored envelope in her hand. "A Mexican person brought this for you, Mr. Whitney. He said it's from Donna Aracela Ortero."

Chapter Thirty-six

Joel Whitney looked baffled as he turned the envelope over in his hands, as though he expected it to impart all its secrets without him having to read what was inside. "Who the hell is she?" he said finally. He was looking at Charlie Packett, but the question was really directed at Ironside.

"She's Don Manuel's daughter."

"Why would she write a letter to me?" Whitney asked.

"Open it and see," Ironside said.

Whitney ripped open the envelope and read the enclosed note. "She's inviting me to dinner tomorrow evening at the hacienda."

"It's a trap, boss," Packett said.

"Could be." Whitney motioned at Ironside with the note. "Why dinner with her and not her pa?"

Ironside was forced to admit that he was stumped.

"What does she look like?" Whitney said.

"I've seen maybe three or four truly beautiful

women in my life," Ironside said. "Aracela Ortero is one of them."

Packett, one of the more primitive of Whitney's gunmen, grimaced. "I say it's a trap, boss. Them Meskins will be laying for you at the hacienda."

"What do you think?" Whitney said to Ironside.

"Well, Don Manuel obviously knows you're here because Aracela would've told him. If he wanted you dead he'd bring a dozen vaqueros and kill you right here in the hotel."

Whitney looked at Packett. "What he says makes sense."

"I still say it's a trap."

Ironside rose and put his tray on the parlor table. "If I read the sign right, Don Manuel lost a lot of men when he attacked your Texans. Maybe he wants a peace treaty."

"Then why didn't he send the invitation himself?" Whitney said.

"He's a proud man," Ironside said. "Proud men get others to do their crawling."

"Boss, I'll go saddle the horses like you said, and we'll round up the boys." Packett grinned, his eyes like blue pinpoints of light in his smooth face. "The Mex will serve you a hot dinner all right, because his place will be burning down around his ears."

"Kid," Ironside said, "you're a real charmer. Anyone ever tell you that?"

"Don't push it, pops," Packett said. "I gunned my own gray-haired daddy when I was fourteen, so I ain't gonna lose any sleep if I put a bullet in you."

Ironside nodded. "Damn it, boy, I figured you hadn't been raised right."

Packett was just angry enough to draw, but Whitney's voice stopped him. "No horses tonight, Kid. I'll go see what this"—he consulted the letter—"Donna Aracela and her pa have to say." He threw Packett a bone. "You'll ride with me."

But the Kid wasn't listening. His entire focus was on Ironside. "Pops, never sass me again when I'm in a bad mood, understand?"

"Sure," Ironside said. "I'll keep it in mind."

"And never sass me in front of a man who's paying my wages."

"Got it," Ironside said.

"Let it go, Kid," Whitney said. "You're scaring the old man half to death."

Packett grinned, and waved a dismissive hand. "Well, to hell with him. He ain't worth a bullet anyway."

Ironside picked up his coat from the chair where he'd laid it. "Well, I reckon I'll turn in."

"Sleep tight, Pops," Packett said. "And remember what I told you."

Ironside nodded. "That's something I ain't likely to ever forget."

At breakfast the next morning, Whitney and Packett ate in the parlor while Ironside enjoyed bacon and eggs and the company of Miss Hazel in the kitchen.

There was no letup in the weather, as though the snow was determined to last until the summer of the brand-new year of 1887. The sky that glowered over Estancia was gray and hard, and icicles a foot long hung off the hotel porch. When Ironside brought out his coffee and lit his morning cigar, the snow had stopped, but a few random flakes flitted past in the wind. He looked out on a mother-of-pearl world with no delineation between land and sky, the aborning day wrapped in an air of icy hostility.

Ironside rubbed frost off a rocker with his gloved hand, then sat, his booted feet on the rail. His coffee cup was empty, his cigar smoked to a stub, when he heard piano music from the saloon. At first he gave it little heed, but then even his tin ear recognized, not the tune, but the piano player.

Getting to his feet, with spurs ringing in the winter hush, he walked to the end of the porch and listened. After a few moments he nodded to himself. There was no mistaking Jacob O'Brien's deft touch on the keys. But what the hell was he doing in Estancia? Well, there was only one way to find out.

Ironside left the porch and stepped onto the stretch of snowy, open ground that rejoiced in the name Fifth Street. He was halfway to the saloon when he heard Charlie Packett call out to him from the hotel porch.

"Hey, Pops, where are you headed?"

Without turning, Ironside yelled, "None of your damned business."

He walked on. Behind him, Packett's eyes were ugly.

The saloon's oil lamps were lit against the gloom

of the day, and a stove glowed cherry-red in a corner. Despite a dearth of regular customers, the place boasted a mahogany bar and a fair-sized mirror that had no doubt been shipped from Santa Fe. The bartender, who looked like he'd been freshly tonsured and shaved, had just finished pouring coffee into Jacob's cup when Ironside entered.

Andre Perez, sitting at a table to Jacob's left, grinned when he saw him. "Mr. Ironside," he said, getting to his feet, "what are you doing here?"

"I could ask the same about you," Ironside said.

Jacob didn't immediately turn. He played a few more notes, and then closed the lid on the piano. He turned and smiled at Ironside. "You've had enough of Mrs. Hazel's coffee, too, huh?"

Jacob gave the older man a hug, a boyhood habit he'd never lost, then stepped back. "What the hell's happening, Luther?"

"A lot. What's new with you?"

"Not a damn thing. Andre and me scouted from Lobo Hill to Argonne Mesa and back, and never saw a wooly. So we headed here and rode in early this morning." Jacob smiled. "Saloons always know how to brew real cowboy coffee."

"Would you care for some, mister?" the bartender asked Ironside.

"Will it float a silver dollar?"

"And change."

"Then fill me a cup." Ironside took his coffee and sat at a table with Jacob and Perez.

"Where are Shawn and Patrick?" Jacob said.

"Out trying to protect herders from Joel Whitney and his boys," Ironside said.

Jacob gave Ironside a wry smile. "My brothers have always loved the underdogs, bless 'em."

"Yeah, well it seems to me that maybe Whitney is the one needs saving," Ironside said. "After what I seen yesterday."

Answering the question on Jacob's face, he told about finding the dead Texans and the evidence of a major battle. Then, after lighting a cigar, he said, "Now Donna Aracela has invited Whitney to dinner this evening."

"I don't catch your drift, Luther," Jacob said.

"Well, I can't say it any plainer," Ironside said. "Donna Aracela wishes the company of Joel Whitney, Esquire, at dinner tonight. Said dinner to be served at the Hacienda Ortero."

"Well, I'll be," Jacob said, his face puzzled. "Why?"

"Your guess is as good as mine."

"What about her father?"

"I don't know nothing about him, either."

Perez said, "Mr. Ironside, you said you saw much blood where the Texans died." He waited for the older man's nod, and then added, "Suppose some of it was Don Manuel's blood?"

"You mean he was wounded in the fight?" Ironside said.

"Or killed." Perez shrugged. "Maybe so."

After a few moments silence, Jacob said, "That could explain the invite."

"Donna Aracela might tell Whitney she's surrendering any claim to the Estancia, now her pappy is dead," Ironside said.

"Seems to me she's not the kind to give up so easy," Jacob said. "It's just not her style. I reckon she must want something in return."

"What?" Ironside asked.

Jacob shook his head. "I'll have to study some on that."

The saloon doors banged open, an aggressive fanfare for a man determined to make a grand entrance. Charlie Packett stepped inside. The sneering curl of his lips faded when he saw Jacob and Perez. "I didn't know you was back in town, O'Brien."

Jacob rose to his feet and cleared the mackinaw from his gun. "Well, you know it now."

Packett knew he'd made a mistake, but he'd burst into the saloon on the brag and on the prod, and he couldn't back down now.

He turned his attention to Ironside. "Pops, in future when I ask you a question, you answer me, and you put 'sir' on the end of it. Understand?"

The Memphis Kid had killed too many men too easily, and he'd learned arrogance. But he had not followed Ironside into the saloon for the draw-and-shoot. Bullying an older, gray-haired cattleman appealed to his warped sense of humor.

"Yes, sir," Ironside said.

Jacob looked at him appalled, and Perez's jaw dropped, unable to believe what he'd just heard.

"Then remember it." Packett smiled and framed another question. "Will you remember it? Tell me, now."

"Here," the bartender said, "that won't do. That man has friends in here."

The young gunfighter ignored the man and stood smirking, waiting for Ironside's answer. But when it came, it was not what he'd expected.

"Yes, sir." Ironside pushed back his chair, stood up. After a short pause he added, "You sorry piece of Tennessee mountain trash."

Packett didn't like the odds he faced, but backed into a corner as he was, the draw was his only option. His hand dropped for his gun. But Ironside, covering the space between them in a couple of long strides, grabbed the young gunman's wrist in his left hand as the Colt cleared leather. He hit Packett with a straight right, his work-hardened fist crashing into the younger man's face. The Kid's head snapped back on his neck and blood fanned from his busted nose.

Packett's revolver clattered to the timber floor, and Ironside kicked it away. He didn't let the younger man fall, but held him upright as he dragged him to the bar.

Ironside yanked Packett's face close to his own. "Now, are you listening to me?"

The young gunman's head rolled on his neck,

blood from his nose streaming over his mustache and chin. Ironside shook him hard. "Do you hear me?"

Packett nodded and tried to focus his rolling eyes.

"All right, here's the story," Ironside said. "You're the most uncivil, disrespectable young feller I ever met, and I've done my best not to get riled enough to put a bullet into your hide. Understand?"

Packett finally focused on Ironside's stony face. He said nothing.

Another violent shake, then, "Do you understand?"

The young man nodded, and Ironside said, "Say it out loud, and put a 'sir' on the end."

"Yes, sir," Packett said, his voice hollow.

"Good boy," Ironside said. "'A soft answer turneth away wrath,' the Good Book says. Now get your duds off."

Packett had regained his senses enough to say, "Huh?"

Ironside's gun came up very fast and the muzzle bored its way into the young man's left nostril as the hammer triple-clicked back. "Get 'em off, all of them."

"Luther," Jacob said, grinning, "what the hell are you doing?"

"Me? I'm gonna cool this young feller down. He's way too hotheaded."

If Charlie Packett thought he had any choice in the matter, he didn't let it show. Ironside's gun still pointed at his head, he stripped to his long johns.

"Them, too," the older man said.

"No, I won't, damn you," Packett said.

"All right, then," Ironside said. "I'll just shoot you."

Packett quickly stripped to the skin, his eyes fearful.

"Now, listen up, young feller. It was in my mind to use that poker you see over there by the stove as a running iron to burn the Dromore brand onto your ass." Ironside shook his head. "But I won't. A brand is a sacred thing and not to be profaned by the ass of a tinhorn like you."

Ironside spun the naked man around, grabbed him by the back of his neck, and said into his ear, "I'm giving you a chance, boy. You won't get another."

He ran Packett to the door and helped him on his way outside with a boot in the butt. Ironside stood at the open door, and after a few moments yelled, "That's right, son, run to the hotel and get Mrs. Hazel to put a poultice on your sore ass."

When he came back inside he piled Packett's clothes, boots, and gun on the bar. "He'll be back for these," he said to the bartender.

"Wasn't you a shade hard on the boy?" the man asked.

"He has to learn," Ironside said. "It might have been worse—I could've killed him."

"Well, mister, you've made a bad enemy," the bartender said. "From now on I'd watch my back if I was you."

Chapter Thirty-seven

Dromore, January 1887

"How far south did your men ride, Samuel?" Shamus O'Brien said.

"All the way to Chavez Draw and then some."

"Nothing?"

"Not hide nor hair of them," Samuel said. "They didn't see any sheep, either."

"I don't like this one bit." Shamus rolled his wheelchair to the window and looked outside at the gray morning and falling snow. "I told Shawn to stay north of the Estancia." He thumped the arm of his chair with the flat of his hand. "I bet this is Luther's doing. He was a heller during the war, and age hasn't changed him. He charges into things headlong, and those sons of mine are easily led."

Thinking of Jacob, Samuel didn't agree with that last statement, but he said nothing.

"I keep getting the feeling something bad is

happening down there, that Luther's gotten my boys into trouble. I should be in the Estancia Valley, Samuel, not sitting here in this damned wheelchair."

"Pa, I can ride down there and see what's happening."

Shamus went quiet, weighing that in his mind. If he lost Samuel, the whole future of Dromore would be in jeopardy. On the other hand, he had no one else to send.

The Apache lance head in his back caused Shamus pain, but it was nothing compared to the agony he felt as he made his decision. "Ride to the Estancia, Samuel. Find them."

Shamus turned his chair away from the window, frowning, as though he'd suddenly found the view outside distasteful. "Call out all the hands. Take the three best with the iron with you, and order the rest to keep watch along Chavez Draw. What I told Shawn still stands—I want no woolies on Dromore land."

Samuel laid his coffee cup in the saucer and rose to his feet. "I'll have the men saddle up right away."

"Samuel," Shamus said. "Bring yourself back with the others."

After his son left, he stared moodily out the window again. He felt depressed, afraid, and suddenly old. All his sons would soon be in harm's way, and a sense of dark, Irish foreboding weighed heavily on him. The wind around the house wailed like the banshee wails when she warns of coming death and mourning.

Shamus shivered and pulled his shawl closer around his shoulders.

* * *

Samuel O'Brien and his three vaqueros were a
mile south of Chavez Draw when they heard gun-
shots. Ahead of them lay a rise thick with juniper and
piñon, a few boulders scattered along its crest. The
day was bitterly cold. Snow and ice lay everywhere.

He reached into his saddlebags and pulled out a
pair of field glasses. Motioning to his men to stay
where they were, he dismounted, then topped the
rise and kneeled among the rocks. He put the glasses
to his eyes and stared down into a wide expanse of
valley lashed by wind and snow. A half-dozen riders
milling around four men huddled in a group, their
hands in the air, caught his attention.

Suddenly one of the four made a break. He ran
through a sheep herd, the frightened woolies scattering ahead of him. The man didn't get far. A rifle
barked and he pitched forward on his face, then
tried to rise. A second shot fired. The man's body
jerked and he lay still. All the riders fired, and one by
one the other three men dropped to the ground,
sprawled and undignified in death.

It had been cold-blooded murder and Samuel was
horrified. He watched the riders laugh and slap each
other on the back. Clouds were pressing down on
the valley and the scene below played out in a gray
haze, flecked with flurries of white.

A vaquero kneeled beside Samuel. "We heard

the shooting, patron, and thought you might be in trouble."

Samuel passed the glasses to him. "Take a look down there."

The vaquero did, and after a few moments he said, "I see dead sheepherders. One . . . two . . . I count four of them."

Samuel nodded. "Killed by the riders you see congratulating each other."

"Are those the hired Texas gunmen of Joel Whitney, the man the colonel spoke to us about?"

Samuel nodded. "That would be my guess. Whitney lays claim to the whole Estancia valley and he wants the herders off his land."

"What manner of men can kill like that?" the vaquero asked.

"The kind of men my brothers are facing. And right now that thought is laying a world of hurt on me."

A pair of wagons hove into sight and the riders formed up then led them southwest, as though they intended to drive deeper into the valley.

"What are your orders, señor ?" the vaquero said.

"I don't have any," Samuel said. "As of now, we have no quarrel with Whitney and his men, even those killers down there. Our main task is to find my brothers and Luther Ironside."

"Then we will find them," the vaquero said.

Samuel nodded, his face grim. "That we will. We'll find them."

Chapter Thirty-eight

"I trust your journey was not too arduous, Mr. Whitney," Donna Aracela said.

"Apart from snow, wind, and darkness, it was bearable."

"Then you must spend the night here at the Hacienda Ortero. I wouldn't dream of sending you out again on such a night."

"That's very kind of you, I'm sure," Whitney said. "But I'll decide that for myself later."

Aracela smiled, but she realized she'd seriously misjudged this man. With his small bald head, and thin body wrapped in an oversized fur coat, he looked like a seedy little rat. But she sensed steel in him and a will that might be on a par with her own. Seducing him wasn't going to be as easy as she'd thought.

She wore a dress of green silk emphasizing the lush curves of her body. Her shoulders were bare, her cleavage so deep that slim arcs of pink areolas were slightly visible. The simple cross on a silver chain hanging between her breasts was her only jewelry, chosen to suggest modesty and girlish innocence.

"The wine is to your liking?" Aracela asked. "We import it by the cask from Spain."

"I prefer French wines," Whitney said. "The aged reds of the Rioja region, like this one, have never been favorites of mine."

"Then we must bring you some French wine immediately." Aracela raised her hands, to clap for a servant.

"No, not on my account. This is drinkable." Whitney looked around him. "Where is Don Manuel?"

Aracela pretended to be shocked. "You didn't hear?"

"Hear what?"

"My father is dead." She dabbed the corners of her eyes with a tiny handkerchief. "His body lies in the hacienda chapel." She made a little sobbing sound. "Now my father and brother are gone, and I am alone."

Her ploy for sympathy went unheeded. "How did your father die?" Whitney's head emerged from his fur coat shell like an inquisitive turtle.

"He was killed leading an attack on your men," Aracela said. "He wanted the valley for himself, and nothing I could say would dissuade him."

"You invited me here to tell me that?" Whitney asked. "That your father is dead?"

"No, not that, Mr. Whitney. Much more than that."

A servant scratched on the door, then entered. "Dinner is served."

"Shall we postpone talking business until after dinner?" Aracela said.

"If you wish," Whitney said. "But I believe we have little to discuss."

He ate sparingly, saying that he avoided highly spiced food because of an unfortunate disposition to dyspepsia. Despite Aracela's entreaties, he'd refused to part with his coat, its moth-eaten presence undoing the gold and silver elegance of her candle-lit table.

She'd begun to hate the little man with a passion. He seemed immune to her charms and her broad hints that she was sexually available. In fact, nothing she did seemed to please the little rat. If she hadn't needed him, at least for now, he would've been dead before midnight.

"Do please try the strawberry torte, Mr. Whitney," Aracela said. Then as a sudden afterthought, "I baked it myself."

Whitney made an exasperated sound close to a sigh. "I didn't kill them with my own hand, but I'm responsible for the deaths of your father and brother. Now you offer me strawberry torte." He sat back in his chair, his eyes steely. "What do you want from me, woman?"

The man would not be charmed, so she laid it on the line. "I'll renounce all claim to the Estancia Valley in exchange for an alliance."

"I already own the Estancia."

"Do you own Dromore?"

"You mean the O'Brien brothers' place north of here?"

"Yes, the biggest, richest ranch in the Territory. Dromore was spared the worst of the blizzards, and I'm told the land and cattle are now worth millions."

For the first time that evening, Whitney seemed taken aback. "What are you trying to tell me? Do you mean I should take Dromore?"

"Yes, I do, Mr. Whitney. I've been thinking about it for a while. I ask you, why stop with the Estancia?"

"Why indeed," Whitney said after a while in thought. His gaze wandered to the fireplace, as though he hoped to find inspiration in the flames. Finally he returned his attention to Aracela. "This alliance you speak of, you'd need to offer me more than your best wishes."

Aracela looked at him over the rim of her glass, her beautiful eyes calculating. "Money. Hard cash, Mr. Whitney. The continuing returns on my father's foreign investments, enough to hire an army of pistoleros."

Whitney considered what she said. That he was cash-strapped he could not deny. With this woman backing him, taking Dromore was not out of the question. Clear the Estancia, then push his men north and acquire the ranch by force, killing anyone who stood in his way. He'd keep Donna Aracela around until her money dried up, and then get rid of her. The entire scheme was wild and not without its dangers. The humiliation of Charlie Packett that morning by the O'Brien brothers and their foreman was a case in point. But it was doable, and the potential rewards were tremendous.

"Well, Mr. Whitney," Aracela said, "do we have a deal?"

"Perhaps. When can you get money to me?"

"Tonight. I can give you ten thousand dollars on account. And there will be more to come."

Whitney said nothing, but Aracela watched avarice grow in his eyes. "Wait here," she said, "I'll be right back."

Whitney stood as the woman rose from her chair and left the room, her silk dress rustling with every elegant step.

Dromore.

The very name inflamed Whitney's imagination. Soon, he could be the new owner of a ranch worth a fortune. As a member of the landed gentry, he'd be welcome in every high society drawing room in the nation, to say nothing of Europe.

He gulped down a glass of wine to calm his hammering heart, and then smiled. The ragged urchin from the East Boston slums could soon be on his way to the top. All he needed was guts, ruthlessness, and the determination to win.

Donna Aracela returned with a pigskin valise. She laid the bag on the table, snapped it open, and took out a bundle of notes. "It's all here. Do you wish to count it?"

"No, I'll take your word for it." Whitney knew he'd count it later at the first opportunity.

She picked up a decanter and stepped to the side

of his chair. Her thigh pushed against his arm as she said, "More wine?"

"No, I must be going."

"I wish you'd reconsider and spend the night. I could make you so . . . comfortable." She glanced out the window. "Oh dear, it's snowing again."

Whitney got to his feet. Sweat beaded his forehead, but from heat or desire, Aracela couldn't guess. The little man solved her dilemma. "I never mix business with pleasure," he said. "We are now, as you say, allies, so any future dealings between us must be on a strictly formal basis."

Aracela smiled. *Oh, how I'm really going to enjoy killing you, you arrogant little rodent.* "You're right, Mr. Whitney. But how will we keep in touch?"

"I will report to you here from time to time," he said, "and keep you apprised of what's happening."

"Our partnership is on a fifty-fifty basis, of course," Aracela said. "I get half the Estancia and half of Dromore."

"Yes, that goes without saying." Whitney could afford to be generous, since he didn't have the slightest intention of keeping his part of the bargain. "Now, could you have my horse brought around? Oh, and thank you for a wonderful evening."

"The feeling is mutual, I'm sure, dear Mr. Whitney," Aracela said, aware she sounded like the heroine of a bad novel.

Whitney picked up the valise. "I'll assemble my men in Estancia town and hire more Texas guns. By spring, I'll own Dromore."

"We'll own Dromore, you mean."

"Why, of course. That was just a slip of the tongue."

After Whitney left, Donna Aracela's ambitions were soaring, and she was too keyed up to relax. She called for her maid. The girl was a dull, lumpish peon with a bovine acceptance of whatever abuse her mistress inflicted on her. When the girl entered the drawing room, Aracela told her to strip, which she did. When Aracela picked up her riding crop, the maid's black eyes revealed a certain amount of fear, and that pleased her mistress greatly. There was no great pleasure to be had whipping a cow.

"Come closer, child."

The vaquero Otilio stood in darkness and watched Joel Whitney mount his horse and leave. He was certain the little gringo had spent time between Donna Aracela's thighs, and jealously raged in him, painful as a cancer. He had come to consider Aracela as his woman, and she should sleep with no other man, now or ever.

What to do with such a woman? Such a whore?

There was a way, the ancient, honorable way of his people.

His black eyes feral in the gloom, Otilio watched Aracela's window and thought his heart was broken. It felt as heavy as lead.

Chapter Thirty-nine

Joel Whitney opened the door of Charlie Packett's hotel room and warily stepped inside.

"Stand right there, or I'll drop you where you stand," Packett said.

"Damn it, Charlie, don't shoot. It's Whitney."

The sound of a Colt's hammer lowering was loud in the quiet. "I was about to gun you for sure," Packett said.

"Light the lamp. We need to talk."

A match flared, then Packett lit the lamp by his bed. He laid his gun on the table. "I thought you might've been one of them O'Brien clan. I aim to put bullets in all of them."

Whitney wanted so say, *Up until now, you haven't done very well on that score,* but he kept his mouth shut. "You have to ride, Kid. Round up Clay Stanley and the rest of them and bring them here."

"That ain't happening, boss," Packett said. "I was roughly handled and before I ride anywhere I've got a score to settle."

Whitney considered that. Turning Packett loose on the O'Briens might not be a bad idea. Gun the brothers and their hard-case foreman and Dromore could be fatally weakened. But he dismissed the notion. He was certain Charlie couldn't take them, especially Jacob O'Brien, who had a gun rep, and was as mean and nasty as hell to boot. Getting rid of the brothers was a job for Clay Stanley. None of them could match his speed with the iron.

"That will have to wait," Whitney said. "Getting the boys back here is more important."

"Not to me it ain't." Packett lit one of the rolled cigarettes he kept on the bedside table.

Whitney grabbed a chair and dragged it to the bed. "Charlie, you'll get all the revenge you want and then some. I promise you."

"How come?"

"We're taking Dromore, the O'Briens' home ranch." The room was very cold and Whitney sat hunched in his fur coat. "There's millions at stake here, understand? Personal matters must take a backseat."

"Millions for you, you mean," Packett said. "What's in it for me?"

"When I have Dromore here"—Whitney clenched his fist—"you'll get a bonus big enough to keep you in women and whiskey for ten years. Longer than that if you watch your money."

Packett watched his cigarette smoke drift in the room angled with shifting shadows. "What makes you think taking Dromore from the O'Briens will be easy?"

"I didn't say it will be easy. Look . . ." Whitney

picked up the valise from the floor and opened it. He showed the contents to the young gunman.

"It's money," Packett said. "A lot of it."

"Not just money, Charlie. It's a war chest, ten thousand dollars to buy men and arms. Dromore will be mine before the spring melt."

"Where the hell did you get that?"

"From my new partner, Donna Aracela Ortero. And there's more where this came from."

Packett's smiled like a rattlesnake. "And suppose I just take all that money from you?"

A split second later he was staring at the derringer pressed into the space between his eyebrows. "And suppose I just blow your damned head off?" Whitney was not a needlessly profane man, but he was on edge, and his nerves were shredded.

"A joke, boss," Packett said quickly. "Only a little joke."

"A very little joke," Whitney said, ice in his voice.

Packett stubbed out his cigarette butt on top of the table. "I'll saddle up and ride, boss. Bring the boys in like you said."

Whitney eased down the belly gun's hammer. "Stay away from the O'Briens until I give the word, you hear?"

"I hear you, boss."

Whitney rose to his feet and picked up the valise. "If you even think about crossing me, Charlie"—he pointed the derringer at Packett's head—"I'll kill you."

Packett felt a chill. Joel Whitney was more than he seemed, and much more dangerous than he pretended.

* * *

Whitney was too wound up to sleep. He grabbed a bottle of brandy from Mrs. Hazel's stock and sat in a rocker on the porch. A few minutes later Charlie Packett rode out, then disappeared into darkness.

Eventually the Kid would have to go, but that was for the future. Whitney concentrated on the present. He tilted the bottle to his mouth, drank deeply, then lit a cigar, his face scowling his racing thoughts.

He was playing for high stakes, he realized that, and from now on he could trust no one. As he'd previously decided, he would use Donna Aracela, then discard her. The woman did not present a problem. His Texas gunfighters he would pay off after the job was done and he was the new owner of Dromore. To a man they were drifters and wouldn't care to hang around anyway. The way he figured it, the only real problem he had was the O'Brien brothers.

Raised in the worst slums of Boston, where every day he'd faced a new fight for survival, Whitney had an instinct when it came to recognizing fighting men. Clay Stanley was one, Jacob O'Brien was another, and so was that tough old coot Luther Ironside.

As the brandy warmed him, Whitney's confidence grew. Stanley could take care of the O'Briens, he was certain of that. When they were gone, who would be left? He'd heard the patriarch of the family was a cripple confined to a wheelchair, and his hands were vaqueros, not gunmen. Whitney allowed himself a smile. Taking Dromore could be as easy as shooting fish in a barrel.

But then he had another thought. *Why waste my newfound fortune on hiring more high-priced Texas guns?* There were plenty of border riffraff around who would cut any man, woman, or child in half with a shotgun for fifty dollars. Those were the men he should hire, the scum of the earth who'd kill for whiskey and whores. His Texans, braver and aware of their status, would be in the forefront of the fight, so all things being equal, they would be the first ones to die. It was yet another way to save money—you don't pay bonuses to dead men.

Whitney's little head nodded in its fur cocoon. If it all fell apart—unlikely, but a possibility to be considered—he could scamper with the ten thousand, and maybe more. A man, a ruthless, ambitious man, could do a lot in Boston with that kind of money.

All in all, Whitney was pleased with his progress, and he drank to that.

Out in the frozen flatlands, coyotes yipped their hunger to the uncaring night, and snowflakes chased one another in the wind. His wife, God rest her soul, had loved nights like this. Hot from the brandy, he remembered Martha's nakedness, the stark white of her body in bed. He wondered what Donna Aracela looked like without her fancy clothes. But he couldn't picture her in his mind.

He sighed. Ah, well, it didn't matter anyway. He didn't want her body, only her money. And then her death.

Suddenly Whitney's world seemed so simple, so straightforward, that it pleased him immensely.

He didn't know it then, but all that was about to change.

Chapter Forty

"Andre," Ironside said, "can you make out those riders?"

Perez shaded his eyes against the sun and snow glare for a few moments. "*Sí*, those are the brothers of Señor Jacob, and three vaqueros ride with them." He grinned. "All of them relatives of mine."

"Go tell Jacob to get out here."

After Perez hurried inside, Ironside stood against the hotel porch rail and stared into the distance. The snow had stopped, and the morning had dawned bright and sunny. But the cold was still bitter, the wind biting. The breaths of the oncoming men and horses formed a gray mist around them.

After a while Ironside nodded to himself. It was Patrick and Shawn all right, but Samuel was with them. Had something happened at Dromore?

"Hell, you're right. Samuel is with them," Jacob said, standing beside Ironside. "I'd recognize him anywhere. Rides straight up and down like a general on parade."

"I never could teach you to do that," Ironside said.

Jacob looked at the older man. "What do you suppose has happened?"

"I was about to ask you the same thing."

When Samuel rode up to the porch he was smiling, and Jacob took that as a good sign.

"I found a couple of lost souls out there in the wilderness," Samuel said. "They were out of grub, out of options, and riding in circles."

"Hell, we knew where we were," Shawn said. "It was you that was lost, Sam."

All six men looked trail worn, their faces thin and haggard. Patrick, more bookish than the others, seemed more tired than the rest.

"What brings you here, Sam?" Ironside said.

"The colonel was worried about y'all." Samuel stared hard at Ironside. "He said you'd led them astray, Luther."

"He's real mad at me, huh?"

"You could say that."

Samuel swung out of the saddle, as did the others. Patrick staggered a little when his feet hit the ground, and he gave Jacob a wan smile. "I guess I should spend more time riding than I do reading."

"A hoss never teaches a man anything," Jacob said. He called out to one of the vaqueros, "Ignacio, there's a barn out back. You and Ramiro mind putting the horses away?"

The man called Ignacio waved and gathered up reins as Samuel and the others stepped onto the porch. Jacob said, "You boys look all used up. There's coffee on the stove."

"I could sure use it," Patrick said.

Whitney, cup in hand, stepped onto the porch, and Jacob introduced him. "Sam, I guess you haven't had the pleasure of meeting Mr. Joel Whitney. Whitney, this is my brother Samuel."

Samuel nodded, but didn't extend his hand. "Whitney, were those your men I saw up near Chavez Draw yesterday?"

"Could be. What were they doing?"

"Murdering unarmed Mexican sheepherders."

If Whitney was offended he didn't let it show. "I now own the Estancia Valley, and I will not tolerate squatters on my land."

"I reckon your boys are making that pretty obvious," Samuel said.

Before his plans for Dromore, all Whitney felt for the O'Brien brothers was indifference. But now they were enemies and he didn't much feel like engaging them in conversation, especially since the new arrival was so hostile. He'd do plenty of talking later—but with guns.

"Pleased to meet you, I'm sure, Mr. O'Brien," he said. "But please keep out of my business."

"Just so long as your business doesn't endanger Dromore," Samuel said.

Whitney was startled. *Does this man know? It is impossible.* He relaxed, taking his coffee, to the opposite end of the porch, where he sat on a chair and vanished into his fur coat like a snail into its shell.

"It was cold-blooded murder," Samuel O'Brien said, as they were gathered around the parlor table. "They rounded up the herders and just shot them down."

"That's why we were out there," Shawn said. "We hoped to warn the herders to hide in the hills." He made an expressive gesture with his hands. "We didn't find any."

Jacob cupped his hands around his coffee. "The way Whitney sees it, the more herders he kills, the less the chance there is of them driving woolies onto Dromore grass."

"Our range is not in great shape," Samuel said. "We didn't have a big die-off like some other ranches, but the grass suffered. Sheep would just about tip us over the edge."

Jacob smiled. "So, is Whitney our friend or our enemy? What do I do, Sam, hug him or shoot him?"

"We're in the midst of the melancholy dilemma of being unable to make peace, yet unable to make war." Patrick's glasses were steamed up from hot coffee, and his eyes were invisible.

"That's one way of saying it." Jacob looked at Samuel. "Well, do we kick Whitney's ass or not?"

"Hell, Jacob, I don't know," Samuel said.

"What does the colonel say?"

"He says we're to keep sheep off our range. The how-to-do-it of the thing, he left up to me."

"All right, then Whitney is our friend."

"We're making a pact with the devil, seems to me," Shawn said.

Ironside had been silent, but now he spoke. "There is a way. We chase Whitney and his hired guns off the Estancia. The sheepherders stay where they are and go back to what they do best, tending sheep."

"I don't want Dromore involved in a range war," Samuel said. "You know how many men died in the Mason County War? The official count was ten, but at least three times that number were killed."

"Even ten is too many," Patrick said, wiping his glasses with his shirt.

Samuel was quiet, thinking. Then he said, "We do what the colonel said. Now we're all together again, we head north and keep the woolies off our range." He looked around the parlor table. "Anybody object to that plan?" His question was met with silence. "Anybody?" When his question was met with silence a second time, Samuel said, "Then we're agreed. We'll spend the night here at the hotel and ride out in the morning."

"What if it comes to killing, Sam?" Jacob said.

Samuel answered without a moment's hesitation. "We do what it takes."

"Amen." Ironside's eyes were like pieces of blue flint.

* * *

By noon, the sky clouded again, and by three the snow started coming straight down like white paint flaking off the dark wall of the day. The crystalline air was so hard that when a man took a breath he felt as though he was swallowing iron nails. Winter clenched the suffering land in its fist and showed no sign of ever letting go.

Just as the afternoon faded, an old man led a burro through the remnants of the day, walking stiffly as if the cold had rusted his joints. He cradled a Henry rifle in his left arm, and a silver dollar with a bullet hole through it adorned the front of his fur hat. Over the back of the burro, facedown, was the half-naked body of a man—or what was left of a man.

The oldster stopped outside the hotel, the only building of any significance in Estancia, cupped a hand to his mouth, and yelled, "Anybody to home?"

Wilfred Spooner, the desk clerk, stepped onto the porch. He crossed his arms in front of his chest and vigorously rubbed the outsides of his biceps. "What do you want? It's freezing out here." His gaze took in the old man's ragged coat and pants, and said, "We have no rooms available."

"Name's Silas Cade, sonny," the old man said. "I'm lookin' fer an undertaker and a lawman, if'n you have either one o' them."

"We have neither." Spooner shivered, a drip at his nose. He saw the body, and said, "Who is that?"

"I don't know, sonny. I found him up by Buffalo Draw. His boots and spurs say Texas, but the Apaches had been at him, so it's hard to tell who he wuz or what he wuz."

"Apaches?" Spooner said, shocked.

"That's what I said, sonny. I reckon three or four of 'em jumped him, prob'ly broncos who didn't surrender at Skeleton Canyon with ol' Geronimo."

The clerk made a face. "Well, whoever he is, take him away."

"I got nowhere to take him, sonny. That's why I figured to bring him here. Ain't you got a place to bury a man?"

"We'd have to dynamite a hole for him," Spooner said. "And that isn't going to happen. Now, get him out of here."

Before Cade could answer, Joel Whitney brushed past Spooner and stepped to the burro.

"You recognize him, mister?" Cade asked.

The dead man had no eyes or tongue and both his ears had been severed. He'd been scalped, and his body, naked from the waist up, was covered in small burns. Cactus needles, dozens of them, had been thrust into his skin and then set alight.

Suddenly Whitney's mouth was dry, and he felt a green sickness coil in his belly. Charlie Packett had died hard, and it had taken a long time.

"You know him, mister?" Cade asked again.

Whitney nodded. "I know him."

Jacob O'Brien had been watching from his bedroom window. He went downstairs and joined Whitney in the street. Taking one look at the corpse, he said, "Charlie Packett?"

"Yeah, it's him," Whitney said.

"Found him up by Buffalo Draw where I was prospecting," Cade said to Jacob. "Looks like Apaches had been at him for hours afore I came on him."

"Hell of a thing for a man to die like that," Jacob said.

"Uh-huh," Cade said. "But when it comes to Apaches, I've seen worse. Why, I recollect one time down Arizony way . . ."

The old man rambled on, but Whitney wasn't listening. He was worrying. Packett had obviously been killed before he contacted Clay Stanley or any of the others, so his men were still out there. Now he'd have to comb the valley and find them himself. The prospect didn't appeal to him, but he had no other choice. With a bit of luck, he could get his Texans back to Estancia before the O'Briens left. Once the brothers were out of the way, Dromore was as good as his.

Whitney returned to his immediate problem. Cade was still babbling, but he cut the old prospector short. "Where are you headed?"

"Back the way I come, I reckon."

Whitney fished in the pocket of his fur coat, then counted five dollars into his palm. He offered the money to Cade. "Find a place along the trail to leave his body. This will compensate you for your trouble."

"Aren't you going to bury your own dead, Whitney?" Jacob said.

"I'd need dynamite, and I don't have time for that," Whitney said. "Besides, Packett didn't amount to anything." As he stepped away, he said to Cade. "Hide him under a rock or something. There isn't that much of him left to bury."

After Whitney left—in the direction of the barn, Jacob noticed—Cade said, "I cain't really say that I like that feller."

"Not too many folks around here do." Jacob jerked his head in the direction of the body. "If you're staying the night, I'll help you stash that out back until morning."

"I reckon not, sonny," Cade said. "I cain't abide a roof over my head unless I'm in bed with a whore." He rubbed his scrubby jaw. "Let you buy me a rum punch afore I leave, though."

The mixing of a rum punch was within Mrs. Hazel's abilities, and she made enough for Cade and Jacob, and for Patrick, who'd joined them in the parlor.

"Good to feel a fire again," the old man said, sticking out his boots toward the flames. He tried his drink and said to Mrs. Hazel, who was on her way out the door, "My compliments, ma'am. This is an elegant cocktail to be sure."

The woman was as surprised as Jacob and Patrick. Cade, as rough an old man as any of them had set eyes upon, had obviously spent time around high-toned ladies and men with manners.

Patrick, thinking about it later, decided that Silas

Cade was probably one of the old coots who had struck it rich and gone on to make and lose fortunes.

Jacob sat where he could look outside and watch for Whitney's comings and goings. Something about the man's recent behavior troubled him, but he couldn't put a finger on why.

"Silas, the silver dollar on your hat," Patrick said. "Does that have a story to tell?"

Cade grinned, showing toothless gums. "It surely does, sonny. Back in the summer o' '76 I was in Deadwood up in the Dakota Territory, and Wild Bill Hickok, who was showing off to some Eastern folks, says to me, 'Silas, take this silver dollar and hold it up where I can see it. If I shoot it out of your fingers, you can have the dollar and another ten besides.'"

The old man cackled and slapped his knee. "Dang me, if I didn't say I'd do it. Of course, I was drunk at the time, and Bill was drunker. Well, anyhoo, I held the dollar in these two fingers"—he extended his right thumb and forefinger—"and ol' Bill drawed his Navy an' shot the coin dead center. Later, he said to me, 'Silas, that was true blue. Only a white man would've held steady the way you did.'" Cade pointed to his hat. "I've kept that dollar ever since."

Patrick laughed, but Jacob had only been half listening. His face was thoughtful as he saw Whitney ride out with a sack of supplies tied to his saddle horn. The man headed north. *Why? Is he leaving to join his men to again wage war on the herders? Or does he have something else in mind?*

Jacob had questions but no answers, and that troubled him. But, lurking like a malevolent shadow at the back of his mind was one thing he did know— Dromore was to the north. Stripped of its riders, the ranch was something it had never been before . . . . vulnerable.

Chapter Forty-one

Donna Aracela insisted on a night burial. She watched the vaqueros screw down the lid of her father's coffin, then hoist it onto their shoulders, her mouth a tight line under her concealing black veil. Torches were lit, and the droning Father Diego led the melancholy procession out of the chapel and into the snow-draped darkness.

She walked behind the coffin, dozens of wailing women in her wake, and her sigh was lost in the infernal racket. She was already cold, and the north wind continued to tear at her. The old man was already burning in hell, so the sooner they put him away forever, and let her get back to her warm room, the better.

The priest, concerned for Aracela's well-being, sent back an altar boy wearing a white cassock, to help her walk the distance to the family vault, weighed down as she was by sorrow.

She gratefully accepted the boy's help, or so it appeared to the other mourners, as she leaned on him for support. The boy smelled of cow dung and dirty clothes, and she held a perfumed lace handkerchief to her nose, hoping the women who walked behind her would think she was crying.

The procession halted at the bronze doors to the vault, and Aracela fumed when it was discovered that no one had remembered to bring the key to its massy padlock. She stood, leaning on the smelly altar boy, while a servant was dispatched to retrieve the key from its hook in the chapel.

Snow fell around her, making her feet numb. The boy put his hand on her ass, but she didn't slap it away. She smiled. *That's all right boy, feel something you were born never to have.*

Finally a key was produced and she stood aside as the coffin was carried inside. Away from the torchlight, she got a chance to pinch the boy's cheek, pressing hard. The peon danced in pain, and her fingernails dug deeper. Then, bleeding, he cried out and ran into the darkness. The onlookers smiled sadly at one another and whispered that the young ones were always afraid to be around death.

The vault was a large, marble structure built a hundred and fifty years before by one of Aracela's ancestors. When she stepped inside to hear the priest prattle prayers, she was surrounded by cobwebbed coffins, including her brother's. The place smelled dank of the ancient dead.

Finally it was over. Her long ordeal was at an end. The old goat was buried and good riddance.

"Donna Aracela," Father Diego said as they stood

outside in the cold and snow, "if you wish, I will come to the hacienda and pray with you, if you desire to spend the night in holy vigil."

"No Padre," Aracela said. "Tonight I wish to sorrow alone."

The priest smiled. "I understand." He made a sign of the cross over her. "May God bless you, my child, and give you succor in your time of such great sadness and loss."

"Thank you, Padre."

Donna Aracela stripped off her mourning weeds and changed into a nightgown of sheer black silk, imported from Paris. She brushed out her hair so it cascaded black and shining over her shoulders, then poured herself a glass of wine. She'd put off going through her father's papers until he was buried, but her agreement with Whitney made the task more urgent. The little man would no doubt require money again, and she would need to have it readily available.

A fine fire burned in her father's study as she sat at his desk, snow feathering past the window behind her. She piled ledgers on the desktop and picked up a pen, but found it difficult to concentrate. The prospect of ravaging a girl in the tomb had excited her, yet she felt let down, like the aftermath of sex with a man who climaxed too quickly.

With the end of the pen in her teeth, Aracela glanced out the window. *When Dromore is mine, I'll winter there and summer at the hacienda, at least, those years I don't feel like traveling to Paris, Rome, or London.* Finally she had found a thought that pleased her, and she smiled as she opened the topmost ledger.

Someone rapped on the door, and then stepped inside.

"Otilio," Aracela said, "how dare you intrude on me like this?"

The vaquero crossed the floor to the desk, a strange, luminous light in his eyes. "We have to talk."

"Talk? What do you and I have to talk about that can't wait until morning?"

"Our wedding day."

For a few moments, Aracela sat stunned. Then she smiled, and her smile grew into a laugh. "Surely," she gasped, "you don't think for one minute that I'd marry you, a penniless peon who owns nothing but a horse and saddle."

Otilio's skin tightened across his cheekbones. "You're a whore, Aracela. I thought about preserving my honor by killing you, But realized I love you too much for that. Now I offer you marriage, and a way to move from a life of debauchery to my wife."

"And if I don't?" Aracela asked. "If I don't wish to cook and clean for you and wash your stinking rags, what then?"

The vaquero was angry clean through, and failed to see, or chose to ignore, the cold blue ice in the woman's eyes. "If you don't, Aracela, I will go to the authorities and tell them how you ordered me to kill your father," Otilio said. "My silence will be your bride price, and I promise it will be paid it in full."

"Otilio, for a while you amused me," Aracela said, "but now you start to bore me. Know this. I'd rather marry a cur dog off the street than marry a nothing like you."

The young vaquero's hand dropped to his waist and he came up with a knife. "Aracela, please say you'll marry me." His black eyes signaled his torment. "I don't want to kill you. You are my love . . . my life."

Aracela sat back in her chair. She smiled—sympathetically, she hoped. "Come here, poor Otilio," she whispered. "Come closer."

Her hand right hand was in an open drawer. Her scarlet lips pulled back from white teeth as she said, "We will talk about this without rancor. Now put away your knife."

The vaquero's head bent as he readied to sheath his knife. It was all the time Aracela needed. She pulled a Smith & Wesson .38 from the drawer, pointed the gun at his chest, and fired.

Otilio absorbed the hit, but took a step back, his eyes moving from the bleeding wound in his chest to Aracela. Emotions fleeted across his shocked face, surprise, disappointment, sadness, and finally, fear. "Aracela," he whispered, "you have killed me."

"Just so, Otilio," the woman said. She fired again, and then a third time. The vaquero slumped to the ground, disbelief in his eyes, failing to comprehend the reason for his dying.

Aracela heard screams and thudding feet outside her door. She quickly put down the gun, then ripped the nightgown from her breasts. Using her nails, she taloned the front of her left shoulder, drawing blood, leaving five crimson gashes.

"Help me!" Aracela screamed. "Mother of God, help me!"

The door burst open and three male servants ran inside, one of them holding a shotgun. A new maid held back, looking fearfully into the room.

Aracela pointed to Otilio's body. "He tried to rape me!" she yelled. "I begged him to stop, but he wouldn't. When he threw me across the desk, I managed to get my father's gun." She buried her face in her hands. "Oh God, please tell me he's not dead."

One of the men kneeled by the vaquero's body. "I'm sorry, Donna Aracela. But this man is gone."

She wailed, tears streaming down her face. "How could he do this when he knew I was in mourning?"

"He hurt you, patron," the man said. "Your shoulder . . ."

Aracela looked at her wounds and nodded. "He had a knife." She buried her face in her hands. "Oh, it was too horrible."

One of the women had gone for the priest, and Father Diego bustled inside. "What has happened, my child?" he exclaimed, hurrying to take Aracela in his arms.

Her head on the priest's shoulder, Aracela sobbed. "Otilio tried to rape me and . . . and I was forced to shoot him."

She felt Father Diego's head shake. "And I always thought him such a fine boy."

"And so did I, Padre," Aracela said. "But tonight, he was like a crazed animal." She stepped back, letting the priest see her shoulder.

"He did that to you?" Father Diego asked.

"Yes."

"Then I cannot let Otilio lie in the chapel tonight, for surely he is already damned.

"I'll have my men carry him to the icehouse," Aracela said.

"Yes, and then we will tend to your wounds and I will pray with you." Aracela grimaced, knowing Father Diego would take it as an expression of pain. The priest would babble for hours, but it was a small price to pay. She bent her head, as though bowing to the padre's will, but in reality she was hiding a smile.

Yet another obstacle had been removed from her path, a minor one certainly. *But then,* Aracela told herself, *every little bit helps, doesn't it?*

Chapter Forty-two

"If I never see this town again, it will be too soon," Patrick O'Brien said as he tightened his saddle cinch.

"Tell me that a few days from now when you're freezing your ass off up in the high country," Jacob said.

"Herding sheep," Shawn said.

Patrick swung into the saddle. "Well, since the sheep are smarter than my brothers, it just might make a welcome change."

Jacob kneed his horse alongside Patrick. "Since you're so anxious to leave, lead on, brother."

Behind them as they headed north, Mrs. Hazel stood on the porch, a handkerchief to her eyes with one hand, waving with the other. "Yoo-hoo, Mr. Ironside!" she yelled.

Luther drew rein and turned. He swept off his hat and made a little bow. "What can I do for you, dear lady?"

"Will you come back and see me, Mr. Ironside?"

"Of course I will."

"You could write. Just address the envelope, to Mrs. Hazel, care of the Prince Regent Hotel, Estancia. Your letter will get to me."

"Then I will surely pen you a billet-doux just as soon as I am able, dear lady."

As Ironside settled his hat on his head and followed the others, Jacob said to him, "What the hell is a billy doo?"

"Ah, my boy, your education is sadly lacking," Ironside said. "A billet-doux means love letter, in French like."

"Then why didn't you just say love letter?"

"Because French is the language of love, my boy. Something you should keep in mind, but will soon forget."

"I didn't know you could speak French, Luther," Patrick said.

"I can't, but I learned billet-doux from a French whore up Abilene way."

"When was that?"

"When you were still young enough to mind your own damned business, Patrick," Ironside said.

Patrick laughed and the others laughed with him, but Ironside was disgruntled. "I didn't whup you boys enough when you were younkers." He lowered his shaggy eyebrows. "I can see that now."

The Dromore riders were following the bend of Big Draw, walking their horses through falling snow and a rising wind, when they came under fire. Bullets cracked the air above their heads and one kicked up dirt a few feet in front of Andre Perez.

"What the hell?" Jacob drew rein and looked around him. "I can't see a thing."

"There!" Perez pointed to a clump of mixed juniper and piñon at the bottom of a shallow valley. "I saw a drift of smoke from the trees."

"Is it Whitney's men?" Samuel asked.

"Hell if I know," Jacob said. "But I'm going to find out." Without waiting to see if the others were following, he kicked his horse into a gallop and headed for the trees, his Colt up and ready.

Ahead of him, Jacob saw three mounted Apaches break from the juniper. The Indians cut loose with a few ineffective shots, then swung north. Yipping, they held rifles above their heads.

Jacob didn't fire. The range was too great for a Colt, and the Apaches had already vanished into swirling snow.

Samuel drew up beside him. "Those must be the three that killed Charlie Packett."

"Seems like," Jacob said.

"Hell," Ironside said, "are them boys gonna be pests and take pots at us every time we come in range?"

"But Geronimo surrendered," Patrick said.

"Looks like those three didn't get the message," Jacob said.

A string of smoke still lifted above the juniper only to be quickly shredded by the wind. "You reckon they've got a white man stashed in there?" Ironside said. "Or maybe a Mexican sheepherder?"

Jacob lifted his beak of a nose and let the wind talk to him. "Hell, I smell meat roasting."

"Could be a white man staked down over a fire," Ironside said, his voice dark.

Without saying anything, Jacob kneed his horse into motion and headed for the trees. The others followed. The vaqueros, who had even more reason than white men to fear Apaches, rode with rifles across their saddle horns, wary eyes searching ahead of them.

But their caution was for nothing.

The Apaches had cut up a sheep and had been roasting chunks of meat in the fire when they saw the Dromore riders.

"Eat your fill, boys," Ironside said. "There ain't nothing better than sheep meat when a man's hungry."

The meat was blackened on the outside, bloody on the inside, but even Patrick, a picky eater, admitted that it wasn't half bad if a man closed his eyes and didn't chew it much.

They boiled up coffee, and sat under the thin shelter of the trees while Samuel told them what he'd decided. "I reckon we'll patrol a line from the foothills of the Manzano Mountains to the west, all the way to Palma Hill in the east. I'd say that's a distance of about forty-five miles, give or take."

"That's a far piece, Sam," Ironside said.

Samuel nodded. "I reckon so. Anywhere along

that line we find sheep, we'll turn them back south."
He looked at Jacob as random snowflakes sizzled in
the fire. "If we have to use force, we will."

Jacob shrugged his indifference. "What's best for
Dromore, is what I'll do."

"You know, boys," Ironside said, "I've been studying
the Estancia, and it seems to me"—he took time to
light a cigar with a brand from the fire—"that cattle
would thrive in the valley."

"I think we've all noticed that, Luther," Shawn said.
"What's your drift?"

"The colonel could move a big herd down here,"
Ironside said. "Hell, he could double his grass overnight."

Samuel didn't show surprise. "That's a thought for
the future. Right now the colonel feels Dromore is
big enough. But his opinion could change."

"You mean, just take the land for ourselves?" Patrick said.

"Yes, something like that," Samuel said.

"Wouldn't that make us as bad as Joel Whitney?"
Patrick said.

"No," Samuel said. "We're nothing like Whitney.
We're Dromore."

It took the O'Brien brothers and their assembled
vaqueros a week to realize the Estancia Valley sheepherders were under no pressure from Whitney and
his gunmen.

They spoke to several parties of Mexicans and

their stories were always the same—they'd seen nothing of Whitney and their flocks grazed in peace.

Not a single wooly had moved north of Lobo Hill. As one herder told them, "Why go from one winter graze to another when we don't have to? The grass here is poor, but is it not poor everywhere?"

Alarm bells rang in Jacob's head. It wasn't Whitney's style to lie low. What mischief was the little man up to, and did it involve Dromore?

He voiced his fears to Samuel, who said, "Jacob, Whitney won't attack Dromore. He doesn't have the cojones for that."

Luther Ironside smiled behind his coffee cup. "Hell, he knows we'd be down on him like a ton of brick. We'd skin him alive, and he knows that, too."

"There's no one at Dromore, only the colonel." Jacob looked at Samuel over the flames of the campfire. "There's something wrong, Sam. I can sense it."

Like the others, Samuel knew better than to discount his brother's feelings. Their ma always said Jacob had the gift of second sight, a legacy of his Celtic forebears.

Ironside looked around him, counting heads. They were camped west of Rattlesnake Draw under a narrow rock overhang that sheltered them from the worst of the snow and wind. "There's fifteen of us, more than enough to take Dromore back from Whitney." He smiled. "Not that I think he has it."

"I don't think he has Dromore, either," Shawn said. "But if Jacob feels something, then we should take him seriously. Maybe Pa's ill."

Ironside glared at Jacob. "Damn it, boy, you've got us all spooked."

"I know this much," Jacob said. "I'm riding for Dromore at first light."

"And we'll ride with you. We're sure as hell not doing any good here. Besides, I want to see my wife and son and . . ." Samuel's voice faltered to a halt, a look of dawning horror on his face.

"I'm sure they're all right, Sam," Shawn said. But his worried face gave lie to his words.

Chapter Forty-three

"The contract is in front of you, Colonel O'Brien," Joel Whitney said. "And the pen is in your hand. Now, sign it."

Shamus O'Brien threw the pen at Whitney's head, making the little man duck. "You go to hell, you Yankee trash."

Whitney walked past the colonel's desk and stared at the portrait above the mantel. "Your late wife, I presume." Shamus said nothing, his face ablaze with anger at Whitney and rage at his own, utter helplessness.

"Pity she's not still alive," the little man said. "She might have convinced you to see reason."

"Do you really think that piece of paper will hold up in court, you damned fool?" Shamus said.

"Oh but it will, Colonel. I used my legal training to draw it up very carefully. It will stand up in any court in the land."

"Not when I testify I signed it at gunpoint."

"Gunpoint?" Whitney glanced around him. "I see no gun pointed at your head. Mr. Stanley, do you see a gun pointed at the colonel's head? Am I missing something?"

Clay Stanley grinned. "No, you sure aren't, boss."

"There you are, Colonel," Whitney said, "no gun." He picked up the pen from the floor and slammed it onto Shamus's desk. "Now sign Dromore over to me, then you can pack your bags and get out."

"Go to hell," Shamus said.

"Oh dear, has it come to this? I abhor violence, but sometimes it's the only way to make a stubborn old man see reason." Whitney motioned to one of three grinning gunmen in the colonel's study. "Bring the black woman in here."

The man left, and Shamus said, "What are you going to do to Nellie?"

Whitney spread his pink hands. In his fur coat he looked like a malevolent mole. "Why, shoot her dead, of course."

"Harm a hair on Nellie's head and I'll hang you myself, Whitney," Shamus said.

"Why, you useless old cripple, you won't hang anybody," Whitney snapped. He picked up the pen and forced it into Shamus's hand. "Sign it!" he screamed as he tried to twist the colonel's fingers around the pen. "Sign it! Sign it!"

Confined to a wheelchair as he was, the constant struggle to push himself around had preserved the thick muscles of Shamus's arms and shoulders. He drew back his fist and slammed Whitney hard in the mouth.

The little man staggered back, blood dripping from his mashed lips. "Damn you, O'Brien," he said, his eyes ugly, "you'll regret that blow."

The door opened and Nellie was dragged inside. She looked at Shamus, her eyes pleading. "Colonel, help me. I'm sore afeared."

"They won't harm you, Nellie," Shamus said. "I'll hang any man who lays a finger on you."

Whitney grabbed the woman by the arm and held her. "Will you sign?"

"I'm warning you, Whitney," Shamus said, "leave Nellie alone."

"Will you sign the contract?"

"Go to hell."

"Clay," Whitney said, "place the muzzle of your gun against this woman's head."

Stanley drew and shoved the muzzle of his Russian into Nellie's temple. The woman shrieked. "Help me, Colonel. Oh, please help me!"

Shamus tried to rise out of his wheelchair. "Whitney—"

"Will you sign?"

"Damn you, Whitney!" Shamus roared, still trying to rise.

"Kill her!" Whitney cried.

Stanley pulled the trigger.

Blood, bone, and brain haloed above Nellie's head and splashed in a gory splatter across Shamus's desk.

Whitney let go of the woman's arm and she dropped to the floor amid the ringing silence that followed the shot.

"Her blood is on you, O'Brien, not me," Whitney screamed.

Stunned, horrified as he was, Shamus found himself unable to speak. He stared at Whitney, his hate-filled eyes talking volumes.

"Will you sign?" Whitney said. "Damn you, take up the pen and sign."

"You'll have to kill me," Shamus said. "Or, by God, I'll kill you."

"Damn the rants of an old cripple," Whitney said. "Bring in the woman—what's her name?—Samuel O'Brien's wife. And her child."

"Whitney," Shamus said, his voice like death, "I'm warning you, leave Lorena and my grandson alone." Lorena O'Brien was a slender, blond woman with a pretty, oval-shaped face and expressive brown eyes. She clung to her baby as she was pushed into the middle of the floor where Nellie's body lay. Without a moment's hesitation, Lorena threw herself at Whitney, her baby in her left arm as she struck out with her right. "You animal!" she screamed. "You filthy animal!"

"Hold her, somebody," Whitney yelled, ducking back to avoid the woman's wild blows. A gunman grabbed Lorena and held her.

"Mr. Stanley," Whitney said, "place the muzzle of your gun against Mrs. O'Brien's head."

Stanley had all of a Texan's prejudices. He'd been

raised in the belief that it was one thing to kill a black, but to kill a white woman was a different matter entirely. "Boss, are you sure about this?"

"Are you questioning my order, Mr. Stanley?"

"No, sir, I guess not."

"Then make ready to scatter her brains when I give the word."

"You're scum, all of you," Lorena said. "My husband will kill you all for this."

Whitney spoke past the bloody handkerchief he held to his mouth. "Your husband isn't here, Mrs. O'Brien. Or haven't you noticed?"

That statement brought guffaws from a couple gunmen, and Whitney talked through the laughter. "It's up to you now, Colonel. It would be a pity to blow apart such a pretty head. And then, there's the baby, of course. What of his head, I wonder?"

Dromore was life itself to Shamus, but now it demanded too high a cost. "Damn you to hell, Whitney, I'll sign your paper."

The little man nodded. "What a pity you didn't agree earlier. The black woman would still be alive." He stepped to the desk. "Sign."

"No, Colonel," Lorena said. "Please don't."

Shamus took the pen and scrawled away his ownership of Dromore.

Joel Whitney sat behind Shamus's desk and ran his hand over its polished mahogany top. He smiled at the colonel. "I'm going to enjoy this, being master of Dromore."

"Damn you, Whitney. My sons will hunt you down and kill you like the yellow dog you are."

Whitney took out his watch, thumbed it open, and glanced at the time. "By now, your sons are all dead. And if they're not, they soon will be. My men will track them down."

"Do you think the riffraff you brought down from Santa Fe will stand against men with sand?" Shamus said.

"It was my intention not to hire those ruffians, you know," Whitney said. "But they came cheap, and I thought, 'Well, now I own Dromore, why not?'"

"They're scum, like you are scum, Whitney," Shamus said.

The little man sighed, and sank back in the colonel's cowhide chair. "This grows tiresome. Mr. Stanley, please remove that mess from the floor, and then escort Colonel O'Brien and his kin off the premises."

"What about the servants, boss? There's a bunch of them. And then there's the families of the vaqueros."

"I wish the servants to remain." Whitney smiled. "A man in my position needs servants. All the others"—he jerked a thumb toward the window and sighed—"must be tossed out in the cold."

"And what about horses," Stanley said.

"What about them?"

"Do I give them mounts?"

"Of course not. I need all my horses. And my cattle."
Whitney's smile was close to a pout. "And my land."

"Then I'll start with him." Stanley pointed to
Shamus. "I have the feeling that where he goes, the
others will follow."

Whitney waved a negligent hand. "Do whatever
you have to do, just throw the damned beggars out
of my house."

Forty women and children followed Shamus O'Brien
into exile.

The night closed around them fast. Stumbling
tracks in the falling snow marked their passing. Cold
was the wind, icy from the north, and the hard land
lay around them, indifferent, uncaring.

Lorena passed her son to one of the women, and at
first she tried to push the colonel's chair. But the
narrow wheels snagged on every root and clump of
grass, thumped into every depression, and the woman's
strength was soon spent.

Fortunately, one of the Mexican women had the
foresight to bring a rope. It was tied to Shamus's
chair and the woman and older boys took turns to
pull, one pushing from behind.

A lesser man would've been dejected, wallowing
in despair, but Shamus O'Brien was made of sterner
stuff. He directed his little party of refugees south,
like a rough-hewn Moses leading his people across
the wilderness. He was confident that, somehow,

somewhere, he'd meet up with his sons. He had to. All their lives depended on it.

But after an hour, as the darkness grew deeper, the raw wind stronger, and snow spun through the sighing night, Shamus saw the women around him falter. Their young ones cried from cold and hunger, and he realized that he was a burden. Moving his wheelchair across rough country was a backbreaking task.

He ordered a halt and had Lorena and another woman parcel out what little food they'd managed to bring with them. Gradually the children quieted down, huddling with their mothers in a circle around Shamus's chair.

"If my memory serves me right and I haven't lost my sense of direction, White Bluffs should be a mile to our west," he told Lorena. "There's an old ruined pueblo there where we can shelter for the night."

"Anything to get out of this wind," the girl said, holding her suckling son to her breast. Her face brightened. "Maybe Samuel is there."

"Maybe." But Shamus held out little hope. The country was wide and rugged and his sons could be anywhere. "Will the people make it?"

"Yes," Lorena said. "They're tough."

"I'm a burden, I know that," Shamus said. "You'll lead them, to the bluffs, Lorena, and leave me here."

The woman smiled. "And let you freeze to death? That's not going to happen, Colonel."

"I could order you to leave me here."

"You could, but I'm not one of your cowboys, so

your orders carry no weight with me. You'll go. We all go. You're the glue that holds us together."

"Lorena, without me you might have a chance."

"Shamus, I don't want to hear any more of this. You're going with us, even if I have to push you myself."

"You remind me of my wife," Shamus said, smiling. "She was a strong-willed woman like you."

"She would have to have been, wouldn't she? Married to a stubborn husband like you and four equally hard-headed sons."

Lorena removed her son's mouth from her breast with a soft little *pop!* "It's time to move on, Colonel." She shivered. "I think the snow's falling heavier."

When Shamus O'Brien was close enough to make out the flat-topped bulk of White Bluffs through the snowfall, he swung north, toward what he hoped was the location of the pueblo.

His memory hadn't failed him. Only two ruined adobes remained of what had been a fair-sized settlement two hundred years before, but they represented shelter from the cold and wind and offered the possibility of a fire.

The women and children wasted no time crowding into the adobes. To their joy there was enough ancient, dry wood scattered around for a couple fires.

There was no coffee, but Lorena melted a tin cup of snow over a fire and brought the hot water to

Shamus, who was on guard at the door of the larger building. "Drink this, Colonel. It will warm you."

"Is there some for the others?"

"Yes." She smiled. "We have plenty of cups, but no coffee."

Shamus drank the hot water gratefully, his eyes reaching out through darkness and snow. "I wonder where they are?"

He did not expect an answer, nor did Lorena give one.

Far off, a pack of wolves glided through the high timber like gray ghosts. Lorena shivered when she heard sudden howls that portended a chase and a violent death amid the wind-shadowed night.

Chapter Forty-four

Joel Whitney's renegades struck at dawn.

Two vaqueros went down with the first volley. Luther Ironside, drinking coffee by the fire, fell after a bullet tore into his left thigh.

Jacob and Shawn had just saddled their horses when the first shots split the air and rattled through the surrounding juniper and piñon. They heard shooting in the direction of the camp, but ignored it, focusing on the oncoming attackers. The brothers, and four vaqueros with them, took the brunt of the attack, a dozen mounted bushwhackers coming at them in a headlong charge along a brush-covered creek bank.

Jacob drew, understanding it was a bedrock gunfight. There was no room or time for grandstand plays.

He slammed shots into the horsemen. Shawn and the vaqueros were firing, too. A sound of rolling, racketing thunder surrounded them. Men and horses went down, and a few of the renegades drew

rein, stunned . . . appalled. In just a few seconds
they'd lost half their number, bullets buzzing past
and through them as though they'd kicked over a
hornet's nest.

Whitney had tried to save money by recruiting
border trash, petty thieves, pimps, and goldbrick
artists. Nothing in their experience had prepared
them to fight against men like these. They were
facing gunfighters, and now all bets were off.

The riders in front tried to turn their horses, and
got tangled in those coming from behind them.
More horses fell. Cursing men rolled away from
them, trying to regain their feet.

Their Colts shot dry, Jacob and Shawn grabbed
rifles from their saddle boots and the vaqueros followed suit. One of the attackers, with more sand
than the others, freed himself from his fallen horse,
then stood, a gun in each hand, shrieking war talk.
Jacob shot him, saw the man stagger and shot him
again. The renegade went down and stayed down.

Shawn and the vaqueros worked their Winchesters and pumped lead. It was enough. The surviving
horsemen broke and ran, leaving eight of their
number dead and dying on the ground.

Jacob turned his horse toward the campfire. Ironside sat, one leg drawn up, working his Colt well,
scoring hits. Patrick and Samuel stood side by side
and fired steadily. Five renegades were down, and
another slumped in the saddle, coughing black
blood over his chest.

Jacob killed a rider, and then winged a second. The

vaqueros who'd been closest to the fire hammered shots into the raiders and dropped three of them.

As wise as outhouse rats, Whitney's riffraff realized they were trying to buck a stacked deck. Several of them turned and set spurs to their horses. "And for all I know, they're still runnin' yet," Ironside would say later.

To a man, every Dromore rider that morning was good with a gun, but Jacob and Shawn were first-rate—named men whom other belted men acknowledged were fast and deadly with any firearm.

Whitney's rabble had made a terrible mistake, and one of them explained it in detail.

He was a lanky towhead, the big hands of a farm boy dangling out of the sleeves of a coat three sizes too small for him. He appeared out of the smoke haze and stepped toward the fire. The kid's chest was ripped apart by bullets and his face was covered in blood. He was no longer alive, but didn't yet know he was dead. And he wanted to say his piece.

He stopped when he was several feet from Jacob and the others. "He told us it would be easy, that you was just a bunch of rubes who'd die easy."

"Whitney told you wrong, boy," Samuel said.

"I've never seen the like of you and your'n afore," the kid said, looking at Jacob. "You ain't human, not hardly."

"Best you lie down and die quiet, boy," Samuel said. "Say a prayer, maybe."

But Jacob looked at the bodies of the two dead vaqueros and Ironside grimacing in pain, and there was no give in him. He raised his rifle, shot the boy dead center, and watched him fall.

"Things are tough all over, son."

"Looks like the bullet went right through your leg without hitting bone, Luther," Samuel said.

"Well, that's good news, ain't it?" Ironside said, dry as a stick.

Samuel smiled, "We're taking you back to Dromore right now and let Nellie work on you."

"Spoil him, you mean," Jacob said.

"Shot-up leg or no, I can still outride and outwork you, boy," Ironside said.

"Hell, Luther, you haven't done a lick of work in years," Jacob said.

"Yeah? Well, I've been resting," Ironside said. "Kinda biding my time so I can out-cowboy mouthy young whippersnappers like you, Jacob."

Jacob grinned. "Then let's bind up that leg and get you on your horse, cowboy."

Shawn sacrificed his spare shirt to make bandages for Luther's thigh. The entry wound was bad, raw and inflamed, but the exiting .44 bullet had tumbled and torn away a chunk of flesh. The O'Brien brothers had seen Nellie work wonders on bullet wounds before, but they figured her work would be cut out for her this time.

Luther Ironside was not a complaining man, but he vented his lungs when he was helped into the saddle by a couple vaqueros and his wounded thigh slammed against the stock of his booted rifle. "Damn it, you boys are gonna kill me long before I ever get to see Nellie," he yelled.

"Take it easy there." Jacob grinned. "Mr. Ironside's got a lot of ropin' and brandin' to do and he'll need his leg."

"Jacob," Ironside said, scowling from the saddle, "I swear . . ." But he didn't swear anything, because he couldn't come up with the right cusswords at such short notice.

The two dead vaqueros were loaded onto their horses for return to Dromore, but Whitney's dead men stayed where they lay. Coyotes and buzzards would scatter their bones, and in the fullness of time the bones would turn to dust. A great wind would blow the dust away, and it would fertilize the prairie grass. Such was nature's way of ensuring that nothing was wasted.

Ironside had lost blood and wasn't in shape to spend long hours in the saddle, riding into a north wind that drove stinging sheets of snow at him. Samuel decided to make camp that night in the shadow of Hurtado Mesa. They rode out the next morning an hour short of daylight, anxious to get Ironside into Nellie's capable, gentle hands.

Chapter Forty-five

The big house looked the same, white and pillared against a backdrop of falling snow, as pretty as a Currier and Ives print. Smoke from the chimneys tied bows in the air and a winter wreath of holly hung on the red door.

But Jacob sensed something was wrong, and when Samuel looked at his brother's stony face he felt a stirring of alarm. "What do you think, Jacob?"

"I don't know," Jacob said. "The house doesn't look right, as though the windows are staring at me, warning me to stay away. Somehow, I sense Whitney's hand in this."

"Has he done something to the colonel?"

"Could be. But Dromore doesn't seem like a house in mourning." Jacob shook his head. "Hell, why stand here talking about it? Let's find out."

He kneed his horse forward. Patrick, Shawn, Samuel, and the ten vaqueros spread out on either side of him.

Luther Ironside held back, holding the lead ropes of the dead vaqueros' horses. Lightheaded and fevered as he was, if Jacob was right and something bad had happened at Dromore involving Joel Whitney, it could mean gun work, and he was in no shape for a fight.

As Jacob had said, the windows of Dromore had eyes, but they were human. Joel Whitney saw the riders emerge through the gusting afternoon snow and raised the alarm.

"Get rid of them, Clay," he said to Stanley. "Warn them that they're trespassing on my property."

The Texan grinned. "The O'Briens will fight, boss."

"Well, isn't that what I'm paying you for, to fight back?"

"I just wanted to warn you that there will be dead men to bury come dark," Stanley said.

Whitney shrugged. "That's the cost of doing business."

"Jacob is the fastest with the iron," Stanley said. "I reckon if I gun him it'll take the fight out of the others and they'll quit."

"Do what you have to do, Mr. Stanley," Whitney said. "Just get rid of them." He stared out the window. "They're almost here. Get your men outside."

If the O'Brien brothers had any doubts about Jacob's fears, they vanished when they saw Whitney's gunmen pile out the front door.

Samuel led his riders to within ten yards of the Texans and drew rein. "What are you men doing here?"

Stanley stepped forward. He wore a canvas coat but had it pulled back from the guns strapped to his chest. "This is private property and you men are trespassing," he said, grinning.

"Where is the colonel?" Samuel said.

Stanley waved a hand. "Out there somewhere. He skedaddled after he signed over this ranch to Mr. Whitney."

"Where are my wife and child?" Samuel said, alarm rising in his voice.

"They're with your pappy, boy." Stanley moved his eyes to Jacob. "Howdy, Jake. Can I get you a cup of coffee before you leave?"

"I'm not going anywhere," Jacob said. "The colonel would never surrender this ranch to trash like Joel Whitney. Get that little rat out here."

"Well, he did sign it away, and Mr. Whitney is not receiving visitors today. There's the beginning and the end of it. Now, if you boys will be on your way, I want to get out of this cold."

"We have a wounded man here," Samuel said. "Where is Nellie?"

Stanley said, "She ain't around anymore."

"Is she with the colonel?" Samuel said.

"Nah, she's out back waiting for the spring thaw."

"Clay, what happened to Nellie?" Jacob slowly unbuttoned his mackinaw. His snow-flecked face was as still as a death mask.

"Well, your pa killed her, in a manner of speaking." Stanley was smiling, a man hugely enjoying himself. "See, he refused to sign Mr. Whitney's paper, so he told me to shoot the black gal, which I did." He pointed his right forefinger at his temple. "Right there, Jacob."

Confident of his lightning speed with a gun, the last thing Clay Stanley expected was for Jacob to draw.

Jacob's Colt was up and firing before Stanley even cleared leather. Jacob fired two shots at a range of twenty-five feet and scored two hits. Both bullets crashed into the middle of Stanley's chest, only an inch apart. The gunman staggered back, his eyes unbelieving. He tried to lift his Russians on target, but suddenly the big revolvers felt too heavy to lift. Clay Stanley dropped to his knees, his surprised eyes on Jacob. He died in that position . . . as guns roared his requiem.

But the firing didn't come from the O'Briens and their vaqueros. They were momentarily as stunned motionless by the sudden violence of Jacob's draw as Whitney's Texans. Led by Shamus's black butler, four of Dromore's male servants rounded the corner of the house and cut loose with shotguns they'd retrieved from the colonel's gun cabinet.

Three gunmen went down and a couple more were bloodied by scattering buckshot. The others reeled back from the unexpected onslaught. Backing into those behind them made a couple Texans step wide, their drawn guns coming up as they sought to bring them to bear. Jacob, thumbing fast shots off a rearing horse, dropped one man and the other decided he'd had enough. He threw his gun away, out of it.

The half dozen Texans who were still on their feet raised their hands. They were all named gunfighters, not one of them a coward, but mercenaries aren't expected to fight to the death. They'd had their fill of Dromore and its fast-shooting riders.

Jacob O'Brien was in a killing rage, his face a twisted mask of hate and fury. He swung out of the saddle and ran for the door. Men shrank back from him as they would an out-of-control inferno.

He wanted to kill Joel Whitney—wanted to kill him real bad.

Jacob's search of the house revealed that the bird had flown. Whitney had probably run for it when he saw Clay Stanley fall. When Jacob went outside, there were fresh horse tracks leading from the barn. He followed them until they swung north and headed into a stand of mixed juniper and wild oak.

It looked like Whitney was headed for Santa Fe where he could lose himself in the crowd, but Jacob wasn't about to give up. He was going to track him down.

A flash of red caught his eye at the bottom of the barn wall, between the stone foundation and the old zinc horse trough that had stood there since he was a boy. Jacob stepped to the wall and saw what he at first thought was a large rag doll half buried in snow. He kneeled, wedging himself into the tight space between the barn and the trough, and looked closer. It was Nellie's body, wearing one of her red dresses that she loved so much.

Gently, Jacob brushed snow from the woman's face. Her black eyes stared up at him, no longer flashing wit and intelligence, but as dull and flat as river pebbles.

Whitney had just tossed Nellie away, like a piece of worthless garbage.

It took time to ease the body out of that tight space, but Jacob didn't hurry. He was determined to protect Nellie's dignity, even in death.

Finally he was able to take the stiff little body in his arms. He carried her to the timber chapel the vaqueros had built for their families and laid her out in front of the altar. He stood there, his hat in his hands, and stared down at her, grieving, remembering his boyhood and the kind, loving woman who'd been a second mother to him.

Jacob stood there, in the snow-gloom of the chapel, until Patrick came and gently led him outside.

As they walked toward the house, Patrick handed Jacob a piece of paper. "I found this in the colonel's study." Jacob glanced at the contract that transferred ownership of Dromore, his father's scrawled signature at the bottom. "Whitney skedaddled so fast, he didn't have time to take this with him." Jacob tore the

paper into shreds and let them drop to the ground.
"I'm going after him."

Patrick nodded, but said nothing,

"Where are Whitney's men?" Jacob asked.

"Samuel and the others have them corralled."

"I'm going to kill them," Jacob said, feeding fresh
cartridges into his Colt. "I'm going to kill every
damned one of those sons of bitches."

Patrick stopped and grabbed his brother's arm.
"No, Jacob. There's been too much killing already.
It's over, can't you see that?"

"It's not over while Whitney and his hired killers
are still alive."

"Jacob, Clay Stanley murdered Nellie on Whitney's orders," Patrick said. "Those others had nothing to do with it. Go after Whitney with my blessing,
but don't shoot men down in cold blood."

Jacob brushed past his brother, cold death in his
eyes, but he stopped when he heard the triple click
of a Colt's hammer. He turned and saw Patrick's gun
pointed squarely at him, the muzzle unwavering.

"Jacob, I won't let you gun down those men like
dogs."

It took a few moments, but eventually Jacob smiled.
"You've got sand, big brother."

Patrick shook his head. "No, I haven't. Right now
I'm scared. I saw you shoot today."

"All right, you can let the Texans go, Pat," Jacob
said. "I never cross a man who's holding a .44 on me."

Patrick holstered his gun. "Hell, I wouldn't have pulled the trigger anyway."

"I know you wouldn't. You've got balls, brother. They don't clang when you walk like mine do, but you got them nonetheless."

"So that's what I keep hearing," Patrick said, grinning.

Everything that had stood between him and Jacob was made right again.

The Texans were escorted off Dromore land by vaqueros. They went meekly enough, uneasily aware that the hard-eyed Mexicans were fingers looking for triggers.

After Samuel promised to do right by Nellie, Jacob saddled a fresh horse and rode out after Whitney.

As his brothers watched him go, Shawn turned to Samuel. "I sure wouldn't want to be in Whitney's shoes. Would you?"

"No I wouldn't." Samuel smiled. "Did you know Jacob took his cat with him?"

"Why would he do that?" Patrick asked

"Maybe he doesn't intend to come back to Dromore." Samuel looked at his brother. "Jacob does what he does, and sometimes there's no reason to it."

"What did you think today, Sam?" Shawn stroked the neck of a packhorse loaded with blankets and food.

"About Jacob?" Samuel saw his brother nod. Slowly, as though he was talking thoughts as they came to him, he said, "I think he may be the fastest with a gun there is. Maybe one man in ten thousand can do what he does. Maybe one in a hundred thousand. He's wired differently from the rest of us, is all."

"Is Jacob a killer?" Shawn said.

"He's got some of the killer in him. It would be stupid of me to deny it. But a man who was all killer couldn't play the piano as he does, or cry as he did for Nellie, or fuss over a kitten." Samuel shook his head. "Shawn, I can't tell you what Jacob is. What he's not is an uncomplicated man."

"I can shuck a gun as fast as any of them," Shawn said. "But I'm no match for Jacob."

"Well, like I said, I don't think any man alive is." Samuel glanced at the black sky, and then collected the reins of his horse. "Mount up, you two. Let's go find the colonel and my wife and son."

It was Silas Cade, turning up like a bad penny, who pointed the way to White Bluffs. "Seen your pa over to there, boys. Gave him what I could spare of my coffee an' grub. He's got a passel of folks with him, and a whole scad o' young 'uns."

The O'Briens had ridden up on Cade just north of the V-shaped Arroyo San Cristobal as the old prospector led his burro through falling snow heading for . . . only he and God knew.

"How are they?" Samuel said, his voice unsteady with worry.

"Seem to be doin' fine." Cade frowned. "Colonel told me about losing his ranch an' all. I always knew that little Whitney feller was a bad 'un."

Samuel touched his hat. "Thank you for the information, old-timer. Now we'll be on our way."

Patrick took some money out of his pocket. "This will compensate you for the coffee and grub, Silas."

The old man waved it away. "No need for payment, sonny. I was right happy to do it." He grinned. "The colonel says that when he gets his ranch back, I can come sit by his fire anytime." He jerked a thumb over his shoulder at the burro. "Me and Lucy is sure lookin' forward to that."

Chapter Forty-six

Donna Aracela laid aside her copy of Mary Wollstonecraft's book, *A Vindication of the Rights of Women*, and said, "Enter," to the scratch at the door to her study.

A servant girl stepped inside, her eyes averted from her mistress as Aracela had decreed. "There is someone here to see you, Lady."

"Who is it, girl?"

"He wouldn't say, Lady. He—"

Joel Whitney pushed the servant girl aside and stepped into the room. The shoulders of his fur coat were covered in snow and his face showed the strain of a long and difficult ride. In one hand he carried the money valise Aracela had given him. "We have to talk."

Aracela dismissed the servant, and looked at her visitor. "I think you bring news, Mr. Whitney, and none of it good."

The little man collapsed into a chair, and laid the valise at his feet. "Brandy," he croaked out.

Aracela rose, her green morning dress rustling. "As you wish." She stepped to the drinks trolley and poured brandy into a glass, then handed it to him, Before she sat again, she asked, "What of Dromore?"

Whitney drank deeply. His voice husky, he said, "I had it, and lost it again."

Aracela sat and her beautiful black eyes narrowed. "Why, whatever do you mean, Mr. Whitney?"

"I . . . persuaded Colonel O'Brien to sign his ranch over to me, but his sons took it back. They killed Clay Stanley and half a dozen others."

"I see no wounds on you," Aracela said.

"After I watched Stanley get killed, I got the hell out of there. I'm not a gunfighter." Whitney's face paled. "Oh, my God . . ."

Aracela said nothing. Waited.

"The contract O'Brien signed . . . I left it at Dromore."

"How very careless of you."

Whitney got to his feet and refilled his glass. "I'll get Dromore back, you'll see. But I'll need more money."

"Did you spend all the money I gave you?"

"Of course not. Every penny of it is in the valise. The riffraff I ended up hiring I paid with pocket change."

"How much more do you need?"

"Another ten thousand at least. This time I plan to spend every penny I have on an army of men who know how to use a gun and who won't quit on me when the going gets tough."

"Mr. Whitney, you had an army, and lost it."

"I lost it because I ran into a demon by the name of Jacob O'Brien," the little man said. "No man should be able to draw and shoot like him. It's unnatural. Clay Stanley was the best of them, and his gun didn't even clear his holster before O'Brien killed him."

Aracela nodded. "Jacob is a most remarkable man."

"And I am, too, Aracela." Whitney threw himself at the woman's feet. "Come with me to Texas."

"Isn't this rather sudden?" Aracela's smile was as warm as a grinning skull.

"Aracela, all the time I was away from you, I couldn't stop thinking about you," Whitney said. "Your body, the way it moves, haunts my waking hours and disturbs my sleep. I tried to resist, but . . . but it's as though you've cast a spell over me."

"I'm a witch, didn't you know that? Ask any of the peons, they'll tell you."

"I don't care what you are. Come with me to Texas and share my life and my bed. When we return to the Estancia Valley we'll ride together into Dromore as conquerors."

Aracela was silent for a few moments, then said, "Of course I will . . . Joel."

Whiney looked up at her face and smiled. "Aracela, you've made me a very happy man."

"And I am a happy woman."

"Get your vaqueros mounted. I'm sure the O'Briens are tracking me."

"I have no vaqueros," Aracela said. "One of them

tried to rape me, and I was forced to shoot him. The others left after that. They blamed me for Otilio's death, as though it was my fault."

"Damn him. I would've shot him myself."

Aracela smiled and stroked the little man's stubbled cheek. "Of course you would have, Joel. Of course you would have."

Whitney chose a fresh horse from the hacienda stable and Aracela mounted a beautiful Appaloosa that had been her dead brother's favorite traveling horse. She wore a split, canvas riding skirt, a man's canvas coat, and a wide-brimmed hat. Under her knee she had a booted Winchester Model 1866 Yellow Boy.

"Riding light, aren't you, Aracela?" Whitney said, seeing that the woman carried no bag, only a small, drawstring purse.

"I have everything I need, Joel. The rest I can buy in Texas."

"But the money? Where is it?"

"I had none on hand, but I can wire my bankers when we get to where we're going and have money sent to us," Aracela said.

"I figure we'll head for El Paso," Whitey said.

"Then I'll send a wire from there, Joel. Now let's ride and stop worrying so much."

"Now we're together, I don't want anything to go wrong this time. I want us to get Dromore back."

"Nothing will go wrong, Joel," Aracela said. "Trust me."

* * *

They rode south, parallel to the snow-streaked Manzano Mountains, their rawboned peaks lost in black cloud. Around them lay broken country, wild and lonely, flayed that morning by snow, wind, and grim cold. Juniper and piñon thrived in the lower flats among shoulders of granite rock and higher, closer to the mountains, grew pine and higher still where the air was thin, aspen and then ponderosa near the timberline.

Whitney rode in front and chose the trail, his breath clouding. Behind him Aracela rode with slack reins and let the mountain-bred Appaloosa pick its way. She was freezing cold, her toes numb in her boots, and the sight of Whitney hunched over in his fur coat and hat repelled her. He looked like an overgrown rodent, lifting his wet, red nose every now and then as though sniffing cheese.

She figured she'd had quite enough of this charade.

Easing the Winchester out of the leather, a round already in the chamber, she thumbed back the hammer. By her reckoning they were about a mile north of the ruins of the old Quarai Mission. It was time.

Aracela shouldered the rifle, laid the sights on the middle of Whitney's back, and squeezed the trigger. She saw the man jerk in the saddle, and then he turned his head, his face horrified. She fired again. Whitney fell off his horse, hit the ground, and rolled on his back.

Levering another round, the woman walked her horse closer until she was looming over him.

"Why, Aracela?" Whitney's eyes had a look of utter devastation, like a man who'd just been gut shot by his sweet old granny.

She smiled, her rifle trained on his chest. "You failed me, little man. I wanted Dromore and you lost it." She shrugged. "Oh well, now you're dead and I'll take back the Estancia, so all is not lost."

"I thought you might have loved me," Whitney said.

Aracela laughed out loud. "Love you? You poor fool, whatever gave you that idea?"

Whitney's face turned ugly. "You evil bitch, you've killed me. But, damn you, I'll take you to hell with me." His hand dived into his coat for his derringer.

Aracela let time stretch for a few moments before she pulled the trigger. The pleasure of killing was so exquisite—it should not be hurried. She fired. The big .44 drove through Whitney's right hand and into his chest and he died—all his dreams and ambitions and lusts wiped away in an instant.

She dismounted and removed the valise from Whitney's saddle horn. She stepped into the saddle again, gathered up the reins of the little man's borrowed horse, and headed north toward the hacienda. She was cold, chilled to the bone by snow and wind, yet she'd never felt so alive, as though she could feel the blood surging through her body, pulsing in her blue veins.

After a mile, she became aware of the man watching her from a stand of juniper atop a ridge to her west. He was young, a peon by the look of his ragged serape and straw hat, and he sat astride a yellow mustang.

Someone from the village, Aracela decided. *But why is he out riding on a day like this?* She shook her head. Peons were strange people, incredibly stupid for the most part, so who could even guess? She dismissed the man from her mind and rode on.

Aracela had no way of knowing it then, but the man on the yellow horse was her death.

Chapter Forty-seven

Jacob O'Brien lost Whitney's trail a long time before he rode into the town of Estancia, cold, hungry, and in a bad frame of mind. He knew the man was heading south, but to where? Texas was the obvious answer, but states didn't come any bigger than that, and the little man could easily go to ground and vanish.

Jacob stepped into the hotel lobby. Mrs. Hazel stood behind the desk.

No, she had not seen Whitney, but Mr. O'Brien looked exhausted and would he like something to eat and a room and, by the way, how was that nice Mr. Ironside?

Jacob told the woman about Luther's wound. "My brothers plan to bring a doctor from El Paso, so I'm sure he'll be fine."

Mrs. Hazel sighed. "I won't sleep a wink worrying about him. He's such a fine, distinguished gentlemen."

"Yup, he's all of that." Right then Jacob was a little

chagrined. Eve was purring in Mrs. Hazel's arms and she seemed to prefer the woman's company to his own. Well, he always knew females were fickle, and that obviously also applied to the cat.

"I have a roast in the oven, if you'd care for some," Mrs. Hazel said.

"Maybe later," Jacob said. "I'm going to check at the saloon, see if anyone's seen Joel Whitney." He rubbed Eve's pointy ears. "Do you mind keeping her until I get back?"

"No at all, Mr. O'Brien. She can stay here as long as she wants."

"I have the feeling she'd like that," Jacob smiled. "She's not much of a cat for long, cold trails."

Jacob led his horse into the barn and forked him hay and a scoop of oats. Then he crossed the street to the saloon under a gray sky that offered not even a hint of blue.

The bartender hadn't seen Whitney, either. In fact business was slow.

"It's the weather," Jacob said. "Everybody's holed up until spring."

"Seems like," the bartender said.

Jacob refused a drink but accepted coffee, then another cup.

He took his cup, stepped to the window and looked outside. It was snowing again. He'd read a newspaper that said it was the worst winter on record and that the cattle industry from Mexico to Montana had been devastated. "Blizzards of '87 Spell An End To Open Range Ranching" the editorial trumpeted.

Staring gloomily into the blustering snow and the ice-bound valley, Jacob could believe it. He figured ranchers would keep their herds fenced and close, and that would not only spell the end of the open range but the sound of the wind through barbed wire would sing a requiem for the cowboy way. A pity, Jacob thought, because it was a good way. But time makes changes and no man can halt its march.

Depressed, he stepped back to the bar.

"That feller Whitney," the bartender said, "you hunting him?"

Jacob saw no reason to lie. "I aim to kill him."

The bartender didn't flinch. He'd heard that kind of talk many times before. "Where you figure he's headed?"

"Could be Texas. Or the Arizona Territory or Old Mexico." Jacob smiled. "Take your pick." His smile slipped. "Hell, maybe my hunt ends right here in Estancia."

"Has he kin hereabouts, this Whitney feller?" the bartender asked, refilling Jacob's cup.

"No kin, only enemies," Jacob said. "And one of them is Don Manuel Ortero, another man who wants Whitney dead."

"Not anymore he don't. Didn't you hear? The old

man's dead, killed in a gun battle, I hear. They say it was with Texas outlaws, but I don't know about that."

Jacob was stunned. "Are you sure?"

"Sure as I'm standing here and you're drinking free coffee."

Jacob felt that sixth sense niggle him. With the old man out of the way, had Whitney made some kind of devil's deal with Aracela? Was he with her now? Nah, that was unlikely. And yet, it was just possible.

It was a long shot to be sure, but it was the only lead Jacob had and a sight better than hanging around Estancia kicking his heels. He rang a dollar on the counter. "For the coffee."

He turned away as the bartender said. "You don't have to do that. The coffee is free."

Jacob stopped at the door. "Times are hard and coffee is expensive. I like to pay my way."

"Sure you can keep her, Mrs. Hazel," Jacob said. "Eve doesn't much like trailing with me. I guess she wants a fire and a place to curl up o' nights and a mouse to catch."

"I'll be good to her, Mr. O'Brien, depend on that. As for mice, I've got plenty of those."

"I know you'll take good care of her." Jacob touched his hat. "Well, so long, ma'am."

He swung away from the hotel porch and headed in the direction of the Hacienda Otero. He had little confidence that Joel Whitney had made a pact with

Aracela and would actually be there. But it was the only lead he had on the little killer and he had to check it out.

Besides, if nothing else, it would be a real pleasure to see the beautiful Aracela again.

Chapter Forty-eight

The maid cried and tried to turn back when she saw that Donna Aracela was dragging her toward the Ortero crypt. Aracela stopped, slapped the girl hard across the face, then grabbed her by the hair and pulled her to the tomb door.

"Be quiet, you little bitch." Aracela took the key from the pocket of her dress, clanked it in the lock, and swung the door open. She pushed the whimpering girl inside and closed the door behind her.

Dusk had fallen and the inside of the tomb was dark. Aracela struck a match and lit the candle that stood beside her father's coffin. In the shifting, yellow light she saw the maid had wedged herself into a corner, her eyes wide and terrified. That pleased Aracela greatly. She'd ravaged and whipped this girl before and it hadn't brought her much pleasure. But the memory of the thrill she'd experienced when she killed Whitney still lingered, so tonight would be different. She'd kill the stupid peon with the whip and feel that thrill again. She must feel that thrill again.

"Take off your clothes," Aracela said.

"No, Lady, please don't whip me," the girl said.

"Take off your clothes," Aracela said again.

The frightened girl did as she was told and stood naked and shivering against the cold tomb wall.

Aracela threw off her cloak and tossed it over her father's coffin. She tapped a riding crop into the palm of her hand, then smiled. "Come to me, child."

"No." The girl made a dive for the door.

Aracela intercepted her and used the riding crop to lash her back to the wall again. A cut with the whip had opened up the girl's left shoulder.

"Child, you will die for my pleasure tonight," Aracela said. "I can bestow on you no greater honor."

Tears ran down the girl's cheeks. "Please, Lady, let me go. I'm a good girl." Then she tried a threat. "I will tell the padre."

"You'll be dead, so you'll tell no one." Aracela dug her fingers into the girl's hair and raised the crop. "I am giving you an honorable death and yet all you do is defy me."

The crypt door creaked open.

Aracela froze, her whip raised. She turned slowly, an unholy fire in her eyes. "What the hell do you want? Get out of here."

"My name is Juan Hernandez and I want you, Donna Aracela." The young peasant stood in the doorway in his ragged serape and straw hat. In his right hand he held a knife.

"Get out!" Aracela cried, feeling a start of fear. "I don't know you."

"You knew Pilar, the girl I loved . . . and still love. You dishonored her, and then, unable to cope with her shame, she walked into the snow and cold, and died. Pilar was to be my wife, and I grieve for her. That is why I am here to kill you."

"Ha, you need a woman, that's all." Aracela grabbed the naked girl by the arm and pushed her toward the youth. "Here, Juan, take her, take her now." She smiled. "And after her, you can have me. Tonight all your dreams will come true, Juan. I will deny you nothing."

"All I want is to send you to hell, Donna Aracela." He took a step toward the woman, his knife up and ready.

Thoroughly frightened now, Aracela backed to the tomb wall. She tore open the top of her dress, exposing her magnificent breasts. "Take me, Juan," she said, panting. "Take me now."

The boy's knife plunged into her chest, between the breasts she'd offered to him. She sank slowly to the floor, her back sliding down the cold marble of the crypt wall. The pain was great, the knowledge that she was dying an even greater pain.

She looked up at Juan and struggled to find breath. "Goddamn you, you stinking peasant pig!"

Her eyes were still open, filled with hate, as she died.

The maid screamed and shrank away from Juan, her gaze on the haft of the knife protruding from Aracela's chest. She tried to speak but couldn't form the words. It was to be the peasant girl's destiny that she would never be able to speak again.

"The girl was struck dumb by the horror she'd witnessed," Padre Diego said. "She may never regain her power of speech."

"How did it happen, Father?" Jacob spoke in the same hushed tones as the priest as they sat in the candle-lit chapel where Aracela's body lay.

"The vaqueros were all gone, so Donna Aracela was alone, but for a few servants," Padre Diego said. "As far as we can piece the events together, the peasant boy Juan Hernandez had dragged Donna Aracela's maid into the tomb to rape her. He'd raped and beaten a girl before, a beauty named Pilar. After she was dishonored, Pilar was so ashamed she walked into the snow and killed herself."

Jacob nodded. "Yeah, I remember that."

"What we think is that Donna Aracela, an exceedingly pious woman who was devoted to her father, went to the tomb to pray over his body. Unfortunately, she caught Juan Hernandez in the act and he killed her."

Padre Diego sighed. "Perhaps the girl in question

will be able to talk again and we'll have the full story. Until then all we can do is grieve for Donna Aracela and honor her memory." He looked at Jacob with sad eyes. "She was a fine woman."

"And a beautiful one," Jacob said.

"Yes, we always seem to lose the ones we can least afford to lose, don't we?" Padre Diego said.

"And what of the murderer, Father?" Jacob said.

"Gone. We sent men out looking for Hernandez, but they came back empty-handed." The priest glanced at Aracela's body, then brought his black eyes back to Jacob. "The peons are a simple, ignorant people and they don't believe, or don't want to believe, that the boy murdered Donna Aracela." He shook his head. "I don't think they searched too hard."

Padre Diego laid a hand on Jacob's forearm. "They say they did find a body, though. But it was not that of Juan Hernandez."

Jacob's interest quickened. "Did they describe it?"

"There wasn't much to describe. The poor soul was much torn about by coyotes. He was a small man and there was not enough of him left to bury, they said."

"Anything else?"

"The peons think the man had been killed by Apaches. There are still a few around, doing mischief." Padre Diego thought for a moment. "A fur coat. Yes, they said the dead man had worn a fur coat, but it too was much torn and tattered."

Jacob knew with certainty that his hunt for Joel Whitney was over and it left him feeling empty and unfulfilled. It had to be the little man's bones that were scattered over the prairie like so much garbage. The Apaches had done Jacob's job for him, but they'd robbed him of his revenge, and that hurt like the devil.

Padre Diego faced the altar, his thin fingers on his rosary beads. His lips moved for a while as his eyes roved around the empty chapel. "Where is my flock?" he said finally.

"I was wondering that myself. Maybe the snow is keeping them indoors." Jacob rued Whitney's demise and was only half listening to the priest.

"Failing to attend a wake for a holy and devout woman could be an occasion of sin. I will say masses for Donna Aracela, and that will bring them out."

"I am sure it will, Father." Jacob rose to his feet. "I got to be riding."

"God bless you, my son," the priest said, making a cross in the air. He smiled. "Yet one thing more that reveals Donna Aracela's great piety. I went through her papers and found her will. She said that in the event of her death, everything she owned should be bequeathed to Holy Mother Church."

"Did that include her claim to the Estancia Valley?" Jacob said.

"Everything."

Jacob was sure that Whitney had relatives back East who would dispute that. But it shaped up to be a court battle, not a range war, and it could drag on for years. Best of all, the sheepherders would stay where they were and end any threat to Dromore.

Candlelight slanted the chapel with dark, shifting shadows as Jacob stepped beside Aracela's bier. Even in death she was beautiful, as serene as a sleeping nun.

Suddenly Padre Diego was at Jacob's side. "Before you take your leave of her, there was another item in her will. She asked that the lid of her coffin not be nailed down." The priest smiled. "She said that come her resurrection, she did not wish to waste time breaking free from a nailed casket." His smile saddened, then faded. "Ah, indeed, Donna Aracela was as devout a Christian woman who ever lived."

Chapter Forty-nine

Dromore, February 1887

The clouds had parted three days before, and the sun shone from a blue sky, adding a sparkle to the streaks of snow that surrounded Dromore. The wind was cool, but soft and smelled of high peaks and tall timber; of cattle and horses and the musky scent of smoke from the log fires inside the big house.

Shamus O'Brien and Luther Ironside, his wounded leg sticking straight out in front of him, were in wheelchairs that had been pushed outside the front door so their occupants could catch the sun.

Patrick had sat down beside them for a while, but since the colonel and Luther were trying their hardest to outdo each other in crankiness, he'd closed his book and left them to it.

Samuel was spending time with his wife and son, and Shawn was off somewhere to meet with a girl he was sparking, so Patrick had the library to himself.

He sat in a chair by the fire, and renewed his acquaintance with Mr. Kingsley's *Hereward the Wake*. After thirty minutes, Patrick became aware of the icy draft that was chilling his neck and shoulders. The library window was at the back of the house and faced north in the direction of the prevailing wind. Reluctantly putting his book aside, he rose, stepped to the window, and slammed it shut.

He glanced outside . . . and saw Jacob.

His brother sat his horse on a rise about fifty yards from the house. As always, he sat his saddle like a sack of grain. Even at a distance, Patrick made out his shabby, ragged clothes and the great beak of a nose that overhung a cavalry mustache he seldom trimmed.

Jacob watched the house intently, as though he was trying to make up his mind about something. Patrick stood motionless at the window, afraid he'd be seen.

After a few minutes, Jacob swung his horse away and vanished into the pines.

"Good luck, brother," Patrick said aloud. He stood watching the trees for a long time, then went back to his chair and picked up his book.

J. A. Johnstone on William W. Johnstone
"When the Truth Becomes Legend"

William W. Johnstone was born in southern Missouri, the youngest of four children. He was raised with strong moral and family values by his minister father, and tutored by his schoolteacher mother. Despite this, he quit school at age fifteen.

"I have the highest respect for education," he says, "but such is the folly of youth, and wanting to see the world beyond the four walls and the blackboard."

True to this vow, Bill attempted to enlist in the French Foreign Legion ("I saw Gary Cooper in *Beau Geste* when I was a kid and I thought the French Foreign Legion would be fun") but was rejected, thankfully, for being underage. Instead, he joined a traveling carnival and did all kinds of odd jobs. It was listening to the veteran carny folk, some of whom had been on the circuit since the late 1800s, telling amazing tales about their experiences, which planted the storytelling seed in Bill's imagination.

"They were mostly honest people, despite the bad reputation traveling carny shows had back then," Bill remembers. "Of course, there were exceptions.

There was one guy named Picky, who got that name because he was a master pickpocket. He could steal a man's socks right off his feet without him knowing. Believe me, Picky got us chased out of more than a few towns."

After a few months of this grueling existence, Bill returned home and finished high school. Next came stints as a deputy sheriff in the Tallulah, Louisiana, Sheriff's Department, followed by a hitch in the U.S. Army. Then he began a career in radio broadcasting at KTLD in Tallulah, Louisiana, which would last sixteen years. It was there that he fine-tuned his storytelling skills. He turned to writing in 1970, but it wouldn't be until 1979 that his first novel, The Devil's Kiss, was published. Thus began the full-time writing career of William W. Johnstone. He wrote horror (*The Uninvited*), thrillers (*The Last of the Dog Team*), even a romance novel or two. Then, in February 1983, *Out of the Ashes* was published. Searching for his missing family in the aftermath of a post-apocalyptic America, rebel mercenary and patriot Ben Raines is united with the civilians of the Resistance forces and moves to the forefront of a revolution for the nation's future.

Out of the Ashes was a smash. The series would continue for the next twenty years, winning Bill three generations of fans all over the world. The series was often imitated but never duplicated. "We all tried to copy The Ashes series," said one publishing executive, "but Bill's uncanny ability, both then and now, to predict in which direction the political winds were blowing brought a certain immediacy to the table no one else could capture." *The Ashes* series would end its run with more than thirty-four books and twenty million copies in print, making it one of the most successful men's action series in American book publishing. (The Ashes series also, Bill notes with a touch of pride, got him on the FBI's Watch List for its less than flattering portrayal of spineless politicians and the growing power of big government over our lives, among other things. "In that respect," says collaborator J. A. Johnstone, "Bill was years ahead of his time.")

Always steps ahead of the political curve, Bill's recent thrillers, written with J. A. Johnstone, include *Vengeance Is Mine, Invasion USA, Border War, Jackknife, Remember the Alamo, Home Invasion, Phoenix Rising, The Blood of Patriots, The Bleeding Edge,* and the upcoming *Suicide Mission.*

It is with the western, though, that Bill found his greatest success and propelled him onto both the *USA Today* and the *New York Times* bestseller lists.

Bill's western series, co-authored by J. A. Johnstone, include *The Mountain Man, Matt Jensen the Last Mountain Man, Preacher, The Family Jensen, Luke Jensen Bounty Hunter, Eagles, MacCallister* (an Eagles spin-off), *Sidewinders, The Brothers O'Brien, Sixkiller, Blood Bond, The Last Gunfighter,* and the upcoming new series *Flintlock* and *The Trail West.* Coming in May 2013 is the hardcover western *Butch Cassidy, The Lost Years.*

"The Western," Bill says, "is one of the few true art forms that is one hundred percent American. I liken the Western as America's version of England's Arthurian legends, like the Knights of the Round Table, or Robin Hood and his Merry Men. Starting with the 1902 publication of *The Virginian* by Owen Wister, and followed by the greats like Zane Grey, Max Brand, Ernest Haycox, and of course Louis L'Amour, the Western has helped to shape the cultural landscape of America.

"I'm no goggle-eyed college academic, so when my fans ask me why the Western is as popular now as it was a century ago, I don't offer a 200-page thesis. Instead, I can only offer this: The Western is honest. In this great country, which is suffering under the yoke of political correctness, the Western harks back to an era when justice was sure and swift. Steal a man's horse, rustle his cattle, rob a bank, a stagecoach, or a train, you were hunted down and fitted with a hangman's noose. One size fit all.

"Sure, we westerners are prone to a little embellishment and exaggeration and, I admit it, occasionally play a little fast and loose with the facts. But we do so for a very good reason—to enhance the enjoyment of readers.

"It was Owen Wister, in *The Virginian* who first coined the phrase *'When you call me that, smile.'* Legend has it that Wister actually heard those words spoken by a deputy sheriff in Medicine Bow, Wyoming, when another poker player called him a son-of-a-bitch.

"Did it really happen, or is it one of those myths that have passed down from one generation to the next? I honestly don't know. But there's a line in one of my favorite Westerns of all time, *The Man Who Shot Liberty Valance*, where the newspaper editor tells the young reporter, 'When the truth becomes legend, print the legend.'

"These are the words I live by."

GREAT BOOKS,
GREAT SAVINGS!

When You Visit Our Website:
www.kensingtonbooks.com

You Can Save Money Off The Retail Price
Of Any Book You Purchase!

- **All Your Favorite Kensington Authors**
- **New Releases & Timeless Classics**
- **Overnight Shipping Available**
- **eBooks Available For Many Titles**
- **All Major Credit Cards Accepted**

Visit Us Today To Start Saving!
www.kensingtonbooks.com

All Orders Are Subject To Availability.
Shipping and Handling Charges Apply.
Offers and Prices Subject To Change Without Notice.